Not to be Forgiven

a Novel

Nancy Mayborn Peterson

Hugo House Publishers, Ltd.

Not to be Forgiven
by
Nancy Mayborn Peterson

ISBN: 978-1-936449-38-5
Library of Congress Control Number: 2013930818

Cover Illustration by Gwendolyn Marie Hill
Graphics and Interior Design by DPMediaPro.com

Hugo House

HugoHousePublishers.com
Englewood Colorado
877-700-0616

Publisher's Cataloging-in-Publication Data
Peterson, Nancy Mayborn.
Not to be forgiven / Nancy Mayborn Peterson.
p. cm.
ISBN: 978-1-936449-38-5 (pbk.)
ISBN: 978-1-936449-39-2 (e-book)
1. World War, 1939-1945—Prisoners and prisons, American—Fiction. 2. World War, 1939-1945—Psychological aspects—Fiction. 3. Germans—United States—Fiction. 4. Nebraska—Fiction. I. Title. PS3616.E8435 N68 2013
813—dc23   2013930818

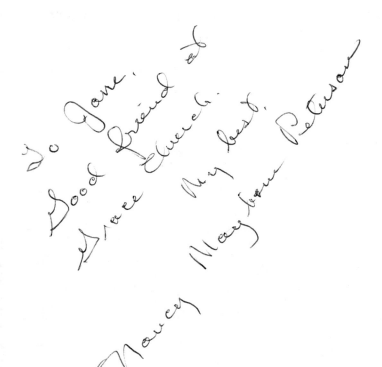

To Jane,
Good Friend of
Grace Church.
My best.

Nancy Marjorie Peterson

DEDICATION

To my highschool jounalism teacher, Irene Auble Abernethy, whose belief in me helped me believe in myself.

ACKNOWLEDGMENTS

My elementary school years were colored dark by World War II. I was in first grade when the Japanese bombed Pearl Harbor and in sixth grade before it was over. While I have certain vivid childhood memories of growing up in those tense times, I needed to consult many sources before I could write the story of the Greggory family. I am deeply grateful to those people who generously shared their memories and knowledge of the era.

Scottsbluff Prisoner of War Camp employees Betty Gilmore and Bonnie Loy told me of their experiences, as did Mary Cook, sister of a POW camp nurse. Mollie Specht, Neil Gatch, and Hugo Schmunk detailed experiences with POWs working on farms.

I am grateful to Marian Laurent, Beth Joines, Irene Auble Abernethy, Ruth Wiberg, Emily Strand and historians Harry and Catherine Chrisman for sharing personal experiences. Catherine documented attacks on the Japanese-owned cafe and the town's resurgence of support afterward. Denver Red Cross volunteer Elizabeth Baylingson, Dr. Lewis Barbato, Fitzsimons Chief of Psychiatric Medicine, and Historian Helen Littlejohn shared their knowledge of Fitzsimons Army Hospital. Yutaka and Rose Yamamoto, Adeline Kano, Moss Sakurada, Louise Kubomoto, Alfred S. Miyagishima, Fred Ikeya and Jenny Hamada Schaffell informed me about persecutions suffered by Japanese-Americans, as well as some kindnesses received.

Newspapermen Stanton W. Theis of the *Scottsbluff Daily Star-Herald*, Frank H. Wisner, the *Gering Courier*, Houston Waring, *Littleton Independent*, and Jack Kisling, the *Denver Post*, enlightened me on the difficulties of publishing newspapers in the war years.

Kenton Forest, Denver Union Station historian, shared his expertise as did bird experts Katherine Hurlbutt and Alice Rumery, who enlightened me on habits of magpies, Yoryeah Roberts shared Greek Christmas customs and Ronald Dreher his knowledge of German.

v

Numerous publications were cheerfully provided by personnel of the North Platte Valley Museum, Scottsbluff Public Library, Denver Public Library, Englewood Public Library, Education Section U.S. Army Military History Institute, Nebraska State Historical Society and historians of the 135th Infantry Regiment.

Files of *LIFE* magazine, the *Scottsbluff Daily Star-Herald* and the *Englewood Herald* were invaluable as was the advice and support of my critique group, Linda Berry, Barbara Fleming, Bonnie McCune, and Betty Swords.

The story is fiction based on fact, a could-have-happened story that created itself in my mind over several years. For this reason I chose to name the town Hiram's Spring. I stayed true to the sequence of events in the North Platte Valley except in one instance. The German prisoners of war were not the first to occupy the POW Camp. Italian soldiers actually arrived first, but I advanced the German arrival to condense the time-line. I believe I remained true to the emotions rampant at the time; our country was at peril in those early years, and no one knew what the outcome might be.

UNCLE SAM WANTS YOU

Early dusk dimmed the western Nebraska hills, filling the hollows with blue shadow and graying the sparse dry clumps of grass. I had been long hours at the wheel, driving automatically as I tried to shrug off the tension that had gripped my shoulders ever since I'd left the capital city mall.

City. I smiled ruefully, thinking how my sophisticated sons would hoot at my calling Lincoln a city. But it was city enough to stifle me with its simulated air and startle me with its parade of tattooed skinheads and black-leathered young people. Their challenging stares came from faces too young to contain such hate-filled eyes.

I opened the window, determined to shake off the shock of realizing what I'd seen as I pushed through the exit of the mall. Entering on my left was a spike-haired young mother. In her arms she held a baby. I had taken a couple of steps on out the door before it hit me. The tiny silver ornaments swinging jauntily below her baby's ears—they were swastikas.

How could she? On her innocent child? Didn't she know of the horror?

It was then I saw the message—painted in washed-out white letters on a weathered board fence along the road.

1

"N o t   to   be   F o r g i v e n"
The fence ended in a dark clump of sage. The arroyos crawled away into the darkness. I had seen it for only seconds, but it was enough. It was as if a hand had stretched out of the past to impale me with a message—was it an accusation or a cry of grief?—on the high, dry Nebraska prairie.

"N o t   to   be   F o r g i v e n—"
I closed my eyes against memories that came tumbling through a door so long unopened. So many years ago. So much blood since. What was the use?

But why was my Grandmother Greggory's voice whispering "everything?" in my mind?

I changed my grip on the wheel and turned up the stereo. It did no good. Nothing could stop the images filling my mind. The shocking emptiness in the narrow bed. The dirt-smudged pages of the small, leather diary. The stricken expression in Horst's eyes.

How had I known, even as a child, the terrible power of forgiveness? The sweet, searing truth that you can destroy your enemy simply by withholding it. Deny forgiveness and you can own his soul.

At eleven, I did not want Horst's soul. Yet I wanted his pain more than I'd ever wanted anything. I thought it would heal my own. It could not, of course. But I did not know that when I was eleven. Nor did I then have the slightest conception of the corrosive dynamics of hatred.

In my bottom bureau drawer, tucked in the cedar box that holds my childhood treasures, I still have the pewter token Horst gave me. The braided leather strap it hangs from, once white, is now dingy gray; the metal itself, nearly black with tarnish.

Now only the raised portions of the gnome-like figure on its surface gleam softly, as if the fingers that soiled the strap had, with habitual rubbings, kept the figure clean. I had examined it so closely that long-ago day in the potato field—the gnome's beard, his peaked hat, his right knee, raised as if to scale the mountain peaks in the background. His right hand, lifted in a cheerful wave, used to stand out in bold relief.

Now, only by tipping the small octagon to the light, can you discern the rest of the figure and make out the words *"ER SCHUTZE DICH"* across the top of the scene. On the back of the token, a road

2

twists and turns up the side of a mountain, rising far above distant fields.

Did Horst once explain its meaning to me? Or was I just taken by the mountaineering gnome and the trail zigzagging up the hillside—so like the Zig Zag Trail up the side of Scotts Bluff that my brother Danny and I loved to climb? What had the talisman meant to Horst, to be carried through years of soldiering and battle and finally to a prisoner of war camp in a western Nebraska river valley?

The Zig Zag Trail is barely visible today, having been filled in by horrified latter-day environmentalists. But we were unaware of such ecological damage in the 1940s and considered the trail the Boy Scouts cut into the east side of Scotts Bluff a public service.

I remember the last time Danny and I puffed our way to its top. That was on a summer-hot Saturday in early September 1942. As I ate my breakfast that morning, a wasp droned and thumped against the window. Wheeling my bike out of the garage, I noticed the edge of the lawn was as crisp and brown as the crust on my toast. When we bicycled down Elm Avenue and out of town, roadside sunflowers stood gray with dust. Over the concrete bridge that spanned the skimpy, sand-choked currents of the North Platte River, we passed cat-tailed seep-water ponds and deep blue pockets made by bottom-land gravel pits. We turned right and headed west up Country Club Road. The club itself sat on the grassy flanks of the Bluff's east face, catering to the aspirations of the future-oriented population. Around the point on the south face, the adobe-style National Monument headquarters spoke to the area's past.

The club commanded—for the "haves" of the community—one of the best views of the valley. We scorned it for the vaster view we knew could be ours for free. Leaning our bikes on a fence post, we helped each other through the barbed wire and crossed the corner of a sugar beet field to reach the small stone archway near the foot of the trail.

A meadowlark threw its flute-like song at the sun and Danny echoed it with a whistle. My mother said he could out-whistle a red bird, and I couldn't count the warm summer nights I'd lain awake in my slant-ceilinged attic bedroom, hearing him serenade the neighborhood on his way home. For as long as I could remember, he'd walked with a spring-legged, exuberant gait. You were never too surprised when he jumped up mid-stride to snatch a leaf from the branch of an overhanging tree or give a store awning a thump.

3

As I expected, he disdained the gradual rise of the twisting trail for an unofficial, eroded path that climbed straight up from level to level. As we scrambled up the steep slope, I panted in his wake, eating tan dust from the dry, clay soil. Stretching to use his footholds, determined to keep up, I grabbed an exposed cedar root when I could, where a small twisted specimen clung stubbornly to the eroded slope. Clumps of yucca fanned their gray-green spikes along the way, but I knew better than to grasp those needle-sharp spines.

"Come on, Sis." Danny took my hand and hoisted me up the last, almost vertical stretch to the foot tunnel that gave access to the west side of the eight-hundred-foot sandstone formation.

There were eight years between us. I was the unexpected pigtail, the tag-along who caught our parents by surprise years after they thought Danny would be the only one. I'd reached for his hand often in my ten years, having learned that while he'd gleefully drop an ice cube down my neck or booby trap his comic book drawer with an open jar of grasshoppers, he'd always stand between me and harm.

Standing in the tunnel entrance, gratefully gulping its cool air, we could see where we'd come from and follow the course of the Platte, lined with cottonwoods that were just beginning to show a trace of yellow, and see the small farm towns spaced along the river's banks.

On the other side of the tunnel Danny started to renew the climb, but my throat was dry. "Let's get a drink from the spring," I urged. Danny grumbled good-naturedly as we climbed down to the spring on the Bluff's back side and knelt to catch the clear, cold water in our cupped hands. He drank noisily, then sat back and cleared his throat. "Sis—" he began.

"Tell me again about Hiram Scott," I interrupted before he could go on.

He gave me his "cross" look, hard to miss because he crossed his green eyes. Then his mood changed and he grabbed me and forced my shoulders toward the dribble of water. "His ghost has come back to take revenge on you!" he teased.

"No, really." I laughed, twisting away. "What did he do? Why'd they leave him here to die?" I saw the glimmer in his eye and I knew I'd caught him. There was nothing Danny loved like telling a story and nothing I loved more than hearing about the days when buffalo watered at the Platte.

"Nothin' bad." Danny splashed water on the back of his neck. "Maybe tangled with a grizzly. Or just got sick at the wrong time and place. You know, in the 1820s there wasn't anything between here and the Missouri River but Pawnees, and fur trappers couldn't figure they'd hand out Carter's Little Liver Pills."

I grinned and picked needle grass from the rolled cuffs of my jeans, thinking how handy it was to have a big brother who knew everything. A tidbit picked up from Danny had impressed a teacher and saved my hash more than once.

But Danny's face grew serious. "Anyhow, somewhere up-river Scott got hurt. The three of them were out of food and racing the winter. Guess the other two decided he was slowing them down too much. One morning he woke up and they were gone."

Danny stood and gazed over the network of ridges and gullies stretching like bony fingers from the foot of the Bluff. "They say he crawled some thirty or forty miles after them before he gave up. All anybody knows is another bunch of trappers found his bones here at the Bluff the next year." He stared into space and a shiver crawled down my spine. "I always wondered how he felt—" Danny's voice trailed off.

Neither of us knew then that a bluff half a world away loomed dark in Danny's future, but I was suddenly sorry I'd mentioned the subject. With any sign of settlement out of sight, I knelt on land altered only by wind and water since long before the trappers' intrusion. I could feel the emptiness, the threat, the panic. And something worse, a dread I didn't want to define.

Then Danny pulled me up and swatted my rear. "And that, Mary Kathleen Greggory, is why you live in a town called Hiram's Spring at the foot of Scotts Bluff."

"Humph," I snorted. "Everybody knows that."

The escarpment Hiram had the misfortune to give his name stands sentinel over the river, an irregular mass of sandstone that has resisted the persistent west wind and sporadic rain. Eroded ridges stretch in various directions from its north-south backbone. From the two small, spaced uprights on the south we kids inelegantly christened Grandpa's Teeth to the fortress-like headland that rears above the badlands along the river is perhaps half a mile.

We renewed our climb to walk the rock-topped highland among ponderosa pine and spreading cedars, few of which were big enough to shade more than the occasional rattlesnake seeking shelter on a hot afternoon. Out on the north point, my favorite place in the whole world, we could see the entire valley.

"Valley of the Nile," the Chamber of Commerce grandly called it. Irrigation canals fed by the North Platte distributed their silty brown riches through smaller and smaller ditches until their burden darkened the soil of the farmers' furrows and disappeared. Platte Valley farmers knew it was futile to pray for rain; they prayed for snow in the Rockies.

The river braided blue channels below us and to the west. To the north and south the country climbed to tableland good for pasture or wheat, but where the farmers could lead water to the soil, the valley produced abundant yields of sugar beets and potatoes.

Up, now, in the pine-scented breeze, we could locate the farm houses by their clusters of protecting cottonwoods. The towns were larger clusters, interrupted by roofs and a water tower. To the east, central to the view and to the economy of the valley, the white silos of the Great Western Sugar factory were bright towers against the sky. The need for beets to supply that factory had peopled the valley with its original settlers.

I squinted my eyes. "I can see Chimney Rock!" I knew its brown spire had guided wagons on the Oregon Trail a hundred years before. Their ruts still skirted the Bluff and were the place I searched most often for the arrowhead I felt destined to find. Refreshed by the cool, dry air, I raced from vantage point to vantage point, picking out the triangular blue shadow of Laramie Peak ninety miles west, the six-story brick hospital on Main Street, the office of the *Hiram Spring Herald*.

"Sis. Sis!" Danny was saying insistently. "We've got to talk."

"No." I backed away, knowing I didn't want to hear.

"Come on, Sis. You can't change something by ignoring it." I stared at the way the sun lit the sandy hair on his tanned arm. "You knew I took my physical last month. I leave day after tomorrow."

"But you can't. The folks need you on the paper. You're going to college. You promised Mom!" Desperately I dredged up arguments I already knew were futile.

6

"I know. But I can't just sit in school with this going on. I've—"
he shrugged. "I've just got to go."

Suddenly the height I'd always gloried in was threatening. I
dropped on the nearest boulder. "But you almost urped that time
you shot the jackrabbit! I saw you!" I protested, ducking my head
as my chin gave a treacherous quiver. "How can you be a soldier?"

"So—I'll have Uncle Sam make me a flyboy." He grabbed up a
pebble beside my foot. "Bombs away!" he said playfully and the
pebble bounced off my head. When I didn't respond, he squatted in
front of me and lifted my chin so I had to meet his eyes. "Listen.
This will be a real adventure. I'll probably get to go overseas. I
might see Hawaii. Or England. Places I never dreamed I'd be. I'll
write and tell you all about everything."

He stood and gave my arm a playful punch. "I'll send you a
coconut—or a Bobby's helmet." Catching his own enthusiasm, he
began to chant. "I'll go to London to visit the Queen. I'll send you
a mouse from under her chair—I'll send you—an hour from Big
Ben's tower." Grinning infectiously, he poked me in the ribs. "I'll
send you a rose from Miss Margaret's nose!"

"Let's hear you rhyme Elizabeth," I challenged, laughing in spite
of myself.

"I'll send you a fan from Elizabeth Ann!" he shot back. "Your
turn!"

"Bring me some porridge from Old King Georidge," I contributed lamely.

But Danny laughed and pulled me up in a hug. "I'll miss you,
Sis," he said. "But cheer up. I'll write and tell you all about the
places I see and what I'm doing. And it's not like I'll be gone
forever."

On Monday evening I hugged my knees in the back seat of our
boxy black 1935 Ford as we drove the seven blocks home from the
depot, hearing again the conductor's "All abooooooooard!", seeing
Mother stand on tiptoe to smooth Danny's ever-present cowlick,
seeing Dad hand him her forgotten shoebox of burnt oatmeal
cookies, watching Danny grab up his cheap cardboard suitcase and
swing up the train steps. Then he was leaning across a seat toward
the window, trying to coax a smile out of me by making Barney
Google eyes as he threw me a salute. I breathed the moist hot steam

spewing from the engine, heard the cars clank into motion. And stared at tracks standing emptier than they had ever been.

I heard the engine whistle at the Elm Avenue crossing, listened to it shriek its warning at Sugar Factory Road, strained to hold onto the sound as it faded away in the distance. And wondered how I could live with such a hollow in my heart.

FOR THE DURATION

Noon was always meat and potatoes time at our house. Even when Danny was in high school across town, he'd bicycled home at noon. Though cooking was never Mother's long suit—she could wreak havoc just opening a box of cornflakes—and our signal to dine was often a cloud of smoke wafting from the kitchen, we all went home for dinner. Everybody did.

With my mother drafted to help Dad at the paper "for the duration"—that gray phrase that rang through our lives like a toneless dirge, allowing no future, admitting no past—it might have been more practical to have our big meal late in the afternoon, before the paper's evening rush. But she insisted this was no time to change, that we should keep our lives as much the same as possible since everything about us was in such turmoil. I was too young to realize adults had their own ritual ways of stepping over sidewalk cracks; her way of protecting her family sugar bowl was to wrap it in familiar routine.

But how could three of us pretend things were the same? Setting the round, oak dining room table the day after Danny left, I found myself with an extra knife, an extra fork, a spoon too many. The sun slanting through the windows over the buffet seemed to focus on the empty seat of his chair. KGKY's noon news, which my father had always strained to hear over our school-day chatter, easily dominated our attempts at conversation, darkening the air like a threatening presence.

Reports of U.S. ships torpedoed off the Florida coast, German armies slicing deep into Russia and Marines fighting futilely on some little island in the Pacific called Guadalcanal came flowing around Mother's china cupboard and under the corner what-not shelf to crease my father's forehead and haunt Mother's eyes.

She only nodded vacantly to my complaints about life in the clutches of Miss Dumbrowski, fifth-grade teacher, principal and god of Longfellow Grade School for untold decades, who did not hesitate to contrast my lackadaisical attitude with Danny's ability to absorb knowledge through his skin. I knew I had no more chance of satisfying her than of impressing my father. After all, who could replace Danny?

But now, even when Mother managed an understanding smile, her eyes kept a distant look. The two of them talked in monotones of Stalingrad and London and the Egyptian desert. I tried not to listen. Listening stirred acid whirlpools of fear deep in my stomach.

When we were four, Danny's vital presence let me keep the war at arm's length; tales of the football coach, near disasters in chemistry class, the high school paper's latest crusade had made it possible to ignore the "Uncle Sam Wants You" poster in front of the post office and the billboard by the depot touting war bonds. Even the last few months, when he'd taken over the sports page for Dad and their three-way dinnertime conversations had focused on getting out each day's edition, my world had held its center.

But now? Now we had only a small red-bordered flag, centered with a blue star, in the front window. And suddenly I realized how much I missed seeing Mother puff up the basement stairs with a basket of laundry or come in from the garden with a handful of larkspur.

I felt like an empty house with curtain-less windows and un-stirred air. I had to make the war go away and get everything back to normal before—before it was too late. There was a poster taped in the dime-store window. Hitler's evil face loomed over the crumpled bodies of a mother and father while a little girl cried in helpless fear. "This is the Enemy!" it warned.

That night, sitting in the porch swing, I ran my fingers down the supporting chain until I found the sharp burr I'd cut my hand on a few weeks before. Gritting my teeth, I pulled my index finger across it. When it was bleeding satisfactorily, I swiveled around in the seat and began to print on the crossbar that topped the slats. It took longer than I expected and I had to squeeze hard to get enough blood, but when I was through I was sure anyone could make out the words "V for Victory!"

"Crucial." The word from the man standing in the flag-draped pickup in the middle of Main Street's busiest intersection Saturday morning sang in my mind, and I wished my father were there to hear it. "We're fighting to save our nation and the world," he shouted, "to save our homes, our families."

I listened intently with the rest of the crowd. "Your sons and husbands and brothers know that," he said, his voice rising. "They're already out there, ready to make every Jap and German sorry he ever heard of America!" The man beside me curled his lip in a shrill whistle, and I stood straighter in my red, white and blue Camp Fire Girls uniform as others cheered. But now the speaker's voice dropped and we had to lean forward to hear. "But our boys can't shoot down Zeros without bullets. They can't drive tanks that haven't been made. Our men are desperate for help." He pivoted with his arm extended, challenging each section of the crowd with his pointing finger. "You must give every scrap of metal you can! Save your sons and brothers from being butchered! This is crucial!"

The word propelled me up and down Hiram's Spring streets, which looked as if the town had turned itself inside out in a spasm of spring cleaning. I loaded rusty toy trucks, dented pans, coal scoops and waffle irons into my red wagon until my legs ached and the hand pulling the wagon blistered across the palm. "Every iron will make two helmets. Every garbage can a thousand bullets. Every shovel—" The words became a litany that would keep Danny safe. The air in my empty house began to stir. I wasn't helpless anymore, waiting for the walls to fall in. I was doing something crucial for the war effort.

But scrap drives didn't happen every day. When I pulled *LIFE* magazine from the mailbox the next Tuesday and spread the large picture-filled pages across my lap, I learned milkweed seed was crucial, too. We watched eagerly for the magazine each week; its vivid photo stories showing what was going on in our country seemed especially necessary with the war on. Reading the article that urged everyone to collect mature milkweed pods, I pounced on the chance to do something more.

I bicycled out the highway east of town and began working my way down the borrow pit, collecting the frost-dried, splitting pods. The sun glinted off the gossamer silk the split revealed, and I coaxed a few strands free. A puff of breath sent them sailing where the breeze willed. Like parachutes. One settled on a puddle and floated serenely. Was that why they used them in life jackets?

I was wondering how many it would take to hold up a man in the ocean when a horn blared and tires screeched. I whirled toward the road. A huge gravel truck skidded to a stop inches from a farm tractor that had pulled out in front of it from a side road. Other cars and trucks swerved and skidded wildly.

I suddenly realized the lines of traffic were crowded with every kind of vehicle. Farm trucks piled with barrels and rocking chairs, pickups filled with shovels and wheelbarrows, a chicken coop mounted on skids, a truckload of hogs, a huge grader, and passenger cars full of families vied for space. I gaped. It looked like half the county was on the move.

Then I saw a soldier, rifle slung on his shoulder, guarding a side road that turned north off the highway.

My heart lunged in my chest. The war was here! Right here in Hiram's Spring! These people all knew. They were fleeing the enemy. I stood frozen, my sack of milkweed pods spilled at my feet.

But when the soldier noticed me, his voice was matter-of-fact. "You better head back for town," he yelled. "This is a Defense Zone. No sightseers."

Sightseers? In a war? Was he crazy? But as I watched he directed a dump truck through the turn and up the side road. A bulldozer followed close behind. And I realized even above the traffic noise I could hear motors grinding somewhere ahead. A long plume of dust and puffs of black smoke spread above a hilltop north of the road. A Defense Zone? What was going on?

My insides relaxed. A half-heard dinner conversation stirred in my mind. Dad had been complaining that the army expected him to be satisfied with a one-paragraph press release. Something about a satellite airport. On impulse I retraced my steps until I reached a small irrigation ditch. I turned north to follow it through the fields.

It wasn't long before I saw what I was looking for, an aged cottonwood whose gnarled branches arched protectively over the easy source of water. I dug my fingers into the deeply fissured, gray bark as my feet scrambled for a toehold, then pulled myself up through the mostly bare branches, higher than I'd ever been. My heart was pounding but the thought of being some good to Dad pulled me higher. Finally, to the east and just visible through clouds of dust, I saw gigantic earth-moving machines puffing black smoke as they cut a long straight swath through the green tops of a sugar beet field. Men and trucks were everywhere, and I could see the skeletons of several long low buildings. Whatever a satellite field was, this was big stuff! I stretched to see more.

A sudden whoosh, a whir of wings, a blur of angry black! My foot slipped and I thought only of hanging on. When my brain turned back on, I realized the dive bomber had been a magpie objecting to my presence. Shaky, willing myself to move again, I inched back down, leaving the tree to the large, feisty bird. My arms were scraped and stinging when I reached bottom, but I was almost glad, imagining Dad's surprise when I reported my news, his respectful glance at my untended wounds.

Then a shrill whistle echoed from somewhere down the ditch. I could see no one, but I heard a voice calling, "Here, Lad, come on boy!" The voice seemed familiar, but there was something different about it. I walked toward the sound. The whistle was louder now, and when the call came again I realized the owner of the voice was close to crying. "Here, Lad. Here, boy."

There was no sign of a dog, but I saw Roger Haycraft looking out over the fields. I'd forgotten he lived out here somewhere. His back was toward me, but we'd sat in the same row of desks for five years now and I knew him coming or going. If I had admitted to liking any boy, Roger would have been first choice. But only my best friend, Betty Hermann, knew I ever entertained such thoughts. I went out of my way to insult him at school, and he seemed to delight in returning the compliment double measure.

I was about to ask him if Lad finally got wise and left for a better home, when he turned and I saw tears running down his cheeks. Looking shocked and humiliated, he whirled around and scrubbed at his face with his hands.

I was embarrassed in turn. I knew he wished I would drop off the earth. I didn't know how to do that, and I couldn't think of a thing to say.

"What ya doing out here, Kathaweenie?" he finally asked.

It didn't seem the time for smart remarks. "Trying to see what the army's doing." Then, realizing we could talk like human beings, I ventured the obvious. "Lose your dog?"

"Lost everything," he said. He put a finger beside his nose and blew snot into the weeds. "House. Farm. Crop. Had to leave in such a hurry." He shrugged.

"I noticed you weren't in school."

"Had to help Mom pack the house stuff. Help Dad herd the cows. Crate up the chickens. Lad got left behind. Every time we came back for another load, I looked, but I guess he followed after us and couldn't keep up."

"You think he'll come back here?"

"That's what I been hopin'." He sighed, then picked up a clod and threw it into the field.

"Where you living now?"

"In a little house in Bayard. Dad's looking for a new place."

"How'd you get here?"

"Rode with Dad. He's combining beans over there." He waved at a distant truck engulfed in dust. "At least they were ready to harvest so we didn't lose the whole crop. A lot of our neighbors weren't that lucky." Roger jammed his hands in his overall pockets. "Dad says we'll live through this. That an air base is more important than our farm. That I can get another dog."

His voice broke on the last phrase and he cleared his throat. "And I guess he's right. I got two uncles in the Pacific. Guess they're more important than any old dog." The truck horn sounded four short blats. "I'm supposed to be helpin' Dad. Gotta go. See ya, Kathaweenie."

"See ya," I said. And he was gone. But I heard his whistle, shrill with desperate hope, twice more before I got back to the highway.

My breathless news about the air field did not stop the *Herald* presses. Instead I stood on my ankles by the teletype, while Dad gave most of his attention to the clattering AP wire. He'd already reported construction was underway. If I ever read anything but the comics I'd know that. What else could I tell him? How many buildings? One story or two? How about a hangar? What direction did the brown swath take?

I gave him more "I don't knows" than Miss Dumbrowski got in three days. With her at least I could take a chance and create an answer. I wouldn't have dreamed of serving up imaginings for my father's news columns.

The only thing that saved me from disgracing myself with tears was Mother's sympathetic wink across the newsroom. Did he ask her questions she couldn't answer? For the first time I wondered how she felt when she started to work as a reporter. Could she have been scared? Suddenly I was looking at a stranger sitting there with the telephone receiver to her ear. But she was my mother again when I passed her on the way out and she pressed the mouthpiece to her chest long enough to say, "Don't worry. He wouldn't have printed any of it anyway because of the voluntary press code. He just wants to know."

For days we'd been watching for a letter from Danny. The narrow black box hanging from the porch bannister was empty again. I banged the lid, my disappointment keen. Had he forgotten us? Was he already a stranger, like one of those stern men who march in the newsreels? Then I caught sight of a blue uniform far up Elm Avenue. Mr. Kelly was just working his way north. I sighed. He was old and slow—like the gray-haired man who bagged our groceries now, and the milkman who trudged up the steps every morning. Every business in town posted proud honor rolls listing their young men in the service.

I went inside and twirled the radio dial, wondering if even the Lone Ranger was off fighting the Germans, but he had just "Hi-yoed" Silver into view when I heard the hollow thump of a step and the clatter of the mailbox lid. What was inside was worth the wait. I started to tear it open. Then wondered if I should. Then finished the job.

Sept. 27, 1942

Deep in the Heart of Texas
Dear Folks and Sis,

Greetings from Camp Wolters in the great state of Texas. It's been a great two weeks. Yours truly has been shipped, stripped, shot (only needles, so far), poked, prodded, tagged, tested and categorized. I am now just so many holes in my qualification card.

*A nameless eight-digit number. They welcomed us to
Fort Leavenworth with a band and shortly thereafter
stole all our clothes.*

I felt a wonderful surge of relief. He was the same irrepressible
Danny.

*What you get in return fit army style. The supply
sergeant said if the clothes move when we move,
they're our size. Funny guy! And you wouldn't believe
the canvas leggings we have to wear! They're a real
pain to put on. I never expected to look like a Dough-
boy.*

I made a mental note to ask Mother what he meant.

*Am anxious to get out of camp and see some
of Texas. Was kind of let down to see it looking much
like home—except the hills are rollier (is that a
word?) But it's dry and the cedar trees look familiar.
We're close to a little town called Mineral Wells, and
Fort Worth is on east.*

*The camp is huge. Thousands of men. My home is
now a cot in a tent with five other guys. Tent tops spread
for miles with good old military monotony. Makes me
want to fly a red flag over ours. Sure easy to get lost.*

*What struck me first was the smell of wood smoke.
Wood stoves heat our tents and gigantic wood piles
are everywhere you look. Pretty chilly tonight, and
the smell makes me think of our campfires at Lake Minatare or the Wildcat Hills—of sitting around the
coals roasting marshmallows as the fire dies—putting
off the drive back to town. I can see Dad patiently
getting his a perfect golden brown and Mom waving
her torch on high and Sis trying to do three at once
and losing them all in the process. Oh, well. Guess it
will be awhile before we can do those things again.*

Sorry this is short but when they say "Lights out!" around here they mean it.
Keep the home fires burning!

Love,

Danny

I read it in a gulp and then read it again. So he was in Texas! Just like the Lone Ranger. I'd write and ask him if he'd seen Tonto. That would make him laugh. Living in tents—building fires—sounded like fun. It must be kind of like his Boy Scout camp-outs. But miles of tent tops? I couldn't imagine that. I'd ask him to send us a picture. In the meantime, I realized, my parents would want to know we'd gotten a letter. I went to the phone and asked the operator for 292, the paper's number.

When my mother answered, I told her about Danny being in Texas, about all the tents and fires like Boy Scout camp.

She broke in. "But what does he say about training? Did he get in the air corps? What kind of base is it?"

I skimmed the letter, finding nothing. "All I can see is his new address. It says Camp Wolters, Infantry Replacement Training Center."

"Oh, God," Mother said. There was a long silence. Then the receiver clicked in my ear.

17

IT'S YOUR PATRIOTIC DUTY

"We should figure out a place to hide if the Germans come," I said as I moved rakes from one corner of Kay Miller's tool shed.

"Yeah. Like in the closet. Or the basement," Betty Hermann agreed. She and I had been tuned to the same station ever since kindergarten. She was the one who'd changed my detested Mary Kathleen to M.K. I'd helped her name her dog Schnoz when he was a pup and was sure I held second place in his affections.

"And keep some blankets there to hide under. And some food." Kay, my second-best friend, was always the practical one.

My mother said we made good stair-steps, with Betty a good head taller than I, her short dark curls a contrast to my blond braids. Kay was almost a head shorter, her brown hair in a sensible Dutch bob. On class-picture day both she and I had to stand in the front row, but it made me feel a little better not to be the shortest one of all.

"How about some ketchup to smear on, so if they find you they'll think you're dead," I offered. "Then we could sneak out later and meet here to join the underground."

"What underground?" Kay tended to be a dead weight Betty and I had to drag through "let's pretend."

19

Betty rolled her eyes and said, "Kay, if the Germans get here, there will have to be an underground to fight them. You know, like in the shows about France?"

Just then Schnoz interrupted the proceedings with a fit of sneezing. His family tree had mysterious branches; while he was about the height of a collie, his snout had the size of a Saint Bernard and it was always where it didn't belong. The granddaddy longlegs he'd nosed out of a flower pot in the Miller's shed canted to 45 degrees in the gale, and the picture of the flag I'd pushed on a nail above waved in the breeze. We'd only just finished clearing out the corner and called our first Victory Club meeting to order. We "*ge-sundheited*" Schnoz and got back to business.

"Maybe I can get some old ketchup from the stockroom," Betty said. Her family lived in what I considered a fascinating house, four rooms that ranged along the side of Jacob Hermann's corner grocery store, a block from our house. The Jacob's Market entrance was on Locust Street, over a wooden sill worn down by years of neighbors stopping in for bread or milk or a package of his special ham loaf. Two doors on the side street led into Betty's house, and I knew the roses in Mrs. Hermann's rug as well as the violets in my mother's.

"Good idea," I said. "And we should practice so we can get here fast."

"Okay." Kay leaned over our orange-crate table and wrote "No. 1. Practice for invasion." She looked up. "What else?"

"Spies," Betty urged. "We need to watch for spies."

"Where do we look?"

"Everywhere. Could be anybody. You never know."

Betty explained. "They signal each other with lights. Or those dot, dot, dash keys. Or leaving a window shade a certain way. I heard that on the radio last week."

As Kay added "Watch for spies" to our list, she had second thoughts. "If we're going to do dangerous stuff like that maybe we need some boy members."

"Yuck," Betty and I said in unison.

"Nancy Drew works with one," Kay insisted. "How about Roger Haycraft? He's pretty smart."

"Roger's gone," I said, realizing for the first time it was true. "The air base took their farm. I guess they've moved to Bayard."

"Gee, kid," Betty said. "It must be twenty miles to Bayard. I guess you won't ever see him again."

"Probably not," I said with real regret. "Let's finish our list before we decide."

Enlarging the list was easy. We should learn to identify enemy airplanes. Make balls of tinfoil from gum and cigarette packages. Learn Morse code for signaling. Collect books and magazines for the Red Cross. Earn money to buy War Savings Stamps.

"What about Schnoz?" Betty asked. We looked at our mascot, the dust on his snout illuminated in the one shaft of sunlight reaching through the small, grimy window.

Kay said, "He could guard the club house. The army uses dogs."

"Yeah," I said. "And I bet we could train him to carry messages if we put a box or something around his neck. And maybe he could learn to track spies. That nose has got to be good for something."

Schnoz seconded the motion with another sneeze.

The next Tuesday I woke late and hurried downstairs, expecting to see the solitary place Mother now set for me in the breakfast nook before she left for work. It was there, along with my corn flakes (at least the war had liberated me from gagging on oatmeal lumps) but propped against the cereal box was the *Hiram's Spring Herald*. There was a red circle around one story and the word "Mine!" in Mother's hand. It was a first, I knew, her first front-page story. Had she graduated from women's club and church circles and PTA meetings? I was momentarily jealous.

But the story was a good one. The army was finally talking, as the town had been for weeks, about its new air field, and Mother's story was full of words like "urgent," "critical" and my old friend "crucial." The engineer in charge said the Hiram's Spring base was one link in a chain "vital to the country's defense." Then he added a new word to my war-time vocabulary. "We have a schedule to meet and it is imperative that we do not fall behind."

Imperative. I tried it on my tongue. If ever there was a word you could shake your finger to, it was "imperative." I tucked it beside "crucial" as one of my favorites.

But the runways were behind schedule. And—I knew now why Mother had got this story—the superintendent of schools had agreed to dismiss 100 senior boys from class half-days to help with construction. Applicants had to weigh at least 130 pounds and keep passing grades, but the work was "a valuable contribution to the war effort." At one dollar an hour, they would also make more money than they'd ever seen. I could imagine the cheering in the high school halls.

The engineer went on to say that if construction fell farther behind, the War Department would call on all the town's citizens "to pitch in and assist in the effort."

Compared to the excitement of building the air field, my classes did not seem at all crucial that day, but since I was neither sixteen nor a boy, I knew it was imperative I be there. Miss Dumbrowski and I immediately had a difference of opinion about the vital nature of learning my nines. After dinner I dropped a blot of ink and ruined a penmanship exercise. I waited impatiently for the afternoon dismissal bell.

When it came, I was free. But for what? Baby-stepping the three blocks home I imagined myself sweating shirtless in the sun, leveling concrete under the impressed eye of a beribboned major, triumphantly printing "V for Victory" on the edge of the completed runway. But even a self-imposed game of Simon Says couldn't last forever and eventually I trudged up our steps. I was immediately sorry I'd dawdled. A letter from Danny waited in the mailbox.

Oct. 11

Dear Folks,

Tell Sis not to feel bad. I'm still taking out the garbage. Only there's a lot more here than there. You wouldn't believe the size of their pots and pans. I got echoes from one I scrubbed. They really do peel potatoes, just like in the cartoons. But I never thought about who breaks the umpteen zillion eggs for chow. Not egg-zactly the way to start the day. Ha.

My bible is now the "Soldier's Handbook" and the army has a statistic for everything! The depth of a man is supposed to be 12 inches. Good luck if you're a deeper character. Our sarge is regular army and obviously thinks we're a hopeless bunch. (He says I walk funny! Calls me Bouncing Bobby!) He'll make soldiers *out of us or kill us trying. He makes it plain he doesn't care which.*

It sounded like the sarge and Miss Dumbrowski had a lot in common. I knew just how Danny felt.

> *There are all kinds of guys here—oil workers, ranch hands, car salesmen, bankers, teachers, store clerks. The first thing everybody wants to know is where you're from. One Italian guy from Chicago thinks Hiram's Spring is the funniest name he ever heard of and now the guys are calling me Hiram. I kind of like it. I'm getting to know one guy from Montana and one from Utah. We Westerners have to stick together.*
>
> *Classes are less "chickenshit" as the guys say—all the pesky rules and regs—and more things we really need to know, like map and compass reading.*

I reread that sentence. "chickenshit!" Another wonderful word, and this time one that made me laugh. Nines were chickenshit. Spelling lists were chickenshit. School and the army sounded more and more alike.

> *Finally got out on the rifle range. I'm glad I've had some experience with a gun. But this lefty can't use his "entrenching tool" (shovel to you) the way the sarge wants. Of course, if I had a chance to entrench the sarge, I could get the job done right quick. Ha.*
>
> *I thought I was in pretty good condition, but at night I'm just bone tired. And I thought Coach Fitzgibbon was tough! Some of the men are just barely hanging in there. Don't think they'll all make it. Sometimes at night you hear a fellow crying. One of the favorite commands is "As*

*you were." I don't guess any of us will ever be just
"as we were" again.*

Write soon.

Love,

"Hiram"

I thought of Danny's jaunty walk, his voice ringing through the house. Not even football practice had slowed him for long. It was hard to imagine him being tired. I hunted up my tablet and wrote an answer, telling him all about the Victory Club and how I felt about my nines.

Then, at loose ends, I picked up the new issue of *LIFE* magazine. Every week now I was poring over its countless pictures. Somewhere in the North Atlantic, a Canadian destroyer sank a U-boat. Then, the battle won, the crew slid the body of an eighteen-year-old sailor into the gray sea. On the homefront, Somerset, Kentucky, draped the county courthouse with flags for a speech by a hometown flier who'd downed eight Jap planes.

I spent a long time studying the week's "Pictures to the Editors." Under the headline "Getting Tough," the camera looked down on tiny figures struggling through an Army obstacle course. A white line traced their route—scaling a seven-foot wall, leaping hip-high benches, hand-walking down a suspended ladder, walking a narrow, head-high beam, up and down hills and ladders, over and under barriers, crawling through a long tunnel. They had to do it in two minutes. Off to the side one man knelt on all fours, his head hanging down between his shoulders.

So that was what Danny was doing. With sales clerks and cowboys and teachers. Soldiers crying at night, he said. I couldn't imagine soldiers crying. I couldn't remember Danny crying. Well, once, when he'd fallen out of the elm tree and landed on his shoulder. As I closed the magazine I wondered, does he feel like crying now?

My father wrote discouraging headlines. "Nazi Tanks Pound into Stalingrad.... Rommel Out-Duels the British in Egypt.... MacArthur Somewhere in New Guinea...." The Office of Civil Defense piled copies of a handbook titled "What Can I Do?" on a booth in front of J. C. Penney. More than 150 copies were gone in fifteen minutes.

Outside of town, field after field of potato vines lay curing under the sun, their round, brown tubers ready to be dug and gathered for market. And still hidden in valley soils, sugar beets responded to the cooling weather by stockpiling their energy in huge, white roots. Sugar content was nearing 15 percent. Harvest could not be delayed. Nearly two-thousand county students were working in the fields, and still farmers pleaded for field hands, loaders and haulers.

My father reported that the large air base at Kearney, Nebraska, was well under way and another at Alliance, sixty miles north of us, had received its first contingent of troops. But the Hiram's Spring field was behind schedule.

"I know it's important. But how can you possibly find the time?" Mother's rising tone pulled my attention from my Superman comic book.

"I can't find time. I'll just have to take it." My father's voice was equally sharp. "The Junior Chamber is recruiting two hundred businessmen to divide the swing shift between four p.m. and midnight. I'm supporting them editorially. I can't ask people to give their time if I'm not willing to give my own."

"But you're working fifteen-hour days as it is! You're going to kill yourself! And there's no way you can be out there between four p.m. and midnight, even if just for four hours."

"I know that," Dad said. "I'll just have to go to an afternoon paper for a couple of weeks."

"An afternoon paper!" I couldn't have been more shocked if Superman had stripped to his costume in front of Lois Lane. Mother was standing open-mouthed. Putting out afternoon papers, we'd heard often enough, was like warming up left-overs when you wanted something fresh and hot—like chewing yesterday's gum.

"Would you really do that?" Mother asked. "Can you really do that?"

"It won't be easy. But I think Dave and the shop crew will work with me. I'll probably cut the number of pages."

"That would help stretch the newsprint supply, anyway," Mother said.

"It won't help our budget any. But this is only until the emergency is over," Dad said emphatically. "The army says we may have the most critical labor shortage in the country right now, between harvest and the air field. They've scoured the country to find more workers. They've got to get the runways done before the ground freezes."

But November was less than two weeks away. Frost had long since blackened the hollyhocks and leaves dropped steadily from the elms. Lawns lay brown and dormant. We reached for jackets in the crisp mornings and welcomed their warmth again well before sunset. In western Nebraska we considered ourselves lucky if we didn't have to trick or treat in the first storm of winter. Each night the town looked east at the faint glow of the airfield lights, imagining the broad ribbons of concrete flowing out behind the concrete mixers, surging in front of the leveling machines, creeping across the potato fields, yard by yard. Citizens and soldiers alike stepped out to test the air before bedtime, wondering when deep frost would strike.

We knew now that the finished runways would be broad and long enough for the biggest bombers, that our satellite field would provide the final phase of training before crews were sent overseas. Here pilots, navigators and bombardiers would be welded into a team, learn to know and trust each other. As soon as the concrete was dry.

I didn't see my father for days at a time. A pile of dirty work clothes in the bathroom told me he'd been home for a few hour's sleep the night before. He and Mother seldom made it home at noon. Mother began to learn to run the Linotype.

One night I woke to the sound of their voices.

"He was so white. So white."

"Oh, how awful, dear. I'm so sorry."

"He wasn't much older than Danny. Had a wife and a baby."

"But you did everything you could."

"God, it was awful, Bess. Digging his head out of that big cement hopper. Trying to clear the powder out of his mouth and nose. I was afraid somebody else was going to get buried. The fire department had to pull him out with ropes. They used the resuscitator on him for an hour."

"Try not to think about it. Come to bed."

"No. I can't sleep. I might as well go down to the office and write it up."

I turned onto my stomach and tried to go back to sleep. The pillow kept pushing into my nose. I flipped over to my back. The sheet blanket wouldn't stay out of my face. Sometimes Danny had teased me and held me down until I thought I couldn't breathe. But he always let me up when I yelled "uncle." What if something held you down and never, ever let you up? Even if you were a big, strong man?

"Mom?" I whispered from her bedroom doorway. "How long does Dad have to work at the airport?"

"Sis? Are you awake? What's wrong?"

"Mom, am I too big to sleep in your bed for a little while?"

She rolled over and lifted the covers so I could crawl in. I snuggled into the incredible warmth, pulling it around me until the picture of white-faced death faded and I could sleep.

JAPS SHAVED HERE. NOT RESPONSIBLE FOR ACCIDENTS.

If you stood in the center of Hiram's Spring in 1942 and walked eight or nine blocks east, north or south, you found yourself in a farmer's field. One side of the road was town, the other country. From our school windows we could look across the playground, and where the gravel ended a green field began. That autumn I did not appreciate the clarity of such a boundary, expecting life would always provide such obvious choices. My eyes saw only black or white, you were either friend of foe, and every question had an answer.

"They're Japs! Look at the Japs!"

The words from Harvey McDougall broke my happy concentration on my nines. I'd just realized I could picture nine piles of chickenshit, or nine times nine, if I wanted, even when Miss Dumbrowski wasn't out of our classroom on her principal duties. I'd almost begun to enjoy multiplication.

I'd gotten off on the wrong foot with Miss Dumbrowski the very first day because of her ear lobes. Ever since I'd seen *Dumbo* the year before, I'd been obsessed with ears. The baby elephant who could fly with his ears had got me to looking. I'd never realized that my father's were oblong and flat against his head, as if he preferred

29

to stay a little out of reach. And Danny's slanted back a little, kind of playfully, and he could wiggle his left one when he wanted.

But Miss Dumbrowski's were the closest to Dumbo's I'd ever seen. They were like huge question marks, with the dot at the bottom stretching down a good inch, waggling there, just waiting to catch you in an error. Her hair, pinned in a tight gray roll around the back of her head, had not the slightest chance of hindering her ears' mission in life. The first time she called on me, I was busy trying to stretch my lobes as far as hers, and before I knew what I was saying I'd called her Miss Dumbo. Her mouth made the grim line I'd seen so often since.

Those clamped lips could immobilize the room without a word, and kept most of us subdued even when she left us for the office. But Smarvey Harvey McDougall was not most of us, and his words sent us rushing to the windows to see where he was pointing.

He was two years older than the rest of us and dumb as the dirt that encrusted his knuckles and elbows. I sighed a big sigh whenever Miss Dumbo called on him to read aloud, spoiling the one shining hour I found in the school day. When he beat me out for shortstop in our pickup ball games, I'd engraved his name on my list of foes.

I began a scornful "Who do you think you're kidd—" but had to swallow the word. In the field next to the playground, a few short, dark men bent over rows of beets that lay loose on the ground. Most of them wore stocking caps, but the faces beneath the bright caps looked like Hirohito's brothers. I was shocked into silence, but questions peppered the air.

"Where did they come from?"

"I bet they're Jap soldiers. Prisoners."

"Then where's their uniforms?"

"Yeah, where's the guards?"

They did not seem to have either. We were stumped.

"Jeez. They can really use those knives."

A broad blade flashed in the sun as one man speared a beet with its hooked end, pulled it against his knee and slashed off the green top. "Banzai!" Harvey laughed. "It's hari-kari in the beet field."

We all laughed, but Sarah Jane Rivers said, "I'd hate to meet one in a dark alley."

"Yeah. They'd slash through you just like they slash through the jungle all the time."

We all shuddered.

"And I wouldn't want to eat any of those beets."

"Yeah. I bet they got poison on that hook. I bet those beets are poison now."

"You don't eat beets, stupid." Harvey said. "They cook them and make sugar."

"Well then, I wouldn't eat the sugar." Sarah Jane pursed her lips. "My parents say they would not think of eating the food those Japs serve at the Liberty Cafe on Main Street."

I was only half listening. Sarah Jane was the only one in the fifth grade who wore a watch and was always bragging about the places her rich parents took her. Instead I was noticing that, in spite of all the cartoons and posters I'd seen of drooling Jap soldiers brandishing swords, some of these men were pretty awkward with their knives. Then a chill descended over the classroom and the shade was jerked down to cut off my view. Miss Dumbo had returned. It was back to chickenshit.

But I had a hard time forgetting the men in the beet field. They were like a piece of puzzle that wouldn't quite fit any place you tried. "Are they prisoners?" I asked Mother that night as she washed her hose in the bathroom sink.

"No, they're called evacuees."

"What's evacuees?"

"They lived on the west coast." She squeezed suds through the stockings. "The government thought that might be dangerous, so they moved them inland."

I reached for some bubbles and blew them from my hand. "Oh, I get it. Like the kids they evacuated from London because of the bombing."

"Not exactly. Don't put your hands in there. These are my last two pair and if they get ruined I'll have to start painting them on." She let out the soapy water and refilled the basin. "The children in England were moved to keep them safe. The Japanese were moved because everybody was afraid they'd help Japan." She swished the hose through the clear water.

"But they were right by the school! If they're dangerous, how come they give them beet knives?"

Mother's hands stopped swishing. "The farmers need workers very badly. I heard some of them volunteered to work the harvest so they would not have to go to the camp."

"So they're going to live in Hiram's Spring?"

"I don't think so. Probably with the farmer—just for beet harvest."

"You mean they'll move around like the Mexicans?"

"No. I think maybe these men are from a camp in Colorado or Wyoming. Nobody's saying much about it. They were moved there with their families."

I was trying to put it all together. "You mean they can't leave even if they want to?"

"No. There's a fence. And guards."

"Then they are prisoners."

"Oh, Sis." Mother rubbed her nose on the back of her hand. "Yes, I guess they are, in a way. It's hard to understand." She pulled the plug and began squeezing the stockings in a towel. "Some people think it's wrong." Her hands worked the towel. "I don't know what to think. It seems wrong, but the government says it's necessary for our country's safety." She shook the stockings out slowly. "In war, I guess that has to come first."

Suddenly I remembered what Sarah Jane had said. "Then how come they don't lock up the Japs from the Liberty Cafe? They could be poisoning people."

"Oh, Sis!" Mother sat back against the rounded edge of the bathtub. "That's different. The Japanese family that owns the Liberty has been in the valley since the 1920s. Billy Tanaka's a good friend of ours and when he served your father the day after Pearl Harbor, tears were running down his cheeks. He hates this war more than anybody—he has friends and family on both sides, but this country is his home."

"Then it's all right to eat there? Sarah Jane said—"

"I know," Mother cut in. "People are saying awful things. It used to be the busiest restaurant on Main Street, but since December seventh it's like a morgue half the time. And that," Mother stood up with a stern look on her face, "I know is wrong. They're fine, hard-working people."

"Then why are people afraid of them?"

32

Mother shook her head. "People are afraid of everything right now. When people are scared and hurt and angry, they don't know what to do and sometimes they make bad choices."

I went up to bed feeling that instead of one puzzle piece that didn't belong, I now had two.

Late Saturday afternoon I wove through downtown sidewalks crowded with farmers in town to do their weekly shopping. Families grouped around cars parked in front of Woolworth's, coordinating schedules, and a mother dragged a reluctant boy into Clem's Shoe Store. But only a few husky, sun-bronzed laborers lounged against the marble front of the First National Bank, and license plates from far-flung states had mostly disappeared. The first week of November was nearly gone, but only that morning had the *Herald* been able to report the last yard of concrete in the three long air base runways was poured and leveled.

My father had gratefully climbed out of his grimy work pants and returned the paper to a morning schedule, celebrating the completion—in an amazing forty-seven days—in a proud editorial. But he'd found space for a sidebar describing the sacrifice of a young laborer and his family, reminding his readers, "A man who falls victim on the home front instead of the battlefield receives no medals except the gratitude we owe him."

I pushed open the *Herald's* door, more than ready for Mother's promised treat—a hamburger at the Liberty Cafe to celebrate our return to a semi-normal life—to find Dad leaning over the teletype, calling out a bulletin. "Bess! Listen to this! We invade French North Africa tomorrow!" He slapped his hand down on the table in satisfaction. Then he added, "Thank God we're back on mornings!"

Shirley, Dad's girl Friday, jumped up from her desk with a shriek. My mother hurried to look over his shoulder and I squirmed my way under his arm, trying to read the capital letters racing across the face of the rolling paper.

"Dateline Washington, Nov. 7." Dad read snatches of copy over the racket of the machine. "Sunday, Nov. 8. Combined American and British forces...Both Atlantic and Mediterranean coasts... Lt. Gen. Dwight Eisenhower commanding... U.S. Navy and Air Force supporting... A major effort. . . Landings in Casablanca, Oran and Algiers."

33

"Africa? You mean like Tarzan's jungle with apes and crocodiles and snakes—?"

"No, Sis," Dad answered impatiently. "North Africa—it's mostly desert. Go look at my map. This is great! I've got to make room on the front page." He ripped the copy from the machine and strode to his desk.

I went over to the wall where he had put up several old *National Geographic* maps to follow the action of the war. A few pins in Britain stood against a European coastline solid with Axis thumbtacks from Scandinavia all the way to the Black Sea. More thumbtacks fanned out from Japan, sweeping down the China coast and east all the way into the Aleutians. Others obscured the tiny points of land in the Pacific they were intended to mark. My father had printed their names on slips of paper that stuck out from under the tacks.

Bataan, one said. Corregidor. Tulagi. I'd heard them often on the noon news—strange, dark, threatening words that evoked images of tangled jungles and Jap snipers lurking in coconut trees. They made my stomach queasy. On a few islands, fragile pins challenged the thumbtacks, but the great expanse of the northern hemisphere belonged to the invincible thumbtacks.

In a moment Shirley was beside me, tracing the northern coast of Africa with her Patriot-red fingernail. Thumbtacks stretched from Morocco on the west all the way across to Egypt on the east, where a few pins showed the British were beginning to push back. "Good news. At last!" she said. "We're fighting back. 'Praise the Lord and pass the ammunition!'"

By now the news had reached the composing room and Dave, Dad's pressman, ran in to look at the map. "Where is it? Where are they?" His ink-blackened finger followed mine. "It's about time we gave Hitler some of his own medicine!" His fist punched the air as he hurried back to the shop.

Excited, I reached for the pin box and planted three or four pins along the Mediterranean coast, where the names read Algeria, Tunisia, Libya. "Look out thumbtacks, here we come! Isn't it great, Mom?"

Mother stood waiting to run the next page of copy from Dad's typewriter to the Linotype. She was staring over my head at the map. She didn't seem to hear my question.

That night I dreamt Danny was swinging on an endless vine, sweeping grandly from tree to tree, giving Tarzan's triumphant yell. I could feel the rough texture of the vine, the brush of branches against his legs, the rush of the dank, heavy air, see the jumble of waffle irons, toy trucks and coal scoops rusting away in the debris of the jungle floor far below. Then the vine he grasped was turning into a snake, and Cheetah was swinging behind him screeching a warning and Mother's voice was calling up the stairway, telling me I'd be late for Sunday school.

In the muted, gray light of a November morning, I focused my eyes on the familiarity of blue nosegays marching up my wallpaper and the comfort of Grandma's pink sunbonnet quilt. The sound of my father's coal scoop rose clearly up the register, and I could hear Mother's mules tap across the kitchen floor. Gratefully, I shook myself back to the real world. But the dream seemed to color the whole week as we waited to hear what was happening in Africa.

Even Danny's letter, which came in the morning mail Wednesday, was not my usual antidote for the blues. Mother was reading it to Dad and me at dinner and she began strongly enough, with a chuckle in her voice at Danny's funny story about his weekend pass to Mineral Wells, otherwise known as the home of the famous *Crazy Water Hotel Radio Show*. How he and Montana Ted had finally found a place to sleep in some teacher's living room and how a soldier and his new bride had rented the spare bedroom and how the spare bedroom was between the living room and the bathroom and how they'd have to holler "comin' through" when they got desperate.

But her voice got serious when she read that the soldier expected to be shipped out "any day." And then she said "Oh, dear," and we could see she was reading ahead.

My dad finally reached over and took it from her. He scanned the page, glanced at me, then with a kind of "that's the way it is" shrug, read in a flat voice.

> *Things are getting serious here. Started training under fire. The sarge didn't need to keep reminding us those bullets zipping over our poor prone bodies were for real. It was pretty scary at first, in and out of trenches, with dynamite charges blasting out of the*

ground around you while you're trying to squirm under barbed wire on your back. Nothing but noise and smoke. Some guys froze.

One started to cry. I got my pants caught in the wire and had to tear them free. I ended up trying to slide on the back of my helmet, sweating like a dog, coughing like mad. Then I stopped to catch my breath and calmed down. Realized I needed to think about the course, not the bullets. The guys started helping each other through the wire and into the final trench.

When we got the whistle to come out, we all cheered and clapped. We did all right and it wasn't so bad after all. We felt kind of proud of ourselves.

I'm writing on Sunday as usual, our one day of rest. I'm developing callouses on my callouses, but feeling stronger every day.

My boots are finally broken in so they don't hurt when we march. And do we march, 20 miles or more, with everything we own on our backs. Can be 50 pounds or more. I feel sorry for the smaller guys and some of the city slickers. But we're all toughening up, and most of them manage to grit their teeth and get the job done.

Love,

Dan

Mother listened, chin in hand, her forefinger pressed against her upper lip. "'Love, Dan,'" she said, almost to herself. "Our boy's growing up, Hal."

"They all do, Bess. You know that. And it's time."

"Yes, I know. But this way? Why does it have to be this way?"

I opened the next week's issue of *LIFE* to read of a triumph. Boys from Iowa and Texas and the Bronx were showing the world how the American war machine could work. We were acting like

Americans again—doing things big, doing them right. We'd sent out a great convoy of 850 ships, and Casablanca, Oran and Algiers were ours. With Rommel retreating from Egypt into Tunisia, British General Montgomery was quoted as saying, "The *Boche* is completely finished." *LIFE*'s editors promised us the Allies were "In the delightful position of pushing the Germans into the sea."

Although nineteen hundred American men were dead or wounded, twelve thousand Germans had been captured. Having Axis prisoners was a new experience for the army and such numbers posed a difficult problem. Somehow they'd have to be fed and housed. Nobody knew yet how or where. It made me feel wonderful to see them with their hands in the air—Germans could lose, just like everybody else! I tore the picture out. I'd look at it every night, I decided, and have good dreams.

Then, as I flipped through the rest of the magazine, a colored painting in a full-page ad grabbed my attention. An empty noose hung from a pole silhouetted against a somber gray sky. "Try this for size. . ." the text read. Five people, one a woman, dangled from another scaffold in the distance. The noose would fit us all—men, women, old and young—I read. The Germans liked to use such nooses on conquered people. We could be next.

Our country could lose this war, it said in boldface type, unless we realize it is up to each of us to "do everything humanly possible, now, to save our necks." I felt a quiver in my stomach. My breath came fast and I slapped the magazine shut. But I could still see those five dangling bodies. What was happening? Were our soldiers the best—the bravest—about to push the Germans into the sea? Or were the Nazis on their way to hang us all? Who should I believe?

HE'S WATCHING YOU

I hurried in for dinner the next Monday noon to hear a banjo plinking and voices humming, "Juanita." Then a man was saying in honeyed tones, ". . . that because a woman is thirty-five, and more, romance in life need not be over . . .."

I pushed through the swinging door into the kitchen as a round-bottomed woman emerged from the depths of the refrigerator. I judged her to be thirty-five, and more. She straightened, which didn't take long as she didn't have far to go, and faced me with a smile dominated by two of the largest front teeth I'd ever seen. But the teeth were somewhat balanced by two rolls of hair, one pinned above each side of her forehead, and her face was friendly.

"You must be Mary Kathleen."

I hedged. "My friends call me M.K."

"Okay. M.K. it is. I'm Agnes."

The man's voice was talking about the brilliant, handsome lawyer Gil Whitney.

"Your mom wants me to help her out. Wanted me all day. But I told her. I can only come part time."

Now Gil and Helen were discussing somebody named Cynthia Carter Swanson Whitney. They didn't sound happy.

Agnes nodded toward the radio blaring in the living room. *"Romance of Helen Trent.* Wouldn't miss it." She straightened her apron and reached for some plates. "Here, you can set the table."

I distributed plates and silverware for three. My father always listened to the noon news on KGKY. My mother detested soap operas. This promised to be an interesting noon hour.

I heard them coming up the back steps. They opened the back door. Their eyebrows shot up to their hairlines.

"What's that thing doing on?" Dad directed the question at me, but I only tilted my head at Agnes. "It's her favorite program."

Helen was crying softly now, telling Gil they must part, that Cynthia Carter Swanson Whitney would never set him free.

My father looked as incredulous as Gil sounded. Mother was urging him through the kitchen. As soon as the door swung shut behind them they began to whisper.

"Now, Hal. We need somebody. It's taken me a month to find her. If she doesn't like it here, she can get a dozen other jobs. You know how independent people are nowadays."

"I can't help it. I won't have it."

"They say she works like a beaver."

"Funny they'd choose that particular simile."

The conversation died as Agnes brought in the food. Insidious gossip columnist Daisy Parker was spreading lies about Helen. The kitchen door swooshed shut again. Dad started to rise.

Mother put her hand on his arm. "She's supposed to be a good cook. Taste your meatloaf."

He tasted, took another bite and wavered for a long moment. But Helen was nobly assuming a lifetime of misery to buy Gil five minutes peace. He stiffened. "I tell you this is my house, and I'm not going to listen to that rubbish!"

As Mother shrugged in resignation, he stalked to the radio and reached for the dial. The music swelled as Helen and Gil put their sorrow away for another day. Dad got KGKY just in time to hear how the barrows and gilts were doing on the Omaha hog market. We ate in silence, while the Sons of the Pioneers gave us harmonious advice about drifting along with the tum-bul-ing tumbleweeds.

At that moment, Agnes poked her head in the door. "Time for *Our Gal Sunday.* Do you mind?" She didn't wait for an answer. She twirled the dial and we were hearing what chance a little girl from the mining camp of Silver Creek, Colorado, had of finding happiness as the wife of England's richest, most handsome—most unfaithful—lord. The chance seemed to be slim or none.

My father choked on his coffee. Mother began to laugh. "Maybe we'd better give Lend Lease a second thought. I'll talk to her, Hal. I promise. I'll see what I can do."

I think two things kept Agnes at our house that fall. My mother discovered another station gave forth *The Romance of Helen Trent* later in the day. And my father was loath to part with her meatloaf. So they tolerated *Our Gal Sunday* at 12:45. Dad could eat, have his news and be on his way back to work before Lord Henry Brinthrope could insert another dagger in the tender heart of the little girl from the West.

Talk of our first air raid blackout swirled from the barber shop to the drugstore counter to the corner grocery. Nine states were to go black simultaneously on December fourteenth, and the Hiram's Spring Civil Defense team would face its first test.

"I suppose you're busy getting ready for the big blackout?" It was Sarah Jane's mother, Mrs. Rivers, talking to Betty's mother as Mrs. Hermann weighed her head of cabbage on the thick, round glass of the Jacob's Market scale.

"We're to be blacked out at least twenty minutes," Mrs. Rivers went on. She's just like Sarah Jane, I thought, always telling people things they already know. "Everybody must be off the street. Cars must pull to the curb. And block wardens will be out checking for any speck of light." Her second chin quivered with excitement. "Even lighting a cigarette is forbidden."

As Mrs. Hermann rang up the cabbage, she cocked her head with a skeptical expression I'd thought she reserved for Betty's and my latest schemes. "Isn't that a little far-fetched? Nebraska getting bombed? I mean how could enemy planes get all the way over the ocean already, let alone clear to the middle of this country?"

"Well!" Mrs. Rivers said. "I don't know exactly how, but I know our government thinks it could happen or they wouldn't be making all these plans. I don't suppose people in London ever expected they'd have to sleep in subway tunnels to survive the night."

"But the German bombers are just twenty miles from England. I think it's a little farther to Hiram's Spring."

Mrs. Rivers drew in her chins and a third joined the original two. "I really don't think it's anything to joke about. They're about to open an air base five miles from where we stand, and my husband says that makes us a prime target."

I stared at her with new respect. The air base. I hadn't thought of that. Of course the Germans would want to bomb it!

Mrs. Rivers was going on. "I know I'm going to cut blackout curtains and make my front bedroom our 'safe room.' I've already got food, blankets and the flashlight and radio together in a box."

"Oh, just turn out the lights for twenty minutes," Mrs. Hermann said as she whipped open a sack with a flick of her wrist, a skill I'd long coveted. "We should make special curtains yet?" She gave a laugh. "And you got a toilet in your safe room, Mrs. Rivers, like they say you should? Or are you going back to a chamber pot, maybe?"

"Well, really!" Mrs. Rivers' face flushed. She dug in her black cloth coin purse for what she owed, dropped it on the counter, and snapped the little purse shut with a click that made me think it would not open again in Jacob's Market. Through lips nearly as tight as the purse top, she said, "I think it's important we all do our utmost to help the war effort. I'm going to make sure my house does not leak one particle of light. I'd think you'd want to do the same." She snatched up her sack of groceries and banged out the door, making the "Open" sign flip over to "Closed."

Mrs. Hermann sighed and shook her head. I gave her the dime I owed for the loaf of bread Mother needed and turned the sign back before I pulled the door shut behind me. I felt strange. Mother said Mrs. Rivers was a busybody who should M.Y.O.B. Mrs. Hermann was my best friend's mother. Yet I thought Mrs. Rivers was right. We were even having air raid drills at school now, learning to dive under our desks when the fire bell rang. Even Harvey McDougall jumped when that bell shrilled out during class and tried to fold himself under his desk. There was a big poster in the bank window that said "Remember Last December." Why didn't Mrs. Hermann see how important it was?

Betty seemed to understand. That Saturday morning the Victory Club prepared for the blackout. Kay's father was a block warden, and since he'd volunteered too late to get an official one, we spent an hour transforming a round, white ice cream carton into a passable helmet. But he said he wasn't wearing it and he didn't want to hear any more about it.

42

Frustrated that we were not old enough to be junior air raid wardens, we elected ourselves unofficial block messengers. We could cover three blocks, with Betty reporting to me, me to Kay and Kay to her father. Crossing streets during a blackout was forbidden, but we decided dogs probably didn't count. Schnoz could carry the messages between us.

However the dog did not seem to fathom the crucial nature of his duties. Try as we would, we could not find a box he did not immediately scratch off his collar. Then, fondling his long furry ears, I thought of a snood, the stylish fishnet bag even women who had never seen the inside of a factory were using to hold back their long hair. Kay borrowed one from her sister's dresser and we cornered the dog. In a moment a message was safely tucked in the white snood along with his ears. For about three seconds he gave us a soulful look that reminded me of Hedy Lamarr. Then, with us at his heels, he was racing wildly through the neighborhood trying to rub it off.

Schnoz never sat up on command without a treat in sight, but his desire to be rid of the snood evidently outweighed his principles. Agnes, out hanging up our wash, must have seemed his only hope. He panted to a stop at her feet and rose in supplication. We arrived just in time to see her collapse into the bushel of wet laundry.

Seeing both Agnes and wet clothes spilled over on the brown grass, I figured I was in trouble. But she only sat there laughing. "Looked just like Aunt Ida," she gasped, "With that nose and that net. Just like Aunt Ida." We made ourselves scarce before she recovered.

Leaving Schnoz for another day, we turned to other preparations for an attack. We had managed to round up three pair of swim goggles, a good supply of gauze bandage, adhesive tape and six empty toilet paper rolls. While Betty fashioned three gauze bags, I taped two paper tubes together for each of us and fastened them to the bottom of the bags. Kay taped the resulting product to the goggles and we pulled them on.

"What do you think?" I peered through my goggles at Betty.

"Swell, kid!" The gauze bag over her nose and mouth ballooned in and out with satisfying realism.

Kay surveyed us and said, "Try this." She tucked the end of her dangling cardboard hose under one arm.

"Perfect." I pronounced. "When we paint it khaki it will look just like the real thing. We'd better make one for Schnoz."

His sleep disturbed by the mention of his name, the dog opened one eye. Then both. Every hair on his spine came to attention and he was on his feet, barking like I'd never heard him bark before.

"It's just us, Schnoz," Betty comforted, her cardboard snout swinging past his nose.

His barks rose an octave. They multiplied as they bounced off the shed's walls and hammered our ears. Just then a ray of light fell into our corner and we looked up to see Kay's mother standing in the toolshed door. She peered into the gloom. "What's going—"

Evidently she found our gas masks as unsettling as Schnoz did. Her words ended in a scream that caromed around the tiny room. I thought she'd never run out of breath.

But when she did, she ordered us to "Get those morbid things off before you suffocate." Before we knew it, the Victory Club was summarily adjourned. Betty and I walked home through the November chill.

"What do you suppose got into her?" Betty asked.

I shrugged. "You got me. But I bet my mother would say she'd better quit listening to so much *Inner Sanctum.*"

I no sooner got in the door than I realized coming home was a big mistake. Agnes lay in wait; the basket of laundry had to be redone, and since she was sure I'd agree to "trade service for silence" she'd decided to wash all the curtains in the house while she had my help.

Capable as Agnes was, she had yet to master the use of our electric wringer. She was farm bred and used to a hand crank. She could keep me open-mouthed with tales of braving furious mother sows and watching Sunday dinner run headless around the chicken yard, but poking clothes into those grasping rollers without catching her fingers seemed beyond her.

Mother always used a piece of old broomstick to pick the steaming clothes from the washing machine and start them through the wringer to the first rinse tub. I watched Agnes hold the stick at arm's length and, like a squat d'Artagnan, try to thrust the wet curtains into the wringer. It easily parried the blow, stubbornly refusing to accept anything into its rollers. Then suddenly, while Agnes

44

shrieked, it ate both stick and fabric before springing its safety catch and releasing its relentless grip.

Not anxious to spend the whole afternoon in the basement, I took over as wringer stuffer. Actually, I always enjoyed a joust with those formidable rollers. Disdaining the stick, I liked to see how close I dared hold a corner of fabric. I usually made it more interesting by pretending the clothes I offered up were the bodies of my current enemies. Miss Dumbo had made many trips through the wringer—with satisfying squawks—and recently I'd taken indecent delight in squashing Harvey McDougall.

We were nearly finished, and I was putting Harvey through his final agony, when I heard the doorbell. I opened the front door to find two strange young men on the porch.

"Are you moving soon?" one asked. "We'd sure like to rent the house."

"Moving?" I stared at him blankly.

"Yeah. We need someplace to live and we hope you'll give us a chance. Doesn't matter what it costs."

I went back to the last word I'd understood. "Moving?"

"Sure." The other one spoke up now. "We saw your curtains down and figured you must be leaving soon."

When my response was, "Leaving?", he evidently despaired of our achieving intelligent conversation and began talking over my head to Agnes, who had puffed up behind me. When she made it clear no departure was imminent, their faces fell. But they didn't give up.

"Then how about renting a room? Have you at least got an empty bedroom?"

Agnes and I looked at each other, seeing Danny's empty room and unused bed.

"We're defense workers out at the canning factory. We can pay real good."

"I'm not the lady of the house," Agnes said. "You'd have to talk to Mrs. Greggory."

They said they'd be back.

When my parents came home for supper, Mrs. Greggory did not seem to hear my question. Instead she posed questions of her own in a rising voice. "She washed my sheer living room panels in the machine?"

"Like I said. All the curtains. That's why—"

But I was talking to air as Mother disappeared down the basement stairs. I heard a series of moans and the next half hour she crawled around the living room, hanging wet curtains and sliding metal rods into the hems, with fervent prayers that the weight of the hem rods would restore the panels to some semblance of their former selves. I thought there was a good chance, as they were only about a foot short, but my mother didn't seem hopeful.

When she joined us at the table, my father was the one who reopened the subject of renting Danny's room.

"We talked about this before," Mother said, laying down her spoon.

"You ought to think about it again," he said. "Between the air base and defense workers, people are plain desperate for places to live. We ought to help out. It's the practical thing to do."

"Well, I won't think about it. Not for a minute."

I said, "But it's for the war effort, Mom."

She stared at me, then at my father. "I can't believe you two. That's Danny's room and it's going to stay that way. If he gets home on furlough, his room is going to be right there ready for him."

"We don't know if that's going to happen," my father said. "We could put his things in the attic, where they'd be safe until he wants them again."

"You mean you'd want strangers in our house?"

"Want? No, it's not what I'd choose. But people need a place to sleep. And frankly, we could use the extra cash."

Mother winced, but she said, "I'm not so hard up I'd sell my son's room."

I saw Dad stiffen. "That's not fair, Bess."

Mother relented. "I didn't mean that. It's just that—I just can't put strangers in his room." She leaned toward him. "Can't you understand? I've got to believe he will walk in the door someday and hang his pants on the closet doorknob and flop down on his bed and—I want his room to be there—ready—just like it's always been."

"Dear," my father said after a moment, "you won't tempt the gods by letting someone else use Danny's room." When Mother did not respond, he drained his coffee cup and stood up. "But if it bothers you that much, we'll forget about it."

That evening on my way to bed I stopped in the doorway of Danny's room. I could almost see him sprawled on the brown chenille spread studying his chemistry, a bowl of popcorn beside him, stopping to lob an occasional kernel at the ceiling light. A picture of the high school football team crowded the collection of small bronze horses on his bureau top, but the room never really changed. I decided my mother was right. I didn't want strangers in Danny's room. It was like not telling a bad dream before breakfast. You couldn't risk making it come true.

REMEMBER PEARL HARBOR

"Why don't I drive up on the Bluff?" Mother asked as she cleared the supper table. "It's the best way to see the whole valley."

Dad took out his little mother-of-pearl pocket knife and began to dig at the black line under his nails, the only hint that he spent long hours in the shop, where you could nearly breathe the ink and grease. He finished one hand before he spoke. "I guess that would work. You could call me from the nearest phone."

To be on top of Scotts Bluff National Monument during the blackout!

"—but I can't let you do it. I don't want you running around like that. Especially in a blackout."

"What else can we do? There's no room in the Civil Defense observer plane." Mother carried a load of dishes to the sink.

"It's either the roof of the hotel or the monument. You can get a better look from the Bluff, but if you go up yourself, you'll have to drive clear back before you can start writing."

I began sending Mother mental messages, but she was concentrating on Dad. "It's the only thing that makes sense. You'll need Frank at the control center and Jerry to drive the streets. You need to be in the office to take their calls and pull the story together. I

49

can't run the Linotype like you can, or set the heads, but I know I can do a good job of reporting. And if you send Dave up there, he'll tell you the lights went out and it got dark."

Dad failed to suppress a grin, but he said, "No, it's too dangerous. The park rangers close that road at sunset."

"I'll get special permission. They just don't want idiots wandering around up there and falling into the badlands."

I took over clearing the table so she wouldn't be distracted. She sat back down and faced my father. "I took a load of Camp Fire Girls up there last summer. Remember?"

I turned up the power of my message sender and filled the dishpan without being asked.

"And Sis could go along to help. She certainly can't stay here alone."

I was halfway up the road!

Then my father said, "Sis! What help could she be?" He blew out his breath in frustration. "Lord, I miss Danny."

I bit my lip. I knew he was right. Danny would have been real help.

"There's not much point in wishing for the impossible." Mother's voice was level but her words were clipped.

My father was silent. I could sense Husband Greggory wrestling with Editor Greggory. I was almost done with the silverware before I knew who had won the struggle. The victor did not sound pleased with his success.

"All right," he said at last. "You can give it a try."

My mother and Mollie were not close friends. Perhaps the Ford felt a woman who had to sit on a pillow to peer between the steering wheel and the dash lacked authority. And Mother was more apt to call Mollie "that dratted car" than the fond name Dad had bestowed. Her hands tightened on the wheel as she braked at the crossbar blocking the road up the Bluff.

At our honk, a figure stepped up to the car; I was surprised to hear a woman's voice. "This is highly irregular, you know. You'll have to take complete responsibility."

"You explained that," Mother said. "But these are irregular times. Did you ever dream we'd be worried about air raids in the North Platte Valley?"

"Not even in my nightmares." The woman chuckled ruefully.

50

Mother lowered her voice. "To tell you the truth, I never expected to be a reporter. Did you ever expect to be wearing that uniform?"

The ranger leaned on the window frame. "No, I hoped maybe someday I could prove what I could do. But I really expected to spend my career behind a typewriter."

Mother laughed. "Well, for me the typewriter beats the kitchen sink. And I'm still proving to my husband that I'm up to the job."

"I know what you mean." She stood back as if she'd made a decision. "You can go ahead. But be careful. Stay well back from the edge. It's pitch dark up there."

She opened the barrier and as we pulled away she called, "Tell you what, when you get down you can use my phone to call in your story."

The road climbed gradually, swinging to the left in a broad curve, but as I sat up on my knees and looked back the museum lights were already far below. Then Mollie's small headlights picked out the mouth of the first tunnel.

"Honk!" I pleaded and Mother obliged with a long ooga-ooga that echoed nicely in our wake.

Even before we were out of the tunnel we were curving back right, reversing our direction, and when we emerged we could see the lights of Mitchell Valley. We were on the west side of the Bluff, climbing faster now and nearly to the second tunnel. Mother ground the gears a little as she pulled the shift back and searched for first gear. Dad always drove when they were together and recently Danny had been eager to have the wheel. Mollie's motor whined in the quiet night.

The headlights probed the narrow, curbed road, finding the black hole the second tunnel cut in the sandstone cliff. The engine worked harder as we climbed higher, ooga-ed through the final tunnel and felt out the steep curves. On our right our lights barely lit the buff-colored cliff side laid up in layers through eons of time. I knew there was nothing but space on the left side of the road, and I was glad we were on the inside for now.

Only after we pulled to a stop against the log barrier in the parking area did I realize how cold and dark the night was. I grasped the flashlight in mittened hands and Mother patted the pocket that held her notebook and pencils. As soon as I put a foot out on the running board I felt the cold north wind. It brought tears to our eyes when we faced into it to reach Observation Point. I hunched my shoulders and played turtle to protect my ears.

We lost the trail several times when it crossed smooth rock and finally decided just to head north for the rim. We knew we were there when the lights in the valley opened at our feet. We felt out the low boulders that marked the edge.

"Shine your light on my watch."

"Ten to nine. Ten minutes 'til Zero hour." I began to jig with excitement.

Mother helped me see the traffic on Highway 26, which wound through Hiram's Spring and on west. The sugar factory silos, the Platte bridge, the seven-story hotel on Main Street just a block from the railroad tracks, even the lights at the air field east of town could be identified with a little effort.

"It's all laid out," she said quietly. "It would be so easy."

I was thinking how clean and sparkling it all looked, the street lights twinkling in tidy squares, when those squares blinked off and on, off and on, off and on. It was just the way Captain Easy had signaled in last month's comic strip when he'd proved the glamorous Liska was a Jap spy.

"That's the five-minute warning," Mother said. "Now let's listen for the fire whistle."

I thought of Kay's father, out patrolling his block, wearing her white stocking hat for a helmet. I imagined Betty, curled warmly against Schnoz on the potato sacks in the stockroom of the store. (Mrs. Hermann had realized they already had a well-stocked safe room, as long as nobody drank too much for supper.) I pictured Mrs. Rivers and Sarah Jane huddled in her frilly bedroom, black curtains tightly drawn, even the light of radio dial, tuned to the special blackout broadcast, obediently covered.

"Hold your flashlight so I can make some notes," Mother said.

We waited. I un-turtled my ears, straining to hear the whistle. Usually when the whistle blew, everybody tuned to KGKY so the Nelson Insurance Agency could tell us where the fire was. Tonight valley radios would carry the voice of General Uhl, explaining the need for the blackout.

We heard nothing. Mother pulled back her headscarf, exposing her ears to the wind. Then lights began blinking out. One after another they disappeared—the hotel, the bridge, the highway traffic. It was if the wind were blowing out Hiram's Spring, a puff at a time.

Then we began to hear something. But it was not the fire whistle. What we finally heard—ever so faintly when the wind was right—was the dogs howling, first one then another, country dogs picking up town dogs' protest and spreading it down the valley. The blackness appeared to be unbroken.

"How eerie," Mother whispered. "It's like the town disappeared. I don't suppose the valley's been this black since the days of the Sioux." She shivered and re-tied her scarf.

"Where do you suppose Dad is?" I whispered back.

"Probably on top of the hotel." Then, "Why are we whispering?" We both giggled.

We heard the drone of a single engine plane and I picked out its lights. It had to be the observer plane. It passed over our heads, then disappeared to the south.

"Mom," I leaned toward her ear. "Do you think we could really get bombed?"

She reached for me and pulled me close. "I don't think so, dear."

"But Sarah Jane said enemy planes could come up from Mexico. Or down from Alaska. That they'd want to hit Nebraska because we're clear in the middle of the country and it would scare everybody to death."

"That's just a rumor, Sis."

"But it makes sense."

Mother hesitated. "It does make some sense. That's the trouble with rumors. The Japanese are not far from Alaska. There are German sympathizers in South America and probably in Mexico. And it would be a great blow to American morale—people all over the country would be terrified. But that doesn't mean it can really happen. I don't think we need to worry about it."

She squeezed my shoulders and let me go. "Now, try to hold the flashlight under my coat so I can write a note or two."

We knelt and huddled together, trying to find a position that wouldn't leak light. As we jockeyed around I suddenly stepped back into a hole. I threw my arms wide to catch my balance and the flashlight flew from my mittened hand. Its light inscribing wobbly circles, it rolled toward the edge of the cliff. I threw myself after it.

"Sis!" Mother screamed. She dived for my foot and caught it in time to pull me down. I fell heavily on my stomach on a boulder, my arms dangling in space.

The flashlight rolled and bounced down several feet, finally wedging itself in some rocks on the steep slope below. Incredibly, it was still burning.

We picked ourselves up. I rubbed my rib cage and tried to pull some air back into my lungs. Mother sat massaging her right wrist.

"I've got to get it," I said.

"Don't be silly. I won't let you do it."

"But it will spoil the blackout!"

"I don't care. You're not going down there."

I glared at the offensive light. It seemed incredibly bright. I was sure the whole town could see it. "I've got to do something! I can't be the one who ruins the blackout! What will Dad say?"

"Sis, it's only a test. Not an air raid. It's not that important."

But I could hear the observer plane returning. What could I do? In the movies somebody would shoot it out. I grabbed off my mittens and groped around on the ground. I pricked my numb fingers on pine cones, a bristling yucca. Then I jammed my middle finger painfully against a rock. The plane was turning toward us.

I grabbed the rock in both hands and ran toward the edge.

"Sis!" Mother yelled again, as I spraddled myself on the boulder.

But I was listening to the plane. I held out the rock, sighted carefully and let it drop. "Bombs away!" I yelled, but it was more like a prayer.

My aim was not perfect. The rock bounced close to the light and hit it only a glancing blow. But it was enough to flip it from the crevice and send it tumbling on down the cliff side. I was satisfied not even a Jack Armstrong flashlight could bounce that many times and keep burning.

Just then the plane swooped low over our heads. In spite of myself, I ducked down beside my mother. "Help me up," she said, "it's almost time for the lights to come back on."

I reached to grasp her right hand but she gave a little cry and offered me her left instead. "What's the matter?"

"I guess I hurt my wrist. Help me watch the lights. I want to see how long it takes to get them on again."

It wasn't long. It looked as if the whole community stood with hands on light switches, waiting for the all-clear. The street lights flickered on, cars began to move, the hotel grew against the sky, floor by floor. I could imagine doors opening, people running outside, matches flaring for cigarettes.

"That's it. Let's go. I want to get to the phone as fast as I can."

We hurried back towards the car, trying to run in spite of the darkness, stumbling on the rough surface, dodging around pine trees. When we reached Mollie we jumped in and Mother pushed the starter button with her foot. The motor turned over and died. She tried again. No luck.

"Listen here, Mollie! You're not that cold."

The motor coughed to life. But when she tried to shift into reverse she let out a cry of pain and grabbed her wrist.

"Is it bad?" I was frightened.

"Worse than I thought. I don't know how I'm going to drive."

I thought about the road down and suddenly the monument headquarters seemed a long ways away. The wind rocked the Ford. I tried to forget how cold I was and think.

"Maybe I could signal the plane. I know S.O.S."

"I don't suppose the plane will be back over. We better think of something else."

All I could think of was how alone we were and how it was all my fault. "In the morning I could make a signal with rocks."

"It's a long time until morning. We'd freeze by then. But don't worry. I'm sure the ranger lady will come up to look for us eventually." She cradled her wrist against her chest. "It's just that I hate to let your father down."

The wind seemed eager to scour us off the promontory. I was afraid I was going to cry. I tried to think what Danny would do. "We took first aid in Camp Fire to get our Victory badge. Would it help if I wrapped your wrist?"

"It might. Do you think you could?"

"Sure," I said, not sure at all. "We practiced with a scarf."

She pulled hers off and I set to work. I had to redo it twice, but the third time I finished the square knot I was satisfied.

Mother pushed in the clutch and gingerly tried the gear shift. She stifled a moan. "I can't believe this is happening," she said. Then in a stronger voice, "I'm not going to let it happen."

She told me to put my hand on the gear knob. "Do you think you can shift if I guide your hand? You move them in the shape of—. "

"A capital 'H'!" I yelled. "I remember from when you taught Danny."

"Sis, sometimes you surprise me."

We practiced the pattern a couple of times, trying to coordinate clutch and gear. Then I ground my way into reverse and we bucked away from the parking log. Mother strained to turn the wheel with one hand and I reached to help. I managed to find first gear and we lurched onto the road and started down.

"We may just leave it in first," Mother said. "I don't think it could hurt anything." She began to use her right elbow to help turn the stiff wheel.

I thought of the drop just beside us and swallowed hard. "Can't we use the other side of the road?"

"Good thinking, Sis." The driver's-side tires rumbled over the warning bars in the center of the road. I sat on my knees, my eyes just above the dashboard, staring out each curve and willing the car to turn. It seemed forever before we were through the first tunnel. "We're not too fast, but we're steady." Mother chuckled.

She was laughing! I was seeing pictures of Mollie careening off the road—crumpled in the bottom of a ravine—impaled on a rock. I was imagining what Dad would write in my obituary. "Careless Girl Causes Disaster."

Then we were safely through the second tunnel. The car seemed willing to hug the cliff. "We're a pretty good team," Mother said.

I began to breathe. We entered the final tunnel and I helped Mother make the turn. We swung too wide—back across the divider bars—and the tires screeched, but we made it through. I scratched out the headlines in my mind and began to rewrite. "News Duo Survives Scary Ride." "Brave Girl Rescues Mother."

By the time we reached the headquarters, we were racing along in second gear. Mother got Dad on the phone and filed her story. After the lady ranger checked Mother's wrist and called my wrapping very professional, we decided we could drive on home.

Too keyed up to sleep, we waited up for Dad. He was excited, too. "One family was warned about sparks from a chimney and a couple of smokers got bawled out," he said. "But only one house left lights on, and they were out of town. And guess what? We had a blackout baby born four minutes after the fire siren blew."

We were eager to tell our story, too. Once Mother had reassured Dad her injury was not serious, she launched into our tale. She was stingy with information about exactly why she fell, but she re-counted every detail of the trip down.

"Well, I'll be damned," was all my father said. Then, "Sure wish you could have found that flashlight. Not much chance of replacing it with the war on."

IS THIS TRIP NECESSARY?

I gave the Victrola a final crank and we watched the little cardboard record revolve. When the scratching gave way to voices, a raucous, two-voice chorus of "I'm Dreaming of a White Christmas" filled the corner of the dining room.

"What on earth?" Mother said.

"Sounds like they're drunk," Dad said.

Then a strange man's voice, choked with laughter: "From the glittering recording studio of the Crazy Water U.S.O. in the heart of downtown Mineral Wells, we present special guest star PFC Hiram Greggory, otherwise known as—tah-tah—Bouncing Bobby!" There was a grunt of breath suddenly expelled and a whispered, "All right, you guys. Get out of my hair."

Then Danny's voice. Mother's fingers tightened on the walnut cabinet edge. "Hi, Mom and Dad. Hi, Siseroo. How y'all doin'? What do you think of this? I'm a recording star! The preceding so-called music was courtesy of my two so-called buddies, Montana Ted and Tone-deaf Chuck from Utah. Hope it didn't spoil your dinner."

He cleared his throat. "I'm sorry it's been so long since I've written, but we were out on maneuvers and I've been too tired to think, let alone write. Hope you haven't worried."

"Huh!" Dad said. I looked at him in surprise.

Danny's voice sobered. "Maneuvers were pretty rugged. They try to give us a taste of combat and they really do it up brown. We even chalked up some casualties." Then a hurried, "But I'm in really good shape. And eating plenty, Mom.

"Anyway," there was a pause, "I wanted to make you a record because I'm afraid I won't get home for Christmas." Mother, who had been leaning eagerly forward, seemed to shrink back into herself.

"Hope you don't feel too bad, Mom. I'll miss you all as much as you miss me. But I'll have some laughs with the guys and try to call home. Guess I don't have much more time. His words became rushed. "I miss you. Take care. And don't forget—"

There was rustling and then three voices were singing "We're dreaming of a white Christmas...." And then a sweet, vibrato whistle was soaring in and out above the melody as the other voices blended in harmony.

". . . sleigh bells in the snow . . ." A tear dropped on Mother's middle knuckle and rolled toward her narrow, silver wedding band. "May your days be merry—"

The recording cut off abruptly. The needle revolved around the center post in a drunken circle. Finally my father reached over and lifted it off.

Christmas without Danny. It seemed unthinkable. We'd already mailed his presents, just in case. But I'd believed all along he'd really be home. It was three days before I could listen to the record again. After I did, I tried to tell my mother how it made me feel good and bad at the same time.

"They call that bittersweet feelings," she said.

"You mean like lemonade?"

"Not quite. That's sour and sweet. Sometimes sour can almost taste good. Bitter never does."

I set my mouth for a bittersweet Christmas.

But Mother said we shouldn't feel sorry for ourselves. "I think it's time we counted our blessings," she said briskly about a week before Christmas. "After all, Danny isn't overseas. He isn't lying wounded in some hospital. We're really very lucky and we ought to act like it."

My father looked up from the *Saturday Evening Post* and said, "You were out interviewing Mrs. Reynolds today, weren't you?"

"Yes. It was so sad. She's just twenty-three and has heard nothing from her husband since Bataan fell. Yet she's still writing him every day. She says it's keeping the faith, believing someday, somewhere he'll get the letters and know she never forgot him, not even for a day."

Mother stood up abruptly. "She made me ashamed of being upset about Christmas. We need to think of what we can do for somebody else."

What we could do, it developed, was make Christmas decorations for the downtown recreation center the town was fixing up for the airmen. The day before Christmas I was on the sixty-third loop of my seventeenth paper chain when the phone rang.

Mother's face paled when she answered. "Long distance?"

Then she relaxed and began to beam. "It's Danny," she mouthed across the room. "Yes, dear. You're sure you're all right? Can you? Can you really?" Then she forgot about mouthing and fairly shouted. "He's got a pass! He's coming home!"

Then, "Oh, just three days? Not Hiram's Spring? To Denver? I see. Yes, of course. We'll be there. Union Station. About eight o'clock tomorrow? Yes, yes. We'll be waiting."

By now I was at her elbow. "To Denver? We're going to Denver to see Danny?"

She threw her arms around me. "Yes! I can't believe it! I don't know how, but we're going. I've got to call your father!"

When my father came in, he proved a tougher sell. "I know how you feel. But how can we do it? We wouldn't have a prayer of finding space on a bus or train. And with gas rationed now we can't drive. It's a 440-mile round trip. We'd need—let's see—at fifteen miles a gallon—" he stared at the ceiling, "at least thirty gallons. At an absolute bare minimum."

He rubbed his forehead, frowning. "We have about nine in the car. We'd have to use all our ration coupons for this month and January. We can't use up all our gas—how can we cover the news? There's just no way we can do it."

I quit breathing. When my father said "no" there was no appeal. But Mother was speaking again. "We can walk until February. Or ride Sis' bike. Or share rides with somebody. I'll worry about that later. We're going!"

"Now, Bess. Be reasonable. I've got to be able to get to the county courthouse—to the air base. It would be an irresponsible thing to do."

Mother's face had a look of desperation. "How can you be so unfeeling? Your son is arriving in Denver Christmas night. Do you want him standing there alone on that platform looking for his family?"

"Of course I don't," Dad snapped. "But some things are possible and some things are not. Why didn't you stop to think?"

"It was not a thing that needed thinking! I'll be there if I have to hitchhike!" They stared at each other in silence. Then Mother's face began to crumble. "Can't you see? It's that we don't know if—when—Danny might get home again."

Dad turned away from her. When he turned back, he said quietly, "I care, too, you know, just as much as you do. I just see no way we can do it."

Mother, her gaze on the floor, said hesitantly, "I've heard the station out by the cannery will take a few dollars in lieu of a ration coupon. Couldn't we just this once—"

My father closed his eyes. His face looked drained. When he opened them he said, "I can't do that. It's just not right. I can't buy gas on the black market, even for Danny."

The sound of the phone broke the gloomy silence. Mother answered in a tight voice. Then a series of "yeses" climbed the scale until she hung up and turned, her face light with hope.

"That was Dora Johnson, the long distance operator. She heard what Danny said and knew we'd have a problem. She asked around the office and already has a coupon for four gallons. I'm going to call the church telephone chain."

"Use other peoples' coupons? That's not exactly legal."

Mother fixed Dad with a steady stare. "Maybe not. But who would it hurt? I intend to do it, with you or without you."

A suspense-filled hour later between neighbors and the Methodist ladies, we had coupons for twenty gallons. Dad, looking resigned, pulled out the road maps and spread them on the dining room table. Again I was afraid to breathe while his Eversharp pencil traced routes and jotted down mileage. Finally he sat back.

"Well, it's certainly risky. We'll have to use half our January ration. But if we take the dirt cut-off to Kimball, go through Cheyenne, and into Denver by Brighton Road, we should be able to make the station. But it means no running around Denver. We'll have to stay downtown."

I realized he was saying "we'll." Mother gave him a fond smile. "I'll sleep on a bench in the station, if I have to. We can worry about that later."

"There's still the tires," Dad warned. "I doubt they have 450 miles left in them."

But Mother was already pulling Dad's rounded, leather Gladstone bag out of the closet and tugging the top open.

The sky was still black when I gulped down breakfast the next morning. My stomach had the tight, fluttery feeling that usually meant it was June and we were starting for vacation at Grandma's house. But this was Christmas Day and my father was pushing back the garage doors to head for Denver.

Luckily the valley was experiencing a typically snowless Christmas week. With Dad conscientiously observing the thirty-five miles-per-hour Victory Speed Limit, the sun was highlighting the crests of the Wild Cat Hills by the time we wound up Stagecoach Hill. I snuggled down in the back seat. How much had Danny changed, I wondered? Would he be too grown up and no fun anymore?

We bumped off the paved road onto gravel, a narrow country road that climbed and dived through swells of prairie. Finally we turned west at Kimball to travel along railroad tracks that divided endless brown grasses waving in the wind. Snow swirled in white sculptures along the fence lines and across the borrow pits. I watched the delicate shadows play across the drifts, feeling like a bird skimming over the top of the world.

Then a dark spot in the distance grew into a locomotive and gray smoke billowed against blue sky. I sat up to wave to the engineer, then realized I had never seen such a train. Open flat cars trailed the gray passenger cars, and they were loaded with Jeeps, trucks and big guns on wheels. I caught a glimpse of a few soldiers standing guard with rifles, their faces red with cold, long coats whipping in the wind.

"Troop train," Dad said. "This is the main line."

"On Christmas Day!" Mother said. "Bless their hearts. God keep them."

Cheyenne streets were nearly deserted as we rumbled through. "Want to gas here," Dad said. When we found an open truck stop Dad counted out a few of the precious coupons. A young woman came out to man the pump. She glanced at our "A" sticker on the windshield and raised her eyebrows when Dad handed her loose coupons.

My father looked uncomfortable. Was she going to refuse them? Or turn us in to the police? I couldn't let it happen. "We're going to Denver to meet my brother Danny at Union Station because he's only got a three-day pass and can't come home," I said in one breath.

She peered at me over Dad's shoulder, leaned forward to look at Mother and said, "Well, I guess you're in a hurry then." She began to fill the tank.

As we headed south Mother and I tried to play "I Spy," but it was difficult to think of things to spy in the empty prairie. Greeley and the towns along the South Platte were scarcely more interesting, being much like home, complete to the penetrating, sour stench of beet pulp that always made me gag when we passed a sugar factory after harvest. I was trying to hold my breath past the Brighton factory when I saw a line of small men boarding a bus.

"Look, Mom! Japs! Just like in the beet field."

"Japanese, please," Mother corrected me, before turning to my father. "Are they working in the factories, too, Hal? The men from the relocation camps?"

"Must be," Dad answered. "I suppose they're up from that camp they call Amache down on the Arkansas River. Or maybe from Heart Mountain in Wyoming."

I was reminded of something that had bothered me ever since Mother had explained about the evacuees. "What about the little kids? Can't they ever get outside the fence?"

Mother sighed. "I don't think they can now, Sis. But I guess the Japanese who are citizens—and maybe even the aliens—who can prove they're loyal will be allowed to join family or friends who live in states away from the coast."

"Are aliens enemies? Like the Axis?"

"Not necessarily. They're just foreigners."

"So they could be allies?"

Mother nodded. I pondered that. "Why don't they just say the Pledge of Allegiance?"

Dad gave a snort which told me I'd said something dumb. But Mother just said, "It's a little more complicated than that, Sis. But working to help the war effort ought to count in their favor."

"Next stop Union Station!" Dad's voice held excitement I seldom heard and I forgot all about the puzzling Japanese as I pressed my nose against the side window. A welter of streets led us under and over railroad tracks, then into canyon-like streets between tall buildings. I stared with delight as we passed trolley cars running on tracks in the middle of the brick streets, their black power rods snapping along the electric line above.

When we pushed through the doors into the station, I caught my breath. The late afternoon sun shone through a row of great windows arching high above and finally came to rest in the biggest rooms I'd ever seen. Rows of giant-sized benches stood in two sections, like a church. They looked long enough to hold every Longfellow fifth-grader.

Yet nearly every square inch of floor space was already taken. Elderly couples, women with babies, teen-aged girls in saddle shoes, ladies in furs, sailors, Marines and countless soldiers stood in lines, sat on suitcases, leaned against walls, even sprawled sleeping in the corners. Mother grabbed my hand. "How will we ever find Danny?"

Even Dad seemed nonplused. But he guided us through the mob to a spot near the telegraph office. "You stand here. Don't move. I'll see what I can find out."

I was dizzy from watching people by the time Dad materialized out of the crowd. "Bad news, I'm afraid. There's been a mix-up somewhere. Danny's train gets in about eight a.m. tomorrow, not tonight."

Mother stared at him. "Ye Gods! Tomorrow morning? I know I said I'd sleep on a bench, but I never imagined it would be like this. What on earth will we do?"

THESE ARE THE THINGS WE'RE FIGHTING FOR

Dad pushed his hat back on his head and sighed. "Well, if you don't mind staying here alone, I'll check around and see if I can find us a hotel room."

We wandered, watching for a seat. We'd worked our way past the lunch counter when I saw a couple stand up. "Here, Mom!" I shrieked.

I dived over a suitcase to claim the spot, but I'd forgotten I wore galoshes. I fell short and my hands slapped down on the bench with a resounding whack. Embarrassed, I spit on my stinging palms and looked around, but no one seemed to have noticed my fall. We sank down gratefully. There was nothing to do but watch and wait.

As the crowd washed around us, first one way and then another as trains arrived and departed, I watched the procession of shoes—work shoes, platform pumps, cowboy boots, army boots, black overshoes, high-topped size threes—come and go. I looked into countless faces, all of them strangers, preoccupied, distant. I began to feel we sat alone, disconnected, nameless. I started to imagine we might be invisible, Mother and I, sitting there in our winter coats and galoshes, that if I cried out no one would hear me.

A brown push broom swept across my view, tapped out its load, returned for another stroke. Then it paused. "Your boy no come yet?"

He was round and rumpled, his overalls smudged with dirt, but he pushed his broom with muscled arms. We looked up in surprise at his question, so used to anonymity that we felt as if someone had suddenly knocked on the door of our private cubicle of space.

"I see you and little one waiting. Your boy no come?" He was gazing earnestly at my mother.

She blinked herself back to the present and made her voice work. "No. There was a misunderstanding. He's not due until early tomorrow."

"You have someplace to go? This Christmas!"

"I'm not sure. My husband's out looking for a room."

He shook his head emphatically, the ceiling light tracing a bright arc on his shiny bald forehead. "No rooms, Missus. No rooms in Denver."

"It doesn't matter," Mother said. "We're all right. If we have to, we'll just wait here for Danny."

"So. Your boy is Danny? Our boy Dimitri." He smiled, his stiff white mustache framed by deep creases beneath his round cheeks. "He's gone to Pa-cif-ic." He spoke the word slowly, separating each syllable.

"I see." Mother reached up and laid her hand on his for a moment. "This is a different Christmas for a lot of people." Then she sat straighter. "But don't worry about us. We'll be all right."

"You husband back soon, you think?"

"I hope so."

"Okay. We see. I check later." He returned to his pile of dirt, stroking and tapping his way through the crowd.

I watched the minute hand of the big clock over the "To Trains" gate creep imperceptibly closer to the big hand. Then I must have fallen asleep against Mother's shoulder, for the next thing I knew Dad was saying, "I tried all the hotels—the Service Men's Center—Travelers Aid's list of private homes that will put people up. I'm sorry, hon. I don't know what else to do. We don't dare drive around to look farther."

"Sit down," Mother said. "You look frozen. And exhausted."

I got a whiff of clean, cold air as he settled beside her and she began to rub his hands. I sat up and stretched, remembering where we were and why. "Daddy, do you think Danny's going to come?"

"I think so, Punkin. I hope so."

It had been a long time since he'd called me Punkin.

"I guess this isn't much of a Christmas for you, is it?"

"I don't want Christmas. Only Danny."

"I know. Come over here and lean on me. Your mother's tired." The wool of his coat was rough against my cheek. "Maybe Santa will find us yet."

Santa. It seemed like years since I'd believed—fiercely and determinedly for as long as possible. But now? It seemed like childish silliness. Still—the windup toys that topped my stocking were always fun. I was remembering the sweet, gummy denseness of an orange slice when the push-broom man was back again.

"So. No luck with the room?"

My father gave him a startled look, but Mother answered quietly. "I'm afraid not."

He nodded soberly. "I thought so." He stood eyeing my parents quizzically. "So—maybe—my shift over now. You like come home with me?"

Even I could tell he made the offer hesitantly. "We no got fancy house. But warm. And my wife good cook. And lonesome today."

"But surely she'd be sleeping," Mother protested.

"No. She fix big dinner tonight and wait for me." He grinned and shrugged. "It Christmas." Then, looking embarrassed, he made a funny little bow. "'Cuse me. I do this all wrong. My name Kostas Markopoulos. I live Lafayette Street, close to street car. I wish you be guests my home tonight."

Dad was shaking his head. "Oh, no, we couldn't—"

But Mother was giving the janitor a long, searching look. Dad and I stared at her in disbelief as we heard her saying, "Thank you. That's very kind. Are you sure you have room? We wouldn't want to be any trouble."

"Room enough. Little one sleep on couch okay?"

Before I knew what was happening, my hand was encased in his large, calloused grip and he was guiding me through the crowd. Behind, I heard Dad whisper. "Bess, are you crazy? What are you doing?"

I couldn't hear my mother's answer, but the whispered conference had ceased by the time we pulled our luggage from the nearly gasless car.

After a brief walk, I found myself stretching to climb the steps of a streetcar that had just clanged to a stop. Our host showed me how to drop coins into the small box by the driver, who turned a crank and made them disappear. Markopoulos—what a wonderful name. I said it over and over to myself as we rumbled and rocked our way up the street.

Mr. Markopoulos lived in a block of small cottages about two blocks from the streetcar line. In the streetlight I could see a small, steeply pitched roof, its gable filled with rows of blue scallops, topping a doll-sized house. A tiny front step was sheltered by a matching peaked roof and more scallops. It was like stepping into the pages of Hansel and Gretel, except for the service flag hanging in the front window.

But there was nothing witch-like about the slight, energetic woman who threw open the door. "*Hronea polla*," she exclaimed. "Good years to you," and she enveloped three surprised Nebraskans in hugs. "I tell Kostas bring somebody home. We be not so lonesome," she said as she drew us into the warm, bright room.

My mother and Mrs. Markopoulos were talking like old friends before we were even out of our overshoes, admiring pictures of Danny and Dimitri, seeming to share a special understanding. Mr. Markopoulos lit a pipe, and he and my father began comparing notes about army and marine training.

I remember a tantalizing spicy aroma, a heavy white tablecloth that shone in the candlelight, succulent bites of roast pork, our host's deep laughter. He began telling me about Christmas in "the old country" where St. Nicholas Day ("He first belong Greeks, you know!") came in early December. How in January the priest carried a cross from the church to bless the ships in the harbor. How as a boy he'd dived into the deep water trying so hard to retrieve the golden cross. How he'd left for America before he was big enough to reach it.

Then it was time for Mrs. Markopoulos' special Christmas bread. She placed the round loaf, topped with a cross of golden brown dough, before her husband. He murmured a prayer and moved his hand in the sign of the cross.

"The first slice for Christ always," he said, laying the fragrant piece aside. "The next for Dimitri, who is far away."

He cut one for his wife and for each of us in turn. Then he cut yet another slice. "And this one for Dionysios, Danny, son of our new friends." I saw my mother's mouth quiver. We finished the meal with toasts, as they wished us a long life and taught us to say "*Kala Christouyena.*"

"Beautiful birth of Christ," Mother repeated. "It says so much more than Merry Christmas." Afterward, I snuggled down on the couch, realizing with surprise I'd never once thought of presents or stockings.

It seemed I'd hardly closed my eyes when Mother was saying, "Sis. Wake up. It's time to meet Danny." The couple sent us off with more hugs—returned in full measure—and we caught the trolley for downtown.

There, news of Danny's train was the same. Late. Maybe two hours. Now secure enough to explore, I discovered the shoeshine boys snapping their polish cloths, the huge, white-tiled ladies room, filled with women and babies in every stage of dress, and a small railroad man who periodically stepped out near the snack bar and bellowed out something about an arriving train. The sound rose and echoed around the room, the words tumbling together in an unintelligible jumble.

I wore a path back and forth from the stuffy waiting room to the cold-swept top of the ramp that ran down to the outlying tracks. When at last the Texas Zephyr was announced, my parents joined me there in the crush of greeters, and passengers began streaming up the ramp.

I scanned the faces, suddenly shy. So many soldiers. Would I know Danny? Twice I thought I saw him, but had to swallow my yell. Then suddenly he was there, tanned and strong, swinging me up for a hug, engulfing Mother in his arms, grasping Dad's hand as they clasped shoulders. We all began talking at once. About the mix-up in times. About our long wait. I had to tell him all about Mr. Markopoulos and Mother wanted to know how much time he had.

The answer, which came as Dad ushered us out of the station, sobered us all. He had to be back at Camp Wolters the next night. We had nine hours.

Nine hours. We shut our ears to the ticking clock and headed down 16th Street to take in the sights. Danny whistled and Mother blinked at a display of sophisticated lingerie in Daniels and Fisher. I stood entranced at a window where a tottery Humpty Dumpty seemed about to fall into a wonderland of toys. Dad and Danny strolled behind us, talking. With trepidation I pushed my way through my first revolving door and rode my first escalator, quickly deciding being a city kid would have its advantages.

My nose crammed against a big man's overcoat, we rode the elevator up to luncheon set on pristine tablecloths in the sedate Denver Dry Goods Company tea room. Later, on the street again, I gawked as steel doors in the sidewalk opened suddenly at my feet to accept big boxes from a delivery truck.

I tried not to gawk at an immensely fat man with stumps for legs who sat on the sidewalk with a cup of pencils and an upturned hat. He was a grotesque Humpty Dumpty come to life. A small platform on wheels leaned against the wall behind him, and I realized that was how he got around. I pictured him pushing himself along the sidewalk, through the legs of the crowd. I felt as if I'd wandered into a foreign country, one I wasn't sure I liked.

Men in uniform were everywhere, their khaki and blue salting the dark-coated throngs of people who pushed by us, filling wide sidewalks that lined streets noisy with honking taxi cabs, rumbling trucks and clanging streetcars. Through it all, over it all, we talked. By late afternoon we were sitting in a small park at the far end of 16th Street, and Danny was telling us about Texas and some of his buddies, making us laugh.

He was much as he'd always been with me, but he was different, too. I thought he treated Mother with a kind of tenderness. He and Dad talked mostly about the war. Dad asked him questions and listened closely to his answers. It sounded more like the way adults talk to each other, and I felt left out.

My attention was drawn to a cart and horse passing by. A sign on the back said, "25 Miles a Bale." When I listened again Danny was saying, "One got caught by a fragmentation grenade and I heard two were pneumonia."

Dad shook his head. "Three men dead just from maneuvers? I didn't realize." After a moment he said, "Did you ever think about keeping a diary, Dan? To help you remember all you're seeing?"

They sat with legs spread, leaning on their thighs. "I've thought about it," Danny said, twirling his cap in his hand. I could see where his hair swirled to form his cowlick, but it was cropped too close to stand out from the rest. "But it can get you in trouble, especially if you're in the war zone. The brass says it makes it too easy for the enemy to pick up information."

"Why couldn't you keep it buttoned up in a pocket?" I asked. "Your uniform's got all kinds of pockets."

Danny looked up at me as if he'd forgotten I was even there. "What? Oh, sure, Sis. Guess I could."

Dad glanced at Mother and lowered his voice. "Do you have any feel for where you'll be sent?"

"One day the lowdown is England. The next day it's the Aleutians." He picked up a pebble and tossed it at a trash can. "But it's hard to see how it can be anywhere but the front. Could be Europe or the Pacific. It's anybody's guess."

"Dimitri is in the Pacific," I said, but nobody seemed to be listening.

The moment the buildings cut off the sun, cold wrapped around our shoulders. We found our way to a restaurant for dinner and Danny ate as if he'd never eat again. The day had passed so fast. As our hours together dwindled, we grew quiet. It was hard not to think about the future, not to wonder where Danny would be sent and when. We delayed, watching him down a second piece of pie.

When we stepped outside again, the streets had emptied and it had begun to snow. White crystals swirled in the light of the streetlamps and puffed from under my boot as I took each step. I played at catching them on my tongue as we walked along. The snow made me feel like Christmas, even if it was a day late. I began to stamp my feet, admiring the giant footprints in my wake. Then Danny was beside me, stomping even bigger tracks, and we were in a contest, trying to out-stomp each other. He threw his left leg across to stamp in front of my right, and I knew enough to instantly return the favor. We alternated in rhythm as smooth as any of Gene Kelly-Donald O'Connor dance routine. I was giddy with joy as we laughed our way down the street. Inside that uniform—where it mattered—he was still my brother Danny.

The hulk of Union Station sitting athwart 17th Street was a cold dose of reality. Sobering, we crossed the parking lot to where Mollie sat feathered with snowflakes. Danny got his gear out and Mother suggested we say our goodbyes there, in the dark, quiet privacy.

"What will you do?" Danny asked. "Stay with your Greek friends again tonight?"

"No," Dad said, "I think we'll head on home. I need to get back to the paper."

"Wish you had better tires."

"We'll be OK. I'll have Sis sing, 'Comin' in on a wing and a prayer.' "

"That'll do it." He tousled my hair. "Sis, you take care of the folks, okay?"

"You worry about yourself," Mother said. "We'll be fine. And keep writing."

He nodded, gave Mollie's hood a thump, and sprinted away. As I watched him swing through the double doors, I could taste both bitter and sweet. I was afraid the bitter would outlast the sweet.

THE JOB IS
BIGGER NOW

T he year 1943 was five days old when my father's long skillful fingers darted over the Linotype for a small, enigmatic headline. "Army Planning New Project Here." The two paragraphs below said construction materials were already on site, but gave no clue what new plans the army had for the valley.

The Hiram's Spring Air Field was up and walking, if not running. Now, if you kept your distance, you could drive out to watch B-17s roar into the sky from runways your friends or family had helped pour. The blue-green glass windows of the control tower lifted beside a boxy hangar and planes stood in precise rows along the apron. Rows of long, low barracks were filling with trainees and, at the increasingly crowded Main Street recreation center, excited high-school girls chosen to be hostesses named themselves the Bluffettes.

Much had been accomplished in a short time. It was something to be proud of, something we were part of—making sure every available airman had a home-cooked Christmas dinner, donating spare couches and card tables for base recreation halls.

When they read the sparse detail provided in the new army release, those in the know said military men had been poking around the city airport, southeast of the air base. Some of the merchants who occupied the back table at Walt's Cafe every morning for breakfast thought it would be ideal for a gunnery range. Others envisioned a base where engineers could learn to build bridges and roads. One claimed to have inside information that we were to welcome a K-9 Corps, but others scoffed that the new dog-training center up at Fort Robinson made that unlikely.

When the merchants unfolded their *Herald* three mornings later, they learned they were all wrong. The new project was a storage facility of sorts, but it was to be an internment camp for prisoners of war.

Nobody knew what to make of it. Hitler's goose-stepping troopers, Mussolini's loud-mouthed copy-cats, Tojo's slant-eyed fanatics in Nebraska? Right in our midst? Sleeping in hangars at the airport? It made men check their shotguns and women try door locks stiff from disuse. It was not something to take pride in. It made stomachs go queasy.

"Why here, for heaven's sake?" Mother asked, tearing another strip off the sheet we were rolling into bandages. A flurry of lint swirled in the light of the bridge lamp. "It doesn't make sense. We're thousands of miles from either ocean."

My father was home for a late supper before putting the paper to bed, and it was the first chance they'd had to discuss the big news. "That's part of the reason, I think. Isolation. The military wants them as far away from the coasts and vital facilities as possible. They figure even if some escape they can do little damage, and they'll never make it out of the country."

"Escape. That's exactly the point. How about those two German POWs in New Mexico? Got loose and tried to steal that man's car. If he hadn't had a gun who knows what would have happened."

"Well the rancher did have a gun and he killed one and wounded the other. I don't suppose many more will try that."

"We don't have a gun. What am I supposed to do if I walk outside and find enemy soldiers hiding in our lilac bushes?" Mother gave the sheet a rip you could have heard in the basement.

"Bess, I think you're getting yourself all excited about nothing."

"Nothing! Having maybe thousands of enemies at our back door is nothing? It scares me to death."

"But they have to be put somewhere. And I'm sure they'll be well guarded."

Mother stood up suddenly and a bandage unrolled across the rug. "Do you have to be so everlastingly reasonable? Sometimes it's more than I can stand!" She disappeared through the kitchen door where we could hear her banging cupboard doors.

We'd had no word from Danny since he'd disappeared into Union Station in Denver two weeks before. Mother was now calling home to ask what was in the afternoon mail. He'd finished basic training. Had he been assigned further training? Was he already on his way overseas? I'd look at the war maps in the paper and try to feel where he was, imagining him talking to a Bobby on a London street one day, sure he was under a coconut palm the next.

The second week of January arrived with Arctic cold that struck to the bone marrow. There was no wind, only a terrible stillness to the gelid air. Temperatures plunged to twenty below at night, warmed to ten below in the afternoon. "Too cold to snow," people said. Snow already on the ground squealed under our boots at every step, as if anticipating glacial pressures.

To be out more than a moment brought sharp pain to the center of the forehead. We took quick, shallow breaths, feeling immediate frost in our nostrils, afraid to draw such air deeper into our lungs. Men got up in the night to throw shovel after shovel of coal into glowing fire boxes. And still pipes froze and windowpanes glazed over with quarter-inch-thick sheets of ice. In the morning milk sat frozen on the porch, a white column pushing the cap into the air. Cars groaned once or twice under the starter and gave up.

One Sunday Mother and I were huddled near the hot air register, sorting bars of soap, shoe polish, and razors into piles, when the doorbell buzzed. I answered it to find a familiar-looking young woman standing on the porch.

"Let the lady in to talk," Mother called, "and close the door."

As she stepped in and unwound her muffler I realized in spite of pinched white cheeks, her wide-spaced eyes and auburn curls reminded me of Claudette Colbert.

"I'm sorry to bother you, ma'am," she said over my head to my mother, "but I'm out looking for a room."

"In weather like this? What are you thinking of? You shouldn't be out at all."

"I didn't have much choice. I've got to move and I have no place to go." She was trying to rub some warmth into her hands.

"And you thought because we own the paper I might know of one?" Mother's voice sounded guarded.

"Oh, no, ma'am. I didn't know you had anything to do with the paper. I'm just going door to door. I know it sounds dumb, but I'll do anything to stay close to my husband." She gave an involuntary shiver.

"I see. I'm sorry if I sounded rude. You look so cold. I can't offer you coffee, but let me fix you a cup of tea or Postum before you go out again."

She voted for tea and I included myself in for a cup of Postum. The ads on the *Henry Aldrich* show kept claiming it was as good as the hot cocoa I would have had before the war. The same was supposed to be true for coffee. In spite of its inviting foam, I didn't think it tasted a lot better than the hot water the screechy-voiced teenager found himself in every Thursday night on NBC, but I didn't want to be left out. Mother, who didn't think I was really old enough for Postum, raised her right eyebrow at me but left for the kitchen.

"What's your name?" our guest asked as she unbuttoned her fur-collared coat.

I felt suddenly shy. "Ah, Sis. Er, M.K. I mean, Mary Kathleen."

She smiled warmly. "I'm Mary Louise, myself, but they call me Lou." She indicated our piles of toiletries. "What's all this?"

"Stuff for soldiers' kits. People bring donations to the paper. And we've got $187 so far to buy more. Our goal's $400."

"That's a lot of money."

"Sure is. 'Specially when the theater is passing cartons for donations to help the war-sicken people."

"I believe that's war-stricken, Sis," Mother said as she brought in the drinks. "I'm Bess Greggory."

"Mary Louise Weber," Lou said with a smile. "My husband is Sergeant Ira Weber. He was sent here from the air base in Casper, but we're from Arizona."

"Phoenix!" I said.

She looked bewildered. "How did you know?"

"I know all the state capitals. But Miss Dumbrowski marked Arizona wrong because I spelled Phoenix with an 'F.' I didn't think it was fair."

She laughed. "I guess I was fourteen before I could spell Phoenix without stopping to think, and if Albuquerque had been a capital I would have been in real trouble."

I licked at the Postum froth on my upper lip and knew I had found a friend.

As she warmed and relaxed, I again thought of the movie star with the throaty chuckle who was one of Mother's favorites. Lou's hair was longer and not as red, but as she visited with Mother there was something about her wide, quick smile. I could tell Mother liked her.

The smile faded when she talked about her husband's future. "We don't know how much longer he'll be here," she said. "He's been teaching, but he's requested active duty and when this squadron is trained—" she shrugged, as if unwilling to put the probability into words.

"What will you do then? Go home?" Mother asked.

"I don't know. I don't really have a home to go to. I'm a nurse, and I've been filling in shifts at the hospital. I shouldn't have trouble finding permanent work if I want to."

She stood and picked up her muffler. "But right now I've got to find a room. I don't suppose you'd know anyone I might try? I'll take anything. I just need a place to sleep."

Mother seemed to be in deep thought. I supposed she was searching her mind for possibilities, but when she spoke she said slowly, "When we were in Denver for Christmas, we stayed with a lovely Greek family. It made me feel..." her words trailed off and Lou gave her a puzzled frown. Then Mother said, "Would you mind visiting with my daughter for a moment?"

She walked down the hall toward Danny's room and I heard the door close. By the time it opened again I had told Lou all about Mr. Markopoulus. I don't know how my mother came to terms with her fears, but when she came back and I saw her lift her chin and smile at Lou, I knew Lou had found a room.

In spite of her resolve, Mother put off dismantling Danny's room, and we were still boxing up his things the next weekend when Lou arrived, suitcase in hand. She stood in the bedroom door for a moment, watching as Mother reached to take a Nebraska Cornhusker pennant from the wall.

"Please don't do that for me," she said gently. "It's still your son's room. I'd enjoy having some of his things around."

Mother turned with tear-brimmed eyes. "I'm trying not to be silly about this."

"Don't be silly," Lou said in a husky voice. "You're not being silly."

They looked at each other and began to laugh, and Lou's cosmetics joined Danny's bronze horses on his dresser.

For the first week or two we tip-toed around each other. Dad tried not to grumble over sharing the bathroom with another female. Mother tried to say "your room" instead of "Danny's" and Lou kept supplies for a simple breakfast in a corner of the refrigerator, ate early and took her other meals downtown. She disappeared into her/Danny's room early in the evening. It was the argument over bread that finally brought her into the family.

"I can't see what's so hard about it," Dad said one morning as he grumpily scraped black crumbs off another piece of toast.

"I do the best I can," Mother said. "It's just a little over-brown. Don't be so particular."

Their voices were rising in spite of Lou's presence at the kitchen sink.

"I don't think it's too much to ask for unburned toast. A toaster is not designed to toast wedges! Why can't you slice it straight?"

"I don't know why! I try!" Mother said, brandishing the bread knife. "If you want to blame somebody, blame the government. How making me slice every loaf of bread I buy helps the war effort is beyond me!"

"It's supposed to save the bakers time and money so they can afford to operate under price controls," Dad said.

"So help me, if you claim this cockamamie idea is reasonable, I'll—I'll—"

I was envisioning breakfast nook carnage when Lou spoke up. "I think I could help."

Embarrassed, they sat back and looked at her.

"I'm a nurse, you know. I'm pretty good with implements." She took the knife from Mother's fingers and sawed off two incredibly symmetrical slices. Mother shook her head in admiration and Dad began to beam.

"Lou, anyone with an eye that good ought to be a woodworker. When we get time, I'll show you my chisels."

From Dad, whose meticulously organized furnace-room work-shop was hallowed ground, it was the ultimate compliment. I'd spent many wistful evenings perched on the stairs as he worked silently below, absorbed in some project until the growing ash on his cigarette finally baptized his work with a tiny shower of gray. Though Danny's presence below was welcomed, it never occurred to Dad I might want to do more than observe. I tasted bittersweet; my warm, exciting new friend Lou had so easily won my father's unqualified approval.

The news from Africa, which had given us such hope and pride, turned suddenly bad. The Allied push into Tunisia was halted, and newscasts talked about stalemate, with the British at Mateur and the Americans at Medjez-el-bab stalled in muddy trenches haunt-ingly like World War I.

The good headlines were about that war's hero, flying ace Capt. Eddie Rickenbacker, and his crew. They'd disappeared on a flight from Hawaii and had finally been plucked from the Pacific after twenty-one days on two tiny rubber rafts.

His personal account of the eight men's ordeal began running in *LIFE* January twenty-fifth, and Mother was reading me his mes-merizing description of men sunburned like meat on a spit, without water, making their only food—eight oranges—last for six days.

By day the sea sent "billions of sharp splinters of light" into their eyes, by night they shivered convulsively in a cold, damp mist and the fifty-two-year-old Rickenbacker would hear "a cry and often a prayer. . . see a shadow move and twist as a man tried to ease his torture" in the bathtub-size boats.

As I listened to Mother's voice I could sense the tension of the starving men as Rickenbacker reached ever so slowly to grab a sea gull that had landed on his hat. I could hear twenty-two-year-old Sergeant Alex crying again and again for water, murmuring deliri-ous prayers, and finally—during the twelfth night—giving a last, long sigh. I could feel the fear of the other men "with the wind blowing and clouds rushing across the sky, and Alex dead in that plunging raft."

I walked upstairs to a bed that tossed and pitched beneath a scorching sun while a gull screamed tauntingly in the distance.

Three days later we learned that Danny was at sea.

A SLIP OF THE LIP
WILL SINK A SHIP

Mother unfolded the pages eagerly and tipped the letter toward the light coming in the windows over the buffet. Dad and I quit chewing and Agnes hovered at the kitchen door to hear.

> *Jan. 2, 1943*
>
> *Dear Folks,*
> *Greetings from the bowels of a nameless ship.*

"Oh, God." Mother's hands dropped to her lap. She stared white-faced at my father. When she began to read again her voice was strained.

> *Guess this won't be on its way until we dock somewhere, but wanted to write you anyway. Makes home seem closer.*

"So he must already be there. Wherever it is," my father said quietly. We listened to the rest in silence.

The last few days are kind of a blur. When our train got near the port, people stood in their yards to wave. One little old house by the tracks had a sheet tacked on the wall. "God bless you" it said. Made us feel pretty good.

Used to wonder if I'd ever see the ocean and here I am on the deep blue. Hard to believe. Finally got up on top for awhile. Windy and cold, but the air was great! I couldn't breathe it in fast enough. Hated to go below again. Was thrilled to see we have a lot of company. Dark shapes on all sides, moving as one— looking sure and steady and determined. Makes you feel important and tiny at the same time—as if you're part of something really big and historic.

Down "below" we're pretty cozy. Our bunks are hung in layers like the bread racks in the bakery truck and sometimes I feel like a piece of cheese in a sandwich. A grilled sandwich. Not a lot of air down here. I'm lucky to be on top though, with the ceiling just above my nose. I kill time by writing verses and stuff on it.

Don't have any idea where we're headed yet. Rumors change by the hour. Most guys are hoping we have a Dickens of a time landing, as opposed to dry feet, if you catch my drift. Guess we'll find out sooner or later. And guess I should know by now in the army it's always later. Ha.

Love,

Dan

When nobody spoke I asked, "Do you think he's on the Pacific, like Captain Rickenbacker?"

"I don't know," Dad said. "Read that last paragraph again."

Mother did so.

"Well, I don't catch his drift," Agnes said. "Why should they want to have a hard time landing?"

"Yeah. What's good about wet feet?" I thought of all the news-reel pictures of men splashing through the surf to Pacific beaches while shells exploded around them.

Dad reached for the letter and studied it for a moment. "Dickens is upper case," he mused. Then with growing excitement, "Of course. Dickens. England. They hope to go to England. So he's on the Atlantic!"

I breathed a sigh of relief.

"But the dry feet?" Mother asked.

Dad pursed his lips. "Where would it be dry across the Atlantic? I think maybe that's his way of telling us the alternative destination is probably Africa."

I told Betty I was sure it would be England and one of these days I'd be getting a Bobby's helmet. He'd be all right in England. Even if he was in London he could go down in the subway, like Princess Elizabeth. When Mother opened the next letter I half expected a rose from Princess Margaret to fall out. But when he'd written it, he was still on the ocean, still at the mercy of the terrible sea.

Jan. 12

Dear Folks,

They say this ship was a banana boat and with all the men and equipment packed in it's not hard to feel like one of a bunch. Ha. Can't find much to read. We shoot the bull a lot. Of course a lot of guys shoot craps. One of my neighbors plays a mean harmonica and I started whistling with him the other day. Petty soon we had a rhythm section of mess kits and canteens and had quite a jam session going. Felt good.

Spend hours standing in line, so we only eat twice a day. Have our life jackets close at all times. You can't help reaching for yours when you feel the ship make a sudden change in direction.

My stomach plunged. I was seeing Rickenbacker spitting precious rain water, mouthful by mouthful, from his bailing bucket into his Mae West for storage, while the other men jealously watched his Adam's apple for a tell-tale swallow.

"Do they have lifeboats, Mom?" I asked.

"I'm sure they do, Sis. Much bigger boats than a plane can carry. But I almost wish we hadn't read that story."

> *It's always a second before you can be sure it's just the usual zigzag to throw off any subs. They laid down the law about throwing even a cigarette butt overboard. Could bring us unwelcome company. We're blacked out at night of course.*

The U-boats could find a ship from a cigarette butt? Was there anything the Germans couldn't do?

"How long does it take to get to England, Mom?"

"I'd say at least two weeks. Maybe three." She walked to the calendar that hung by the telephone. "Let's see. His first letter was dated the second and he was already at sea. This is the thirtieth. He must be there by now. If nothing happened—"

"Of course he's there by now." We'd been so absorbed in the letter we had forgotten my father was there. "You have his letters, don't you? They couldn't get mailed until the ship got to port. Remember?"

I remembered and felt stupid. Why did I always manage to look dumb in front of Dad?

Mother looked embarrassed, too. "You're right. I forgot. It's just that when I read Danny's letters I'm right there with him. It doesn't seem like they could have been written weeks ago."

"You two live anything you read." He began to grin. "I thought between you, you'd empty the water tower the night you were reading Rickenbacker. But old news is better than nothing. Finish it up so I can read the whole thing for myself."

> *I like to figure out what you're doing at home when I'm writing to you. I guess it's about noon there now, so the noon whistle's about to blow. Suppose Sis is trotting down the street for dinner. Is it clear or*

snowy, I wonder? I can see Dad and Mom pulling into the driveway. Hope Mollie is starting in the mornings. Mom, is the hired girl still cooking? Or are Dad and Sis again at your mercy? JUST KIDDING! Army food—and KP—have given me a whole new appreciation of your skills.

How's the basketball team doing? Do they have a chance to make the state tournament in Lincoln? It seems like ages since I've had news from home. Kind of hard to sleep at night. The engines seem to throb louder and the waves thump against the hull. Most of us are restless, anxious to get somewhere—any-where—and get busy.

Love,

Dan

P.S. They passed out some new reading material today which confirmed our navigational hunches. Sis, it looks like old King George is going to have his porridge all to himself.

"He sounds homesick," Mother said.

"Yes, he does," said Dad, "but just think of all that's happening to him. These are days he'll never forget." I thought my father sounded almost jealous. "What do you make of that last line, Sis? Is it one of your private jokes?"

"No," I said, remembering the sun-warmed day on the Bluff top last September. "It means he's going to Africa."

As the wind flicked snow pellets against my window, I crouched in front of my orange-crate bookcase, hesitating between the *Cherry Ames, Student Nurse* series, which I was re-reading because of Lou, and my newest favorite, *Norma Kent of the WACS,* the latest of the "Fighters for Freedom" series.

I was almost done with it and had been rationing myself to a chapter a day because I hated for it to end. In her very first night in training camp, Norma had seen another recruit shine a mysterious light in the barracks and heard another girl whisper strange foreign words in her sleep. Then a camera disappeared and a strange sub was spotted lurking off Black Knob Island. Trying to decide which recruit was the spy, Norma was in the thick of it right up to the bill of her smart khaki hat.

Norma was living a life even more exciting than detective Nancy Drew, and she had something else special—a father who had stood at the depot and told her how proud he was to have a daughter like her to give for the defense of his country—a girl who could "live like a soldier and die like one, if need be."

It looked like she might need to. I could feel her gallant spotter plane shudder as it took a shell from the lurking sub, imagine the cold sea water closing over my head, hear my voice nobly refusing help until all others were rescued. I could see myself standing straight and tall to receive my medal for breaking the spy ring, see my father's look of awe and respect. Then that picture dissolved and I was watching from a fleecy cloud as my father knelt to lay a red rose and a small flag in front of a tombstone which read "Major M. K. Greggory—She made the crucial difference."

"If only I'd known how brave she was," my father was saying.

"Oh, Sis! Don't you ever learn?" Mother's voice interrupted my daydream. "I wish you'd asked me first."

I turned toward my bedroom door, knowing all too well what expression I'd see on Mother's face.

"You've put Scotch tape all over your wallpaper." She was breathless from climbing the steep stairs. "And where did you get that map? Out of *LIFE*? Your father will have a fit."

"But I want my own map to keep track of Danny. What was I supposed to use?" I flopped back on the bed, my visions of grandeur as lost as the gallant plane. In one move I'd managed to get in dutch with both of them.

"Well it's too late to undo it now, so you might as well keep things as they are. Why can't you use your head once in awhile?"

The buzz of the doorbell saved me from answering. Suddenly I remembered Lou's husband, Ira, was coming for dinner. Mother had decided we should entertain him before all the canned food was rationed the first of March.

The man who stood, hat in hand, in the living room was all angles, from his beaked nose to the bony knees which seemed ready to head in opposite directions. Even his ears appeared at odds, poking out from his head like hooks from a wall. When he greeted us, his voice reminded me of a loose guitar string. He was not at all what I had pictured for Lou, who was looking at him so proudly. Nearer to a Ray Bolger than a Randolph Scott.

Nor did he have Scott's taciturn manner. He started dinner table conversation with the hot topic of President Roosevelt's secret flight to Casablanca in mid-January. Dad told him *Herald* readers were scandalized that the president had been spirited out of the country during wartime, that he'd risked his life on an airplane so he could meet Winston Churchill in a sun-splashed North African garden.

Ira looked pained. "It was the safest way to do it," he declared. "He had a long way to go in a short time. Secrecy was essential. Give us a few years after the war and we'll all be flying on planes."

"Even kids?" I asked.

He grinned at me. "Maybe someday you'll be flying one, Sis. Women are flying planes for the army right now."

"I know," I said, "I have this book about the WACs and—"

"That's enough, Sis." My father was frowning at me. "I don't think Sergeant Weber wants to hear an endless rehash of one of your little books. We want to talk." Red-cheeked, I bent my head over my plate and the talk turned to Guadalcanal, where the Japanese had finally given up the bloody struggle. "It was a long time coming," Ira said. "If they all take that long—" he shook his head.

"And cost that much," Mother said. "I suppose you read about the Sullivan brothers?"

I had. I had looked for a long time at their picture in *LIFE*—five Waterloo, Iowa, boys, in pea coats with dark Navy caps set low on their brows, grinning confidently from a ship's deck.

"I heard about that," Ira said. "They went down off the Solomons, didn't they?"

"It ought to be against the law for five brothers to be on one ship," Lou said hotly.

"I don't think that will happen again," Dad said. "There's been too much outcry."

Mother broke the ensuing silence by urging second helpings of crusty fried chicken. Then she got the sergeant to talk about life at the airfield.

"To tell you the truth, ma'am, it's been pretty rugged. It's so barren out there. We have days of zero visibility from the dust. Sometimes I think the whole base is going to go flying with the dirt. And you can't burn enough coal to keep those buildings warm."

"Do you enjoy teaching the airmen?" Mother asked.

"Not like I used to." He chewed on a wing. "Everybody tries hard, but the whole show is so amateur. The guards are untrained, and even though our commander is old army, he can't get those cooks to turn out good grub. I don't know if they used to be truck drivers or farmers, but I haven't eaten anything this good since I've been here."

Mother tried not to look amazed at the unexpected compliment.

"How are you fixed for equipment?" Dad asked.

"You name it, we're short of it," Ira said as he wiped his chin with his napkin. "Not just weapons, but little things like clothes hangers and ink bottles. You have to tear up a towel to get a rag. It all gets frustrating."

I thought of Norma Kent, standing starry-eyed in her new uniform as the parade ground rang with "Stars and Stripes Forever." I couldn't imagine her worrying about rags. I decided the WACs must be a lot better organized than the air corps.

But Ira was asking my father about the new internment camp. "It's just a couple of miles from the field, but all we know about it is what we read in your newspaper."

"I can't tell you much," Dad said. "You know the army. But they've got a hundred men out there working to get it ready. They must think it will be needed soon."

The camp was the hot topic in my Longfellow classroom. We were deep in discussion one noon hour before the bell rang.

"My mother's afraid they'll bring in Japs," Sarah Jane Rivers said. "She had a bad dream about it the other night."

"Don't be dumb," Harvey McDougall snorted. "The Japs all commit hari-kari." He jabbed an imaginary knife into his abdomen and fell to the floor with appropriate noises. "You can't keep no dead prisoners," he said to the ceiling.

Sarah Jane ignored his theatrics. "Well, my Mom's real upset because it won't have a big wall like the penitentiary in Lincoln. Daddy says there won't be anything but barbed wire fences between them and us."

I nudged Betty. "You've got your own fence, Sarah Jane. I don't know what you're worrying about."

"Yeah," Betty said with a giggle. "If it will keep out us riffraff it ought to keep out the Japs."

The other kids laughed. We'd all stood, at one time or another, peering between its six-foot wrought iron bars at the only house in town that pretended to be a castle. We'd all been told, at one time or another, that we belonged on the outside.

Our laugh was cut off by the shrilling of the bell. We started to move toward our desks, but the bell kept ringing and ringing.

"Stupid bell's stuck." Harvey began to laugh.

"No, it's not." I said with sudden realization, "That's an air raid warning!"

We threw ourselves to the floor and crawled under our seats. My heart was thumping in my chest. Miss Dumbrowski wasn't even in the room yet. There'd been nothing said about a drill.

Then we heard her voice from the doorway. It was high and shrill. "Listen to me, children. You can't stay under your desks today." She sounded breathless. "We're to go to the basement instead. Please move quickly and quietly."

We scrambled out and rushed the door, pushing and shoving, afraid of being last, afraid of being left. My mind fastened on her words. They're sending us to the basement? Maybe this was a real raid! I tried to get a look back out the big windows, but I caught only a glimpse of gray sky before the crush carried me out the door.

ROSIE THE RIVETER

"Single file." Miss Dumbrowski called. "Move right along. Hurry." Too late she called, "No running."

But we were already at the stairway and flowing down, our feet barely touching the treads. I caught a glimpse of Betty toward the front of the line, eyes big in a white face. The hall lights went out and room doors swung shut as we reached first floor.

A teacher pointed and we were on another set of stairs that I'd never seen before, stairs only the janitor got to use. The air was damp and heavy. Big white pipes lined the low ceiling. I smelled oil mops as we all but ran through the dimness toward the kindergarten end of the building. I could hear children crying.

Miss Dumbrowski told us to sit down against the wall and hug our knees. I felt for the floor. The concrete was cold against my back. Acid burned in my throat. I was in the tunnel in London. I could hear the drone of planes coming closer and closer. Imagine bomb bay doors opening. Bombs whistling toward us.

A hand clamped on my arm.

"No, no!" I yelled. "Let go of me! Let go of me!" I jerked away, banging my head painfully against the wall, and jumped to my feet. I was halfway down the hall when Miss Dumbrowski grabbed my shoulders. "See here! Where do you think you're going?" She whirled me around and forced me to a sitting position. "I will not tolerate panic!" she hissed as she shook her finger in my face.

She had pushed me down amongst some sixth graders. A couple of boys began to giggle. I buried my face in my knees and tried to stop shaking. "Scaredy cat!" one of the boys whispered. The giggle spread to others. I could feel my face hot against my legs. Back down the dark hall I heard a scornful snicker. It was Harvey Mc-Dougall.

Slowly I lifted my head. It had been Harvey. That grasping hand had been Harvey's! I'd run from nothing! Harvey had made a fool of me. I'd made a fool of myself.

When the lights finally came back on, I wanted to go anywhere but back to my classroom. I was one of the last people back. Harvey gave me a vicious grin. When I caught Betty's eye she looked embarrassed. Miss Dumbrowski, evidently busy with her duties as principal, did not return for several minutes. Meanwhile I heard furtive whispers about me. I sat with clenched jaws.

When Miss Dumbrowski returned she seemed equally upset. "Boys and girls," she said. "Longfellow has been given a special test today. I've just learned we were the only grade school in Hiram's Spring subjected to this special drill. It seems someone decided to use us as a guinea pig to prove a point about preparedness." Her mouth made a hard line across her face. "I knew nothing about a drill until I received a telephone call. I was told to push the alarm button immediately. I did."

She lifted her chin. "I want you to know we passed the test with flying colors. I'm proud of you all." I thought her eyes were lingering on me and held my breath for fear she would disgrace me further. But she said only, "I'm sorry if any of you were frightened."

The rest of the afternoon I stared at my school books without seeing any words, and when the day was finally over, I hurried back to get my coat. But not fast enough to avoid Sarah Jane.

"That was quite a show you put on, Mary Kathleen. What'd you think? The Nazis were in Longfellow's basement?" She gave a superior toss of her head.

I whirled away from her and nearly ran into Harvey. I pushed past him and hurried down the stairs. But even though I was almost running, Harvey was soon riding his rickety bike alongside me.

"Well, Mary, Mary, quite contrary, so you're not so smart after all."

"Oh, leave me alone," I said. "You don't know anything about it." I searched my mind for something mean to say. "You're so dumb you didn't even know it was an air raid warning."

"Yeah," he said. "Well, maybe not, Miss Smarty Pants. But you didn't see me run like a scared rabbit." He threw his shaggy head back with a loud laugh. Then he stepped hard on his left pedal and sprinted off down the street. I reached down for a rock and fired it after him, but I didn't even come close.

I stomped across the porch and burst in the door to hear Helen Trent reciting her latest woes. Agnes was slowly, slowly polishing the piano, her lips curled in a dreamy smile.

"Huh," I said. "Helen Trent doesn't know anything about troubles."

"Bad day?"Agnes gave me half her attention. I suspected the other half was on the portly sergeant who'd been picking her up after work the last week, but I was in no mood to think about her love life.

"They don't come any badder."

"Look on the radio. Maybe you'll feel better."

A letter from Danny was propped against my grandparents' picture. I walked to the phone as I ripped it open; Mother would want to know right away. By the time she came on the line, my troubles at school had been eclipsed by a larger worry. I had been right. Danny was "Somewhere in N. Africa."

He wrote of a beautiful white city, of Arab men in turbans and women in veils, of donkey carts and goat herds, of little kids who begged for "shawlet and shoongum" and wanted to be American mascots, of red mud and Roman ruins. I flipped to the second page.

> *They say the front is a long ways off. Had quite a wait to see what outfit I'd be assigned to. Seemed like a century. Or at least a third of that, give or take a year. Almost made me give up, if you know what I mean!!!!*

I stopped reading. "Huh! He's got four exclamation marks after 'mean.' Every time I do that Miss Dumbo scratches out three with her red pencil."

"Four exclamation marks? Danny hasn't written like that since he was your age." Mother's tone went from puzzled to excited. "Read that again."

I couldn't see anything to get excited about, but I obliged. Then I started to read on.

"No, wait a minute. I think he's trying to tell us something— like what division he's in. Read it again."

I repeated the sentences with more interest.

"Okay. A third of a century. That's about thirty-three years— give or take a year—"

"What's that mean?"

"Add or subtract," Mother said impatiently. "I wonder which."

"He's got the give underlined!" I almost shouted.

"And four exclamation marks? He must mean thirty-four. The 34th Infantry! I'll check with your father, but I'm sure that division is in North Africa."

"There's holes cut in the paper. It's been censored!" I felt both excited and embarrassed that Danny had written something he shouldn't have. No wonder he'd used code before.

"Well, keep going. We'll see what we can figure out."

> *We're training hard. My outfit spent* ▮▮ *months training in* ▮▮▮▮ *and have been here* ▮ *so I've missed a lot. The guys seem kind of stand-off-ish, not real ready to be friends. Guess it just takes time.*

Mother broke in. "That's surprising. Danny usually makes friends easily."

> *P.S. Would you send me a map? And clippings? I knew more about the war when I was home. And we'd better start using V-Mail. It should be faster.*

We had already stocked up on the special one-page forms and sent our first letter on its way. You could write only on one side. Then you folded it up and addressed the outside. I thought it was exciting to know our letters would be unfolded and photographed with more than a thousand others on a roll of film that would be developed and reprinted overseas. It made me feel like I was part of a spy ring.

My father thought it was an ideal solution for handling the volumes of overseas mail. "Somebody was using their noggin when they came up with that," he said.

My mother didn't like it. "I'd rather know I'm holding the paper he's written on," she had said to me later. "It makes me feel a little closer."

By the time my father came home that night he'd found out that the 34th Infantry was formed from National Guard troops from Iowa, Minnesota, and the Dakotas. They'd been training in Ireland since the spring of 1942.

Mother was standing in the kitchen ironing. "Is that good, do you think? That he's with a Guard unit?" She unrolled a dampened shirt.

"I don't know." My father sighed. "It sounds awfully amateur. But from what Sergeant Weber said the whole show is awfully amateur." He paced back and forth across the kitchen. "God, it's hard to feel so helpless! To think what could happen if his officers are incompetent!"

Mother slammed the iron down. "Hal," she said sharply, "stop that! If we think like that we'll go crazy. We've got to believe those men know what they're doing."

I could smell the sheet that covered the ironing board begin to scorch. Mother reached automatically to sit it up. "You said they've been training a long time. They're good, bright Americans, after all. We've got to have faith—" Her voice broke. "I don't want to hear—" She pressed her hands to her lips.

My father seldom displayed affection, but he moved to put his hands on her shoulders. "I know. I'm sorry, Bess. I shouldn't have said that. You're right, of course."

But as he stared over her head into the reflections in the kitchen window, I could see something she could not. He did not believe what he'd just said.

Two days later I sat on the footstool in front of the radio, tuning in to hear the Lucky Strike Orchestra swing out with the *Hit Parade* theme. Lou was working a night shift, and I'd promised to listen and find out why everybody was swooning over that skinny singer named Frank Sinatra. My choice went to Betty Hutton belting out

"Murder! He Said" or the tongue twister "Mairzy Doats," which always reduced Betty and me to giggles.

But instead of the chant of the tobacco auctioneer, the announcer was introducing President Roosevelt. I reached for the dial to find something else, but Mother said, "No. I want to hear this speech. It's important."

My attention wandered. I turned to playing Tiddlywinks against myself and the red disks were beating the blue when something the president said caught my attention. Mother reached over to tune out encroaching static. He was talking about Tunisia.

I could see it in my mind, there in the middle of my map of North Africa, the place where the pins and thumbtacks pushed against each other. I had looked at it just that morning, wondering exactly where the most important pin, one I'd tied with red yarn to stand for Danny, should really be.

Now the president was saying Allied armies were massing in Tunisia for one of the major battles of the war. I left the Tiddlywinks and went over to sit with Mother. She leaned forward, listening intently.

"Our prime purpose is to drive our enemies into the sea," the president said in his high, sharp voice. I remembered the confident words of the British general: The *Boche* is completely finished. But President Roosevelt was saying "The enemy has strong forces in strong positions."

The great British Eighth Army and French forces were to attack from the south. A combined British-American force would push in from the west. All would be under the command of the young general, Dwight Eisenhower, descendant of Kansas pioneers.

Driving the Axis from Tunisia will cost us heavily in casualties, the president told us. And mothers, fathers and wives of American servicemen "must face that fact now with the same calm courage as our men are facing it on the battlefield itself."

I thought of John Wayne and Humphrey Bogart and all the other brave soldiers I'd seen fighting so determinedly on the screen of the Egyptian Theater Saturday afternoons. I could see Danny beside them, standing atop his foxhole, urging his men into a charge.

"The fires of war are blazing across the whole horizon of mankind…," the president said. "We cannot escape history."

As applause burst on his closing words, I realized he had said we were part of history. For me history had always been men in white wigs and women in long dresses, tipis and arrowheads and Hiram Scott crawling along the Platte. But he was saying Mother and Dad and Danny and I were caught in history right now. We couldn't escape.

I felt a stab of fear that was not at all like the delicious chills I got when the door to "Inner Sanctum" creaked open with such menace on Tuesday nights. That voice inviting me inside "the gory portals" kept me riveted to my footstool, afraid even to glance into the dark corners of the room. But this fear was different, real and deep. I took a long breath.

Spooky Host Raymond always ended *Inner Sanctum* with a gruesome joke that made you laugh and brought you back to the real world. But the president had not brought us back to a warm, safe living room. He had only warned the listening mothers, fathers and wives to be calm and brave. He had not said anything about sisters, but I knew it was up to me to be just as brave, just as courageous, as John Wayne and Danny and his buddies.

The president's message to the country, broadcast that Saturday night, February 13, 1943, was heart-breakingly prophetic. As the week started we began hearing about an "exceedingly strong" Axis attack. "U.S. troops are raw," one correspondent wrote, declaring they were suffering more casualties than experienced troops might in the same circumstances, that U.S. battle tactics had been poor, coordination sadly lacking. This in the face of a tough, experienced enemy, 170,000 strong, who dominated the air and could attack with impunity. The troops are "learning to become soldiers the hard way," he told us.

On February 18, the headlines my grim-faced father spelled out announced a Nazi Blitzkrieg in Tunisia. Stukas bombed and strafed at will. The Germans' huge Mark VI tanks knifed through Allied forces for thirty-five miles, nearly to the Algerian border. Our guns could barely dent their heavy armor. American tanks had been overrun, our troops captured. Three U.S. airfields were in German hands. Our retreat was precipitous. General Eisenhower evacuated Sidi Bou Zid just ninety minutes before German tanks crashed in.

Could Danny be there, somewhere in that chaos? Or was he still training, with the front "a long ways off?" We could only wonder.

RUMORS COST LIVES

"Well, I don't like it. There's altogether too many Germans in this valley." I was following Mrs. Rivers' bulk through the basement of the church, trying to squeeze by as she and Mrs. Simon, my Sunday School teacher, made their leisurely way down the hall after class.

"I don't worry so much about the Germans," Mrs. Simon said. "The Japs scare me more. There's a lot of them around, especially out on the farms. And they must all be dangerous." She fixed Sarah Jane's mother with eyes that reminded me of the muddy color I got when I rinsed my watercolor paint brush. "Why else would they arrest all those people on the west coast and put them in some kind of camps."

"You're right about that. And the FBI sure didn't waste any time arresting that Jap who preaches out in Mitchell Valley. Hindu or whatever he was. That was right after Pearl Harbor, wasn't it?"

A Japanese spy in the valley? I decided I wasn't in such a hurry, after all.

"I think it was, just a day or two. You know he was writing all kinds of letters to Japan. Writing in Japanese, so no good American could read them. They say maybe he was sending short wave messages, too."

"Maybe so, but the short wave transmitter I've heard about is the one in the attic of the Liberty Cafe on Main Street," Mrs. Rivers said.

"Really? Are you sure?" Mrs. Simon stopped dead at the bottom of the stairs. "We always ate there after church, but we haven't been in there for over a year."

"We haven't either. I can't see giving good money to Japs. Let them go back to Japan, I say. I hear they're always hanging around your table, waiting for you to say something you shouldn't. And I've heard they give free Cokes to the airmen to get them to spend time there. There's got to be a reason for that."

Mrs. Rivers saw me waiting and waved me between them. I was about to bound up the steps when Mrs. Simon said, "It's funny you should say that. I was noticing the window in Jacob's Market the other day."

I took the steps one at a time.

"He had the cans arranged in a fancy 'V,' all decorated with red, white and blue streamers. And when the coffee shelf is empty—like it usually is—he puts up that sign, 'Blame Hitler and Tojo, Not Us.' It just struck me funny, him being German and all. Like he was making a point of looking patriotic."

"Patriotic! I was in there one day when she was making fun of the blackout. Like it was some big joke. I haven't spent a red cent there since."

I was at the door now, but I whirled around. "You're both crazy as coots and you should M.Y.O.B.! Betty's dad is no German!"

Their mouths gaped. The door swung shut behind me on Mrs. Rivers' outraged "Mary Kathleen! Come back here!"

"Mom," I said indignantly as I wielded the potato masher, "Mrs. Rivers says Betty's Dad is a German!"

She was stirring the gravy with a vigor that made her good dress shimmy around her knees. "Drat! It's going to lump again!" She stirred harder. "Actually," she said, "I think he's German-Russian. Some people in the valley tend to call them Rooshuns. But you should not."

"What do you mean?" I pushed down with both hands and cut through to the bottom of the pan. "He's an American!"

"Yes, Sis, but he came from a part of Russia settled by people from Germany."

I turned the pan and mashed some more while I took this in. "You mean he isn't a real American?"

"Of course he is. He's a citizen just like you or me. He just wasn't born here. I think both Mr. and Mrs. Hermann came over when they were teenagers. Mr. Hermann lived on the farm with his brother's family."

"Is that why he says Betty can come over *by* my house, instead of come over *to* my house? And why Betty's Mom always says '*Gott im Himmel*' when she trips over Schnoz?"

"I suppose so. Haven't you got those mashed yet? The roast is getting cold."

I dumped in some top milk and gave a couple of stirs. "They're good enough."

My father was methodically re-mashing his mashed potatoes and gravy when I remembered what else Mrs. Rivers had said. "I didn't know they arrested a Japanese preacher for sending secret messages from a radio in his church!"

Dad quit mashing. "What are you talking about?"

"Up at Mitchell. One of those guys that rub the tummy of that fat, ugly statue. Mrs. Rivers says they put him in jail for sending war secrets to Japan."

Dad looked to Mother for help. She frowned. "Maybe she's talking about Father Sato."

Dad tried a bite of potatoes and gravy and began to mash again. "Sis, that is about the most jumbled up mess of misinformation I've ever heard. God forbid you should ever be a reporter. To begin with: Father Sato is an Episcopal priest, not, if I'm interpreting your twisted description correctly, a Buddhist. He was arrested, along with other important Japanese men in the country, the day of Pearl Harbor. As I remember from writing the story, the FBI arrested him on the steps of his church."

"Pearl Harbor Day?" Mother asked. "They must have been watching him."

Dad glanced at Mother. "Did you know the first thing they asked him was did he know judo? And then they wanted to know if he was going to resist arrest."

"Good grief," Mother said. "Tiny Father Sato? He must be in his fifties."

"They say he was writing frequently to the Japanese government in Tokyo. He admits he did. He says he helped other Japanese immigrants with their paperwork. And, of course, he still had family in Japan to keep in touch with."

"Did you ever hear if they proved anything?"

"I don't know," Dad said. "There was a meeting going on in the church. They had a map on the wall with circles around Cheyenne and Denver, both of which have military installations. I find it hard to believe, but—" Dad shrugged.

"Well, I don't believe it for a minute," Mother said. "Where is he now?"

"I don't know. Still in custody somewhere," my father said.

"Imagine," Mother said. "What's happened to his family? There might be a story there."

"There might be," said Dad. "I hadn't thought of them. You can check it out if you want to. But the way people have boycotted the Liberty Cafe, I doubt our readers much care."

The letter that arrived two days later told us exactly what we didn't want to know. We unfolded the V-Mail form to find it was dated two weeks before. Danny's printing, always small and neat, looked even smaller than usual.

> Had a lot of action lately. Tired and dirty but OK. Can't say much. We're doing our damnedest and it's going to take all we've got.
>
> Hilly country—colder than blazes at night. Rugged, rocky ridges between wide valleys. Some wheat fields and olive groves. Petty barren but for patches of prickly pear-type cactus. A little like the badlands by the river. Farmer's fields all chopped up, olives trees all broken, donkeys running lose.
>
> We're fighting for passes, but to take a pass you have to take the hills above it. Arabs call them something that sounds like gebels, but HQ gives them numbers.
>
> We're up and down a lot, mostly in the dark. You dig a hole wherever you drop, dig it deeper every chance you get. Use helmets, knives, fingernails - whatever it takes.

Sorry I can't write oftener, but don't worry. I'm always the first one to hit the dirt. And we all carry sulfa in case we get hit. Sis, you'd laugh to see my bright purple feet—the army's cure for athlete's foot.

Love and miss you all,

Dan

P.S. Dad, I've decided to do what we talked about in the park in Denver.

I opened my mouth to ask my father if the P.S. was about a diary, when Mother said, "He may be right there." She closed her eyes. "Right in the middle of that mayhem."

"Maybe. But maybe not," Dad said. "I haven't seen anything yet about individual units. Maybe the 34th Infantry isn't involved. Or maybe he's still in the rear training. He hasn't even been in six months yet."

"Six months. Just think." Mother waved the letter. "He ought to be writing us about going to mixers after the basketball game and worrying over term papers—" Her voice was rising.

"Bess, you know it's useless to think about that!"

"I can't help it. That's what he should be doing. Instead of learning to be a killer!"

"Right now all I hope is that he's learned to be a good-enough killer!"

"My God, what a thing to hope for your son." Mother sank back and dropped the letter in her lap.

"It's all we can hope," Dad's voice was hard, "if we want to have a son when this is over."

It was a long moment before my mother spoke again. "You're right, of course. But it's just so awful."

Danny—a killer? What were they talking about? My brother was a soldier! My mind whirled with familiar images. Bodies sprawled in ditches, draped over guns, dangling from burned-out trucks—the helmeted skull of a Japanese soldier, burned to the bone when his tank caught fire. The papers and magazines and newsreels were full of them. But they were only dead enemies. To be walked by or pushed aside without thought. One less dirty Jap or stinking German to stand between us and freedom.

How could my parents think Danny, or any soldier who put them there, was anything but a hero?

Betty and I knelt in front of the store's canned fruit shelves. "Put down six cans of peaches," she instructed. I marked the chart in the peaches' column. Then it was my turn to count the pears.

It was only two days before we'd all have to use ration stamps to buy canned food. I'd already helped Mother count what was in our cupboard at home so when we registered at Longfellow School we could tell the ration board if we had over the five items each of us was allowed.

Mother had winced when the official tore stamps from our new books for every item over the limit, but she'd said she was more worried about how I was going to make three pairs of shoes last a year. I was more concerned about the irreplaceable elastic in my underpants, which didn't have a prayer of holding up for the duration. I gave them a hitch now as I reached for the pears.

The grocery stores also had to take inventory of their stock so they could account for later sales. I'd volunteered my help, and Betty's distracted parents had accepted. Permission for me to sleep over and a pancake breakfast were to be our reward.

The two of us had spent the evening inching our way down the canned goods aisle. It was quite late, but we were nearly done. Mrs. Hermann, working on the other side of the shelves, kept urging us to hurry so we could get to bed.

I hadn't told Betty anything about what I'd overheard the Sunday before in the church basement. I was sure those women had to be wrong. But since then, I'd caught myself peering into the dim corners of the back room, wondering what might hide in the darkness. It made me feel guilty. And one noon, waiting my turn at the meat counter, I'd watched Mr. Hermann roll a chicken in white paper and tie it with a string he pulled from the cone on the wall. It would be easy to slip a note in a package of meat, I thought. Or tie a package with a special knot as a signal. Or hide some microfilm in a sausage. I came out of my speculations to realize he was asking me what I wanted. I got so flustered I could hardly tell him, and I'd thought he looked at me very strangely.

"Move, Schnoz!" Betty gave the dog an exasperated shove and began to count the vegetables. "Eight cans of crummy carrots," she said.

I grinned. "Five cans of slimy spinach."

"Three cans of awful asparagus," she answered.

I was trying to think of a word mushy enough for canned peas when the front window exploded into the store. Slivers of glass cut the air all around us, splintering against the shelves and embedding themselves in the dark floor. Mrs. Hermann screamed and Schnoz knocked me over as he leapt, barking, toward the front door.

KNOW YOUR ENEMY

"**G**et down!" Mr. Hermann yelled. "Get down!"

We flattened ourselves on the floor. I felt a piece of glass bite into my cheek. I could hear someone scrambling across the floor and the lights went out.

"Mama!" Betty screamed.

"Stay down!" her mother ordered. We heard a screech of tires, then nothing more except Schnoz' hysterical barking.

"Are you girls all right?"

I jumped. Mrs. Hermann had crawled around behind us.

"I think so," Betty said in a shaky voice. "Mama! What happened?"

"I don't know. Stay down."

I shrank against the worn boards, the odor of oil strong in my nose, listening for—what? Some threat creeping closer beneath the dog's racket? Then the lights flickered on. I blinked and sat up.

Mrs. Hermann helped Betty and me off the floor, turning us around to check for cuts. My cheek stung and I put my hand up to feel a sticky drop of blood. Betty had glass in her hair but did not seem to be bleeding. Mrs. Hermann raised a shaking hand to pick out the glass.

Footsteps crunched gratingly near the window. "Shut up, Schnoz!" Mr. Hermann's command came from the front of the store. We turned to see him examining a chunk of concrete that had landed in the midst of the window display, denting and scattering cans of corn. Red crepe paper streamers dripped liquid that had sprayed from a broken can.

"This is America!" he said. "*Mein Gott*! This is America!" His face twisted and he started to laugh. For a wild moment I thought, "It must be a joke." A giggle rose in my throat. Then I realized he wasn't laughing. He was crying. It frightened me more than the window shattering. I'd never seen a man cry.

"Why?" Mrs. Hermann was saying. "Why would they do this thing?"

Mr. Hermann reached in and rolled the chunk so we could see words were painted on the one flat side. In angry red letters they said, "Fucking Nazi."

I had no idea what fucking meant. But I remembered Danny used it once when I was little and Dad had hauled him off to the basement for a session with his belt. And sometimes I saw it in filling station restrooms, but Mother would only say, "Never mind. It's not nice."

Betty had begun to cry in great hiccupping sobs. "We're not! We're not!" she cried. Mrs. Hermann stood dry-eyed, with one arm around her, her other arm over Mr. Hermann's shoulders. They clung to each other.

She looked at me over Betty's head. "This isn't your business, Mary Kathleen." She stroked Betty's hair. "I'm sure they didn't even know you were here. You'd better go on home. You can take Schnoz with you."

She'd forgotten I was supposed to stay all night. The idea of walking a block in the dark was terrifying, but suddenly I wanted very badly to be home. I nodded numbly and got my coat and pajamas. Then I laced my fingers firmly into the fur on the back of Schnoz' neck and went out the door.

The corner street light threw elongated tree shadows across the sidewalk. They swayed in the cold wind, raking across my path like bony fingers. The night was full of noises. I walked faster, clinging to Schnoz. My heart raced as I came to the alley. It was always darkest there. Something scraped against the alley fence. I was too frightened to look. I yanked Schnoz into a run. My pajamas were slipping from under my arm. I let them fall. Just half a block to go. I sprinted up the back steps. I couldn't open the door!

"Mom! Mom!" I screamed in panic, pounding on the door. Schnoz was barking furiously. I was sure something, someone was just behind me.

It seemed an eternity before Mother opened the door and I fell into her arms.

The mellow clang of the nearby Congregational church bell pulled me into awareness, and my first thought was I would be late for Sunday school. I wondered why Mother had let me sleep so late. Then I remembered the night before. We'd all been up for hours.

My father had questioned me quickly on what I'd seen and hurried off to cover the story. Then he'd called from the paper to question me more closely before he wrote the final copy. In other circumstances, I might have enjoyed the feeling of importance.

"I cannot understand how she could send Sis home by herself." Mother's voice was coming up the stairwell. "After such a terrible experience. And in the dark like that. She was terrified!"

I curled tighter into a ball and pulled the covers even closer. I did not want to think about last night. Mother had heard me first, but Lou had appeared quickly from the back bedroom.

"I suppose they were too upset to think," she said soothingly now, "but it does seem awfully thoughtless."

"Heartless is more like it," Mother said.

I sat up. I'd never heard Mother talk about a friend in that tone of voice.

"Hal said when he got over there she was really strange. Jacob was all broken up about it. Kept saying he was as good an American as anybody. But she was kind of cold. She didn't even want to call the police."

"Why ever not?"

"She said it wouldn't do any good. That it might cause more trouble."

"That's an odd attitude."

"That's what we thought. And she asked Hal not to put anything about it in the paper."

All attention now, I swung my legs over the edge of the bed. My father would never agree to that. Danny and I had heard often enough that news was news with no exceptions. Pleas to ignore business reverses or delinquent children, to eliminate traffic fines and divorce proceedings from courthouse statistics, met stoic refusal. Friends could expect to be treated more sternly than enemies. If Danny or I got in trouble, we knew we would see the news on the front page.

"He said he couldn't make her understand he has to print whatever happens in Hiram's Spring. No matter who it happened to."

"How did she take that?"

"Badly, I'm afraid. She's very angry."

A dreadful fear washed over me when I heard Mother say, "I hope she won't let her feelings interfere with the girls' friendship."

As soon as I had finished breakfast I hurried over to the store. I knew it would be closed on Sunday, but Mr. Hermann was out nailing wood over the broken window. Betty was picking glass out of the dirt. I knelt beside her and began to help. Neither of them said anything. For a while we worked in silence except for the hammering, our heads nearly touching. Then Betty whispered, "Mom's pretty mad."

"I know."

"I don't think I can invite you in."

"That's okay."

"I told her it wasn't your fault."

"Thanks, kid."

Footsteps on the sidewalk behind us paused, and I tipped my head to see a pair of shiny black wingtips. It was Mr. Anthony from down on the corner. Turning farther, I saw that while Betty and I had been busy, three other neighbors had gathered. They stood watching Mr. Hermann work.

Just then Mrs. Hermann came out the store's door. She took in the scene and stood with arms folded, saying nothing. Two of the women held a whispered conversation.

Finally Mr. Anthony broke the silence. "Saw in the *Herald* you'd had some trouble, Jacob."

Before Mr. Hermann could empty his lips of nails to answer, Betty's mother said, "You see, Jacob? What'd I tell you? The damn paper!"

I stared at her in surprise. I'd never heard her swear.

"Won't be anything but more trouble," she went on, her voice rising. "He just wouldn't listen."

The neighbors on the sidewalk shuffled uncertainly. Everyone knew she was talking about my father. I could feel her gaze boring into the top of my head. "I don't know what you're doing here, Mary Kathleen."

I heard Betty catch her breath. "I'm just trying to help," I said.

"We don't need any more help from your family," she said. "Your father has done quite enough."

"Now, Cora," Mr. Hermann said. "It's not the girl's fault."

"What is it? Our fault? Because we're German? He practically hung a swastika around our necks. Betty, come inside now. And you go on home, M.K."

"But, Mama," Betty said.

"Now!" her mother said.

Betty gave me a despairing glance and disappeared behind her mother.

I walked home the block I had run in such fear the night before, sick with the knowledge the shadows that threatened me now would follow me right through my own back door.

My father, preoccupied with his own problems, did not seem to take Mrs. Hermann's animosity very seriously. "Can't be helped," he said shortly. "She'll get over it." My mother said the way things were, maybe it was just as well we didn't play together for a while.

At morning recess Monday, Betty and I sat together on the cement step. "Mama says your Dad has no feelings. He doesn't care how he hurts people."

"Mom said your Mama was heartless, sending me home alone."

"I know. I guess she called Mama. Mama said your mother has never had people throw things through her window."

The step was glass-smooth and I rubbed circles on it with my fingers.

"She says there's lots of other girls I can play with," Betty said.

"Mom said about the same thing."

Betty pulled her coat around her legs. "Dad says when she's got a mad on, she wears it until it's in rags."

The bell rang before we could think of anything we could do.

Agnes wasn't in the house when I got home. I had just fixed the crackers and milk that passed for my afternoon snack when she came in with a package of macaroni under her arm and said, "There's a regular mob at Jacob's Market."

My heart fell to my toes. I grabbed my coat and ran for Locust Street. What could have happened now? Was the other window broken? Were they throwing rocks? Yelling awful things? I wasn't really sure what mobs did. Maybe Betty needed help.

The boarded-up window made me wince. It looked as if the store had lost an eye and was wearing an ugly patch. But to my surprise, the store yard was empty, although several cars were parked along the curb. I pushed through the door to see three or four people in line at the cash register. Mrs. Hermann was busy waiting on customers. Betty sat on a stool next to her, counting and sorting ration stamps. Neither of them saw me come in.

I'd never seen the store so crowded. Back at the meat counter, Mr. Hermann was wrapping a chicken for Mr. Anthony, while three other neighbors waited their turn. "We just want you to know, Jacob, that Hiram's Spring is not that kind of place," Mr. Anthony said.

"That's right," a waiting woman nodded. "Those awful people! I live on the other side of town, but I'll be buying here as often as I have the gas."

Mr. Hermann straightened his white butcher's cap and beamed. "Thank you, thank you," was all he seemed able to say.

My spirits began to lift. My father's story in the paper, brief as it had been with the deadline all but passed, had not caused the Hermann's trouble. It seemed to have helped their business. Maybe Betty and I could be friends again. I squeezed between the big pop cooler and a lady bending over the potato bin and caught Betty's eye. I waved and we grinned happily at each other.

But Mrs. Hermann also saw my wave. She pressed her lips together, shook her head and motioned me toward the door. It was clear her "mad" had a lot of wearing out to do. If I wanted things to change, I'd have to do something.

"All they'll tell me are things everybody can see for themselves," my father said crossly. "'The internment camp is progressing.' How many prisoners it will hold is a military secret. What nationality they'll be is a military secret. I can print it has three compounds because anybody who drives up the road can see that."

"Well, now, you did find out the old airport office will be the hospital." My parents' conversation was interrupted as Lou came in the front door. "Did I hear you mention the hospital?" she asked.

"Not yours, Lou," Mother said. "We were talking about the internment camp."

"Well, that's a coincidence. That's soon going to be my hospital. I've interviewed for a job out there."

Mother looked dumbfounded. "Why in the world would you want to do that?"

"It's good pay, which I'm going to need. And I can work a straight day shift."

I couldn't believe what I was hearing. "But you'll be helping the enemy!"

Lou reached for my hand, but Mother asked, "Won't it be dangerous? Does Ira approve?"

"Ira doesn't exactly know, yet," Lou admitted, "but I'm sure I can make him understand. He sees how young and lost a lot of his men are. I'm twenty-seven, and they make me feel like a grandmother. I don't suppose the prisoners will be much different."

Not different? But everybody knew they were different! Nazi boots crushed little girls dolls in the street. Nazi fists beat up old guys in the French underground. Sneaky Jap snipers in the top of coconut trees shot Americans in the back. They crawled into foxholes at night to stab sleeping GIs. I was too astounded to find any words. I snatched my hand from hers and backed away.

Lou reached toward me and said, "I'll just be helping sick people, Sis. They need help no matter who they are."

I didn't see at all. "But they don't help American men. Just last week in the newsreel they showed Germans shooting a Red Cross truck in Africa! And the Japs stab all the wounded guys."

"But we don't want to be like them, do we, Sis?" Lou was leaning over to look directly into my eyes. I felt as if she could see into my brain and knew I would gladly shoot or blow up or use a flame thrower on any German or Jap I got my hands on. I turned away, sick with sudden guilt and confusion. I knew the Golden Rule. But how could you "do unto others as you would have them do unto you" when they were busy trying to kill you? I could not find an answer. And I could not understand how Lou could want to help such monsters.

Six days later we learned American troops in Tunisia had a new commander. "Old Blood and Guts Takes Over," the headlines trumpeted. Lt. Gen. George S. Patton, Jr., was described as a "rip-roaring, hell-for-leather" general who knew only one command—attack! The fifty-seven-year-old general, pearl-handled revolvers strapped on his hips, was already at the front, leading American troops in a comeback, turning the tide of battle with a major offensive in central Tunisia.

I compared my bedroom map with the paper's and crowded the Germans' thumbtacks into a band along the eastern coast of Tunisia. The blue of the Mediterranean Sea lay just behind them. British pins were pushing up from the south and along the northern coast. And in the middle of the small country, facing the middle of the German lines, I pushed the red-yarn pin I'd fixed for Danny.

For we no longer had to wonder. For the first time the military had released information on which units were where. The men Patton was leading against troops Hitler had ordered to "stand or die" were the 1st and 34th infantries.

KEEP 'EM FLYING

"You just can't tell what's going on." Dad waved a handful of wire copy. "The Office of War Information says one thing, a dispatch from Madrid says another. Then there's Radio France in Algiers and even Radio Berlin. Everybody has a different story."

It was Sunday after church, but we were down at the office to check the AP wire. My father had practically lived at the paper since the Tunisian offensive began.

"One day the British are about to flank the Mareth Line and our boys are only seventy miles from the coast and bombing the Germans to bits." Dad paced from his desk to the map and back. "The next day the British are barely holding on against a counterattack and we're abandoning a town we've held thirty-six hours."

Mother and I studied the map. "Here's that Fondouk they mentioned," I said.

"And Kairouan," Mother pointed. "It's said to be a Moslem holy city. Such strange names. There's the mountain, Djebel el Aoureb."

"Do you think that's where Danny is? On a mountain?" I asked.

"I don't know," Mother said. "I don't know."

"That about sums it up, doesn't it?" Dad said bitterly. "We just don't know what's going on."

We'd been watching the mailbox for weeks, waiting for that certain envelope, the one with "free" written where a stamp would have been. When at last it did come, it was what my father called "old news." It had been written almost three weeks before.

Dear Folks,

Time for a few lines. It's a mixed bunch of men fighting here. Strange sights—the French move their artillery with horse carts. Makes me think of Napoleon. The Arabs fighting for them are a fierce-looking bunch—black beards, leathery faces. Wear dark robes, sort of like bathrobes, but have beautiful horses. Guess they get bounties for Germans they kill. Hear they bring back their ears on a string for proof. Sorry, Mom, guess you'll think that's pretty gruesome.

The army hires them to carry equipment. I've seen them walk through a battle as if the bullets had nothing to do with them. Guess they let Allah decide when it's their time to go. They like to trade for our mattress covers. Then they cut neck and arm holes and wear them! Better than the rags they have, I guess. See them in the middle of a battle selling eggs and live chickens. And afterwards they're quick to strip the dead.

We've seen some Brits. Hear tell they're tough soldiers, but they actually stop when it's time and light fires to make tea! And the Scots march into battle playing the bagpipes! Like Dad says, it takes all kinds.

Nights are warming up a little and fruit trees are blooming. Funny thing. Maybe it was the smell of sage after a rain, but I dreamed the other night of a Scout hike on Laramie Peak. Hope it happens again. Good dreams are tough to come by.

Love,

Dan

"I hate letters," Mother said. "He's not telling us a thing."

"What do you mean, Mom? All that neat stuff about the Arabs and the bagpipes?"

"But nothing about how he is." Mother was staring into the distance. "Nothing at all about himself."

The stories were short, only a paragraph or two, but they found their place on the front page day after day. "Local Boy Killed in Training Crash." "Six die in Casper Trainer." "11 Airmen Die in New Mexico." "Crew of Arizona Bomber Found Dead." "Ten Die in Plane Crash in Colorado."

When Ira could come to Sunday dinner, we talked of other things. I always had questions. "Do the bombardiers really sleep with their bombsights?"

"Not quite. But they have to get them from a special building and carry them back after every flight."

"What makes the building special?"

"It has a big fence around it. And guards."

"So they're always locked up?"

"Always."

"Why are they so secret?"

"Because the Norden is the best in the world and we don't want the enemy to get one."

"What if—" But Ira knew how to turn off the torrent. He'd offer me the chance to pull on his heavy leather flying jacket. I'd snuggle into the creamy fleece lining that always smelled of cigarette smoke and search the pockets for the candy bar or package of gum he never failed to bring me.

Then, often as not, Dad would say he wanted to check something at the paper and Mother would suggest she and I take a walk. The first time she stifled my protests and practically pushed me out the door. After that I knew we were walking to give Lou and Ira privacy so "they can have a good talk."

As the March air softened, offering snowflakes that were big and moist and winds that had less of an edge, crews at Hiram's Spring Air Field were in the air day and night. We grew used to the ever-present drone of motors. Each crew had about ten days to perfect its skills. Lou became tense toward the end of each cycle; Ira still hoped for active duty.

The army warned the public away from bombing and gunnery ranges in Sioux County, thirty miles northwest. However, there were things we could do to help. The base needed radios so radiomen could practice repairs. Gunners needed pictures of war planes, so they could learn to tell friend from foe.

I thumbed through countless magazines. All kinds of companies found reasons to illustrate their advertisements with weapons of war. Silhouettes of the familiar Flying Fortress, the sleek, twin-bodied P-38, Corsairs and Mustangs, the twin-ruddered B-24 became as familiar as Mickey Mouse's ears or Batman's cape against the sky.

Hiram's Spring joined the national drive to "Save a Life with a Knife" after a San Francisco nightclub owner learned troops in the Pacific urgently needed knives. The Elks scoured the town for four-inch blades in scabbards. Nearly every man in the county had a knife that had cleaned a fish or skinned a mule deer; a session with the whetstone assured they would do equally well cutting jungle vines or "dealing with the enemy." One rancher mailed his favorite—its honed edge encased in a beautifully tooled leather scabbard—to the *Herald* with a promise it was a "real Jap gutter."

The draft board added 130 new eighteen-year-olds to its shrinking rolls; the casualty lists took more front-page space. The latest U.S. list was the longest yet: 760 killed; 144 of these in Africa. Local eyes scanned the tiny print for the hometown after each name, then swiveled left to check for friends. A sailor from Mitchell was missing in the Pacific. Another listed was from Minatare. Another from Bayard. My father, who had been trying to find front-page space for Colorado, Kansas and Wyoming boys as well as those from Nebraska, had to narrow his focus to the fourteen from the Cornhusker state. "It makes me feel bad," he said. "As if the other lives don't matter."

The AP wire gave us the larger picture. Two cargo ships torpedoed in the North Atlantic cost 850 lives. My father found space for a story datelined St. Louis: a woman who'd lost her husband and two sons to the war had taken a job in an aircraft factory. "It's what they'd have wanted me to do," she said.

Mother interviewed the high school French teacher, who was leaving for Washington to work as an interpreter, and a secretary who'd quit her job to join the WACs.

One Sunday as we walked home from church, she was excited about a new lead; the organist was joining the weather bureau.

My attention was on the rock I was trying to kick all the way home, and I lagged behind when it veered off into the gutter. I'd just caught up when my father said, "That reminds me. Whatever happened to the story on Reverend Sato's family?"

The Jap who might be a spy. I decided their conversation was more promising than the rock.

Mother took several steps before she answered. "It didn't work out."

I'd given enough ring-around-the-rosy answers to know one when I heard it. Apparently Dad's antennas were also alerted.

"You mean you couldn't find them?"

"No."

"Well? What do you mean?"

"If you must know, I found them in a tiny cottage on the west side of town. They had to give up their big house on Locust, and they're just barely getting by with help from their church."

Dad sounded puzzled. "Sounds like a good little human interest feature. Why haven't I seen it?"

Mother's answer came slowly. "I decided not to write it."

"Why not? It's got possibilities, even if we do get a few irate letters. You know they started drafting Japanese boys last month—some right out of the relocation camps. Maybe it's time somebody talked about what's fair."

"Maybe it is," Mother said, "but Mrs. Sato asked me not to. She's afraid. Someone set a fire at the back door of their church last summer. Their children can be U.S. citizens but the adults are still aliens. They're all afraid. They don't want to attract attention."

Dad stopped in his tracks and I almost ran into him. "You know how I feel about suppressing news. I don't do it for anybody."

That was a given. Betty and I were living proof. I felt a prick of fear. Mother was treading dangerous ground.

She faced him with a determined expression. "It's not news. You just called it 'a little feature.' The world's not going to end if we don't print it."

"Maybe not." Dad's voice was rising. "It's the principle of the thing."

"Sometimes people are more important than principles." Mother matched his volume. I was afraid other people would hear.

"It was my idea. And it's my story. And I'm not going to give that family any more grief! I gave my word."

They stared angrily at each other for a long moment. Then to my surprise Dad turned away. "All right. Have it your way. I guess this isn't important enough to fight about. But after this, don't make commitments for me. I'm still the editor and you're just a reporter. Don't you forget it."

Mother flushed but said nothing. We walked on home in uneasy silence.

I felt like half a person without Betty around to finish my sentences. We dawdled on the way home from school, but hours after school and weekends were hard to fill. I dogged Agnes' steps around the house, complaining of the injustice of it all.

She'd interrupt her humming of "Juanita"—it seemed like she was always humming something anymore—long enough to make sympathetic noises, then give me some handkerchiefs to iron or hand me the dust cloth. Her mind seemed to slip into neutral every time Frankie crooned a ballad, and one noon she served us macaroni and cheese without the cheese.

Even the Friday I scorched two handkerchiefs and spilled the furniture polish she didn't get mad. She only smiled an understanding smile and said, "Why don't you do something nice for Mrs. Hermann? Then maybe she'd forget she was mad."

"Like what?"

"I don't know. Make her something good to eat. You know— 'Do unto others.' It always works for Ma Perkins."

"Will you help me?"

"I don't think I'll be here." Her face took on the blissful look Schnoz got when you scratched his stomach. "I have to talk to your mother when she comes home."

The talk was short, because Agnes had already made up her mind. Her sergeant had orders for a base in Maryland. She intended to follow him. She could get work in a nearby munitions plant that was begging for workers.

"It's good money, ma'am. And I can see Homer on weekends. And I'll be doing something important. Anybody can do housework."

By Monday, Mother and I were on our own.

The trouble was, keeping house was getting to be a challenge even for women so inclined. "The loyal American homemaker will be a soldier, doing her duty at her post, the home front," a government booklet advised. A housewife who conserved food, saved grease, donated rubber and metal and spent 10 percent of the family income on war bonds could glue a proud V-Home sticker in her front window.

With sugar needed for explosives, the patriotic cook used honey, molasses and fruit for sweetening. She made "War Cake" with rye flour, corn syrup and raisins. To save wheat she used corn meal, rice flour or cracker crumbs. A pound of coffee had to last six weeks now; she followed Eleanor Roosevelt's lead and dried the grounds to be used again. With meat and butter rationing imminent, she stretched supplies as far as possible.

"Are you sure this is right?" Mother asked. "This is how she doubled it?"

"I think so. I know Agnes put in canned milk and water."

"And beat it all together?"

"Yeah."

"But it's getting all runny. I'll die if I've ruined a pound of butter. We haven't had any for three weeks."

"That looks pretty yucky."

"Maybe I shouldn't have melted it first." Mother revved up the mixer. Little splatters of white and yellow dotted her apron. I backed away and wiped my cheek.

"Are you sure there wasn't something else?"

"Oh, yeah. I think she put in Jello."

"Jello?"

"Why don't you try cherry?"

"Cherry!"

"Be better than the plain old stuff."

"Why don't you go out and play?"

When I went out the front door it looked like our V-Home sticker was losing its grip on the living room window.

The snow was thick and wet, perfect for a snow fort, but how could I play commando all alone? I stiffened my body and dropped backward, then fanned my arms and legs. What could I do for Mrs. Hermann? The question was never far from my mind. Without Agnes, making something good to eat didn't seem very likely.

I rolled up to admire my angel, but without anyone to pull me up I'd left a hand print under the wing. I could make her a ration book holder. I'd spent hours on one for Mother, sewing pink oil-cloth together with white yarn. But Betty had done that project, too, to earn her Camp Fire citizenship bead.

While some girls earned beads for baking cookies or fixing salads, my home-craft beads usually came from waxing the floor. I could roast wieners over a camp fire and fry an egg on a tin can stove, but building a fire in the yard presented a problem. Besides, I had the feeling Agnes had something better in mind.

Monday after school I was leafing through the newspaper when I saw a recipe I thought might be the answer. Magic pudding, it said. The magic ingredient rated two stars for being extra nutritious. I needed only five other things. Milk, cornmeal, eggs, salt—just everyday things. I did have to go to the store for raisins, and I felt a few qualms when the shelf marker read twenty ration points for a little box. But I was sure when Betty and I were friends again, Mother would think it was worth it. As I tore the blue stamps out of my book and handed them to Mrs. Hermann, I could hardly keep my plans secret.

"Agnes making something special?" she asked.

"Agnes has gone to make bombs," I said. "This is for a surprise." I tipped my head back and squinched my right eye closed like Betty Hutton did when she was making a joke. My left eye could see Mrs. Hermann looking puzzled. I wondered if German people didn't know how to wink.

Back in the kitchen, I cooked the corn meal in milk, like it said, and it boiled over only just a little. While it cooled, I cooked the magic ingredient and faced the task of separating four eggs. I'd seen both Agnes and Mother do this. Agnes used one hand to crack the shell, allowed the white to drool into its bowl and dispatched the yolk to its bowl in one smooth motion. Mother clenched her teeth, gave the egg a whack, used two hands to pry the shell open and said "Drat," when much of the punctured yolk declined to consider a separate destiny. "You use the big pieces of shell to pick out the little pieces," she always told me.

I considered and pulled out the colander. It was a slow process, but eventually the yolks enriched the cornmeal and I had enough whites to whip up a fair froth. I stirred it all together and dumped in the raisins. Then I noticed the recipe said to bake it. I knew that had to be a mistake. We always stirred pudding on top of the stove. They must have meant stir it for thirty minutes. As I stirred, I realized I had plenty for a peace offering for Mrs. Hermann and could still surprise my parents with a treat for supper.

But long before the thirty minutes were up, the pudding was clumping around my spoon. Suddenly the spoon was turning the whole pan. I decided it must be done, but it looked more like cake than pudding. I stared at the lump around my spoon doubtfully, but carved off a chunk and wrapped it in wax paper. Then, with sudden inspiration, I remembered Mrs. Hermann called cake something that sounded like cuuken. I got my tablet and wrote "Magic cuuken for Mrs. Hermann from M.K." and hurried toward Betty's house with my offering.

I lifted my hand and knocked on the kitchen door. Then I felt a surge of panic. What if she thought I was trying to play with Betty? What if she told me to go home? I knelt quickly and put the gift inside the screen door. I could hear Schnoz barking—someone's footsteps. I turned and ran.

My father's supper hours were brief and unpredictable. I had only started cleaning up my mess when they came in the door. They were too busy talking to notice.

"I've been thinking about it ever since Danny asked for clippings," Dad said. "I think we should do it."

"Mail a free paper to every Scotts Bluff County serviceman?" Mother was warming up some leftover potato soup. "I think it's a wonderful idea. But how can we do that and have enough copies for our other subscribers?"

"That's what I've been struggling with. Our newsprint allocation will only stretch so far." He shook the salt shaker over his soup. "There is so much news—so many things people need to know—and here I am printing papers half as big as they used to be. It's driving me crazy." He tasted the soup and salted it again.

"But if we increase our subscriber list—"

Dad reached for the pepper. "We'll have to cut the number of pages."

"But that will cost us advertising." Mother blew on her cup of tea. "How can we afford that?"

"I don't know. It'll be a squeeze. My ad man thinks I'm crazy. What do you think?"

"You're asking me?" Mother looked surprised and pleased. "I think we should do it. We should start next week. We'll manage somehow." She lifted her teacup in kind of a pledge and they smiled at each other across the table.

I thought it was a perfect time to bring out my surprise. I hurried over to the counter, cut off chunks of pudding and presented it with a flourish.

"Dessert?" Mother asked.

"A surprise. I made it myself."

"Really," Mother said.

"It's mostly for Betty's mom, but there was enough for you, too."

"For Betty's mom?"

"Yeah. So she'll like me again. Ma Perkins says it always works."

Mother sighed. "That was sweet of you, dear." They sat looking at their plates.

"Aren't you going to taste it?"

They took tentative bites and seemed to take a long time to swallow.

"Just what is this?" Dad asked finally.

"Magic pudding," I said proudly. "The magic ingredient is oatmeal."

"It's—very good," Mother said, "Isn't it, Hal?"

Dad began to laugh. "Oatmeal pudding! We should send this recipe to Hitler."

"You mean you don't like it?"

Dad was laughing so hard he could hardly talk. "Sis, I'm not sure Hitler is bad enough to deserve this."

The breakfast nook rang with their laughter. I sat in misery, staring at the pudding I'd been so proud of. How could it turn out so awful? How could things go so wrong? Now Mother would have a fit about the stamps I'd wasted on raisins.

Then I thought of something worse. Betty's mother wouldn't understand. She'd think I was deliberately being hateful. That I gave her something awful because I was mad. I jumped up and ran for the door.

"Sis, come back. I'm sorry," Mother called. But I was on the run for the Hermann's house, imagining the terrible scene—Mrs. Hermann, red-faced with anger, Betty in tears.

I had it almost right. A glum-faced Betty was standing in the alley, dropping the remains of my gift in the garbage can. She did not smile when she saw me.

"What did you have to do that for, M.K.?"

"I was trying to make up with your mother."

"Make up? That's a funny way to do it. Now she thinks you were either making fun of us or trying to poison our dog."

"Schnoz?"

"He gobbled down most of it before Mama could grab him. She was trying to make him throw up and he bit her."

"Gosh, kid, I'm sorry. I didn't mean—"

She shook her head sorrowfully. "It doesn't much matter now. Mama's mad all over again. And if she catches us talking, I'm in trouble. I've got to go." She hurried in the back door and I walked sadly home.

When Mother saw how bad I felt, she never said a word about my spending twenty of my forty-eight monthly points for raisins. And I was equally silent when she served 4-point sauerkraut and 8-point beets twice in the next two weeks. She said maybe I should just leave Mrs. Hermann alone for a while, that nobody stays mad forever. My mother was almost always right, but this time I wondered.

GET IN THE SCRAP

"**V**en der Fuehrer says, 'Ve is der Master Race . . .'"

The Saturday matinee audience in the Egyptian Theater gave a cheer. Donald Duck could give a wetter, noisier Bronx cheer than most of us, but we didn't let that keep us from trying. We were more than ready to punctuate each "Heil" of the chorus with our most vociferous razzberries, gleefully aiming them "right in der Fuehrer's face."

From the moment a bayonet prodded Donald awake in a swastika-bedecked bedroom in Nutzi Land, a band oompahed the tune we all knew so well, and the theater erupted in whistles and jeers that outlasted the cartoon.

But the main feature soon had me sober. The title was *Hitler's Children*. It began to show me how the troopers fighting Americans in Africa were schooled and molded. As I watched, uniformed boys little older than I stood ram-rod straight, saluting the Nazi flag. They charged into a group of children from the American Colony School in Berlin, out to play baseball, and pummeled them to the ground while their leader watched approvingly.

Beneath Hitler's picture, their booted teacher decried the wrongs done to Germany and exhorted them to help her reach her glorious destiny. A boy my age was gagged and staked to the ground

129

as punishment for failing in a game of spy. He welcomed the chance to prove his endurance.

I'd never thought of Germans as kids, and I felt a confusing mix of anger and pity. How could their teachers tell such lies? Why did they want to die for someone so terrible? Why couldn't they see how wrong the Nazis were?

Then an older boy in the story began to ask too many questions, to see too clearly, and felt compelled to speak out against Hitler. His reward was a firing squad. I walked home without seeing the slushy streets, wondering if some Germans were good, after all, wondering if all the good Germans were dead.

Spring came more slowly to the North Platte Valley than to the Tunisian desert. Our fruit trees guarded their blossoms well into April, but by the first of the month the icicles that hung in bumpy, yellow columns from the eves were dripping their lives away. Snows were frequent, wet, promising to turn to rain. The ground softened to accept it. A robin hunkered in the snow-laden lilac bush by the kitchen window, patiently waiting.

Out east of town, the internment camp the Army had planted in a beet field was almost ready for its occupants.

"What's it like, Lou?" I asked as she scraped her shoes over a newspaper on the kitchen counter one Saturday evening. I was busy washing out tin cans and tearing off their labels.

"A muddy mess. I thought I'd ruin my pumps just getting to the hospital building," she said.

Mother was pressing my skirt for Sunday. "Don't mention shoes," she said. "Sis has nearly worn through her soles and the new ration coupon isn't good for two months yet." She gave me a meaningful look.

That was not a subject I wanted to dwell on. "No, Lou. I mean what's the camp like?"

"Oh, a lot like the air base. Rows and rows of barracks. But a high, double, barbed-wire fence all around. And more barbed wire between three sections they call compounds."

I cranked the can opener around the bottom rim of a can, thinking of movies I'd seen. "How about big towers with guns and search lights?"

"Towers? Yes, half a dozen or so."

I pushed out the bottom of the can. "And big mean dogs?"

"None that I saw."

"When do the Nazis come?" I began stomping cans flat and discovered I could adjust the rhythm to fit a chorus of "Der Fuehrer's Face."

"Sis, please!" Mother said.

"I don't know. They just told me they'd need me 'soon.' And if I did know I couldn't tell you, you know that." She looked at me reprovingly.

"They plan to use them in the fields, you know," Mother said, her tone dubious. "Helping the farmers. We ran a story last week."

"Nazis? Loose in the fields?" I froze mid-stomp.

"We don't even know if the prisoners here will be Germans," Lou said. "And only those that want to cooperate and volunteer will work. I'm sure they'll be well guarded."

"I hope so," Mother said.

I finished smashing the cans. But the cartoon characters with the huge stomachs and tiny heads I'd been picturing faded before the threatening faces of *Hitler's Children.*

Every week I'd pounce on *LIFE,* hoping for more scenes from the war in Africa. I studied each pictured soldier with the magnifying glass, trying to make him into Danny. But it never was.

Then, when I'd almost given up hope, the flimsy letter would arrive. This time his news was only about three weeks old. He joked about how Patton was fining them $10 if they didn't wear their neckties, how he was in mud up to his "hips" but could shave in a C-can of water, how they rooted for the flyboys when they were in dogfights over their heads. He said he'd lived on D-ration chocolate bars for two days. I thought that sounded great. He described how all his buddies read every word when he got a *Herald,* even though they'd never heard of Hiram's Spring, because it was so good to read about "home."

But he wasn't so happy to read about the internment camp. "I'm not sure I like the idea of Axis soldiers in the valley—even behind barbed wire." I saw Lou frown when she heard that, but she only said, "It doesn't sound as if he's at the front."

"No," Mother said. "I'd like to think he's in the rear, getting some rest." Neither one of them mentioned that the letter was dated March 20, the day before the big spring offensive.

"They're making scrap. Are you collecting it?" The picture showed trucks and tanks aflame in a roadside ditch. The print reminded us America's blast furnaces had an unending need for metal. "Think of every piece of metal as guns to defend your home. There can never be enough."

With basements and garages nearly cleaned out, the salvage effort had turned to new sources. We Camp Fire Girls were on the streets again Saturday mornings, wagons ready to collect tin cans. This time we had special incentive, because the grade schools were competing to see which could collect the most. The school with the biggest pile at the end of a month would win a jungle gym.

As I headed down Elm Avenue, I saw Betty crossing the street a block west on Locust. She had harnessed Schnoz to her wagon, and he wore a cardboard sign, "Slap the Jap with Scrap." We waved and I thought regretfully how much more fun it would be to cover our routes together.

"Like your sign," she yelled, "'Cans are Crucial!' That's great."

"Yours, too," I answered. "See you after the next block?"

By the time we'd covered four blocks we were meeting at the alley to compare progress. Neither of us yet had a full load. The truth was, although most houses had cans ready and waiting in a sack on the porch, only large families had enough ration stamps to buy many canned goods.

The next block was an exception. I couldn't wait to tell Betty all about it.

"No cans at all at the Rivers?" she asked. "But she and Sarah Jane are always bragging how they're such super patriots!"

"No cans out and that big gate was locked."

"I don't know why they don't dig a moat," she said.

"Yeah, to keep out us serfs. But you haven't heard the best part. I got mad and took a can and dragged it along those iron fence posts clear to the corner and back to the alley, and when I got there the cook was waiting for me with this big sack of cans." I poured them out with a flourish. The cans had been rinsed, but were otherwise intact.

"Apricots!" I said in wonder. "Grapefruit juice."

"Pineapple," Betty said. "That's thirteen points. And there's another one. And more apricots. How many people live there?"

"Just three. And maybe the cook."

"Nobody has that many points," she said. "We never sell anybody this much stuff."

We looked at each other. "'Hoarders Help Hitler,'" I said.

"'Victory is Everybody's Business,'" Betty answered. "They must think they can do anything behind their big old fence."

"Yeah," I said. "We ought to do something about that."

We talked over ways to spy on the Rivers and prove they bought on the black market, but couldn't come up with any good ideas. That fence was, after all, just as good as a moat around a castle.

The Desert Fox had broken. Rommel's retreat up the coastal plain of Tunisia was described as a flaming path of death. Some twenty-five thousand Axis troops had already surrendered. Mother clutched the headlines to her chest and breathed a prayer of thanks. But when I moved the pins and thumbtacks on my map, I could see that as Rommel moved his army north he would come closer and closer to the red-yarn pin.

LIFE called it Rommel's "Coffin Corner" and British General Montgomery urged his men to create a German Dunkirk and push the Axis into the sea. But, as April tempted the cherry tree to unfurl its blossoms, we learned the Axis were flying in reinforcements. Rommel was sowing endless fields of mines in his wake, establishing suicide nests in rocky cliffs, digging in to stand again in the mountains that protected the ports of Bizerte and Tunis.

I was sprawled on the floor with the Sunday comics when Lou's voice cut into Li'l Abner's drawl. "Ira's leaving! Do you want to see?" She grabbed up her jacket and was out the back door. I caught the screen door before it slammed behind her.

"Where're we going?" I panted as she strode along.

"The hospital. I just found out."

We were already past Jacob's Market. "Ira's in the hospital?"

"No. I told him I'd be on the roof."

We raced another two blocks. Lou's heels rang on the sidewalk. She looked at her watch. "The message said two o'clock. We'd better run."

We sprinted the last block and ran through the ambulance entrance on the alley. Lou pushed through the doors and raced for the back stairs. The sweet smell of ether and antiseptics engulfed me. Then we were pounding up from floor to floor, our steps echoing behind us, our breath coming in gasps. Lou began to falter. She kicked off her pumps and I grabbed her hand. Together we burst out on the roof.

She pivoted, her eyes on the sky. "He didn't say which way he'd come."

We heard a distant drone of motors. Then we saw it, a lone B-17 swinging in a wide arc north of town. It straightened out and arrowed down Main Street. In a moment the roar of its motors shook the buildings. I covered my ears. I'd never seen one so low.

Then I realized it was Ira. Lou was jumping and shouting. I waved both arms and yelled as it swept nearer. For a deafening moment it was overhead, huge brown wings eclipsing the sun. I was sure I could feel the blast of air from the four propellers, see Ira's face in the nose-gunner's window. I felt light-headed, light-bodied, as if its force were pulling me up, taking me with it. Then its shadow flicked over the edge of the roof and it was climbing, climbing, up across the river, high over the Bluff, to become a spot in the sky. To disappear.

My ears echoed sound in the silence. Lou blew a kiss at the empty sky. "Well, that's that," she said. We headed back for the stairs. We found her shoes on the fifth floor landing. She sat down to put them on and began to cry.

Spring was undeniably with us. The boughs of the cherry tree had changed their lacy white sleeves for serviceable green and the elms were casting dense shadows on the sidewalk before we heard from Danny again.

April 18

Dear Folks,

Sorry I haven't been writing much. Sometimes I just don't feel up to it.

We're having a break for ▮▮▮▮▮▮. The brass doesn't seem to think we are good enough soldiers. What more we could have done I don't know. These guys all grouse a lot, but when the going is rugged they give all they have and then some.

The more we see of Jerry and his ways, the more we realize we have to finish this job.

But enough of that. I'm sitting in a field totally red with flowers. Days are baking hot and some new grass is coming up. Are things greening up at home? Are Mom's tulips up? Funny how you miss things you hardly noticed before. I'm remembering how Mom always has a vase of her garden flowers on the dining room table from spring to fall.

My Lt. has been filling me in on the history here— Hannibal and all. Last time I dug in I realized I was next to a wall the Romans built. What's a guy from Hiram's Spring—a town maybe 40 years old—doing here? That reminds me—been a long time since anybody called me Hiram.

Love,

Dan

P.S. Just moved ▮▮▮▮ *for a change of scene. Lots of purple flowers in grassy fields. More crops around. Kind of like the valley and the Bluff at home, only the hills are higher.*

Letters from Danny always prompted bittersweet discussions. The knowledge that he was all right when he had written the words, that we could share a little of what he was doing, fought to overcome the reality that much could have happened since the day he wrote it.

"He makes it sound so peaceful," Mother said. "What do you think? That he's back somewhere for training?"

"I think he was," Dad said. "But it's my guess from the P.S. they've moved north. North into the coastal mountains."

The newscasts were filled with those mountains' names and numbers. The status of Hill 344, Hill 490, Hill 529 became dinner table conversation. We heard about the British struggle for Long Stop Hill, about the Americans taking and losing and retaking one rocky summit only to face another.

135

The Office of War Information released new casualty lists: 12,855 men killed, wounded or missing since the end of February. Tunisia, we were warned, could cost ten thousand men. Yet every day the Germans could hold off the Allies gave Hitler another day to fortify the European continent against invasion. No effort could be spared.

On May Day dispatches said Patton's men were using bayonets to fight their way up two-thousand foot, mesa-topped *Djebel Tahent* a foot at a time. It was a key position, the hill numbered 609; it had to be taken regardless of cost.

That night I woke to the sound of shots. The night was exploding outside my window. I'd been dreaming I was on the east face of the Bluff, but where the Zig Zag Trail should be someone had painted huge, black numbers—so big I couldn't read them. I was running across the slope with shells exploding around me, trying to make out the numbers. I was desperate to read them. I had to know.

I woke up panting, my heart pounding, and it was a moment before I realized the sounds had a life outside my dream. I crawled over the bed to look out the window. The night was strangely luminescent, as if it encompassed light within its darkness. As I came awake I realized the light source was snow—huge, heavy, wet snowflakes filled the air, absorbing and spreading the glow from the streetlights.

There was a sharp crack immediately to my right. Then a soft, prolonged sigh. Then the muffled thud of something coming to rest. What was happening? I was too frightened to cry out. Were the Germans out there, shooting? Unstoppable? Invincible? Reaching out to kill us in our beds?

Another loud report and a kind of cry, this time between me and the streetlight, and I saw a large branch from our backyard cottonwood shudder and drop slowly through the air, its leaves parting the air with a sigh. I realized the night was full of such sounds, some near, some distant.

I met Mother at the bottom of the stairs, pulling on her bathrobe. "Mom, the trees are crying!"

"Yes, I hear it, too. It's too late for snow. It piles on the leaves and the trees can't support the weight."

"But can't we do something?"

We hurried out on the front porch. The floor was wet and cold. The sounds were louder, an eerie chorus of pops and groans as living branches were torn from their trunks. "It's too late." I shuddered and she put her arm around me. "I think that's the saddest sound I ever heard," she said. We huddled together, listening, held by the awful drama around us.

I curled my feet against the chill of the cold floor. "Mom, do you pray for Danny?"

"Yes, Sis." She pulled me closer. "Every time I think of him."

The big elm across the street gave a cry. "Mom—" This was harder to ask. "Can prayers keep Danny safe?"

"Oh, Sis." She took a deep breath and seemed to search for words. "I wish I could tell you there's some heavenly shield around Danny and all the other fine young men. But I think you know that's not true. War is—kind of like one huge accident." Her arm tightened. "Many good, innocent people suffer."

"Then why do you pray?"

"Because I can't *not* pray. And because sometimes it makes me feel better. And because it's all I can do. And because," she tipped my chin up and her eyes glittered in the strange light, "we have to realize no matter who dies, many others will survive and life will go on."

She cringed at another sharp report, then straightened and said, "Terrible as things are right now, the cottonwoods will grow different branches and underneath this mess I'll bet we find the tulips as perky as ever." She pulled me toward the door. "Let's get back to bed. We'll have a lot to do in the morning."

The morning light revealed the devastation. It looked as if someone had indeed aimed cannons at the town's trees. Streets were blocked and yards littered with branches. Denuded trunks wore scars instead of branches, their symmetry marred by gaping holes.

I stood staring at empty space in our elm tree where I'd reclined so many hours to enjoy a book. Only a jagged stump of the large branch remained. My insides felt as raw as the glaring white timber. Life was going on, like Mother said, but I could see some things would never be the same.

Cleaning up the debris kept us busy for two or three evenings. I had just gathered up the last of the twiggy clutter and gone in to start supper when the phone rang.

"Sis? Is your mom home for supper?" It was Lou's voice. She sounded hushed and hurried.

"Not yet. She called a minute ago to say she was on the way."

"Maybe that's why I couldn't get through to the paper. Listen. This is important. Tell her your dad ought to drive out here right away. He might find a story. Have you got that? I've got to go."

Before I could respond, the line went dead.

SOW SEEDS FOR VICTORY

My first thought was "here" meant the hospital. Then I remembered Lou had started at the internment camp the day before. When Mother drove up, I was at the curb. "Is Dad coming home?"

She started to get out. "No, that's why I'm late. He's working on the press and can't take time. We'll eat without him."

"No. Lou called. We have to go right away." I was climbing into the front seat. "Have you got your notebook?"

"Yes, but what about Lou? Is she hurt? Where are we going?" She stepped on the starter.

"Head east," I said. "Out past the air base."

She negotiated the turn onto Highway 26 and accelerated. "This better not be one of your games, Sis."

"It's not, Mom. Honest injun. Lou called. She said there was a story out at the internment camp if we got there fast."

"We?"

"Well, she said Dad. But you said he's busy and there isn't time to fool around."

By now we were past the sugar factory. "Oh, Mary Kathleen. I should have called your father." She slowed for a moment, then straightened in the seat. "Well, it's too late now. Let's see what's going on."

The sun had set behind the Bluff; Mother pulled out the head-light button. Past the air field, the tires crunched gravel as we turned south onto a county road. Farmhouses along the way began to glow with lights as the dusk deepened.

Mother slowed as she approached an intersection about a mile north of the railroad tracks. "I think I need to go east here," she said. But a Jeep sat blocking the way. We pulled to a stop and a military policeman walked over to us.

"Road's closed now, ma'am," he said. "Can't let you through."

"But I need to get to the internment camp. It's important."

"Sorry. Can't let you through. Not tonight."

He was not moved by entreaty nor intimidated by Mother's press credentials. She fumed. "Your father would know what to do."

As we sat in indecision we began to hear men's voices singing and the sound of feet tramping on gravel. Then, in the dim light of Mollie's headlights, we saw bare legs goose-stepping toward us in disciplined rhythm. Torsos materialized out of the gloom. They were clad in faded khaki shirts and shorts, many of them streaked with dirt, some of them torn. But the men who wore them marched with backs straight and heads erect. Their voices joined in a defiant chorus. With a pang of fear, I realized Rommel's Afrika Korps had arrived in the North Platte Valley.

I stared, mesmerized, as the columns marched out of the dusk. Ranks of tanned men came toward us, wheeled sharply to the right and disappeared down the road that fronted the camp. Boots ground on gravel. My chest tightened; I'd heard that threatening rhythm in the movies a hundred times, ringing through huge, gray city squares, tromping on cobblestoned village streets while resi-dents crouched in their houses in terror. I shrank back against the seat. I could imagine them swinging their arms above their heads and shouting a salute to their all-powerful leader. It was like waking up from a nightmare to find you were already awake and you could not make the specters go away. I wanted to run but I couldn't move.

Then I heard Mother exclaim, "A scoop! I've got a scoop! Help me count, Sis."

With difficulty, I blinked and refocused. The imaginary chorus of "Heil"s began to fade. A US Army MP drove the Jeep that had stopped us. Other American soldiers marched on both sides of the

prisoners, rifles ready. They were doing their job. They would keep us safe.

It was hard to tell in the dim light, but the Germans seemed to be in ranks of ten. We counted one hundred, then another as they strode along, but the light was fading, their feet were stirring up the dust and counting became more difficult. "I've seen enough," Mother said. "We'll get back to the paper and call the camp for more information." She jockeyed Mollie around on the narrow road and we sped toward town.

"What do you mean we can't print anything?" Mother's voice was indignant. "German troops get off the train and march a mile-and-a-half down county roads to the camp and nobody in town is supposed to know about it?"

Dad tilted back in his swivel chair and spread his hands in exasperation. "I got a call five minutes before you got here. The camp commander asked me not to print the story. They don't want the public to get excited."

"Excited!" Mother was almost sputtering. "What's that got to do with it? The Germans are here. We know it. The farmers along the road know it. I bet the party lines were spreading the news before I even got back to the highway. Do they think they can hide several hundred Germans on that flatland?"

"Who knows what they think?" Dad said tiredly. "I'm just as frustrated as you are. I tried to make him understand everybody's going to know, whether we print the story or not. Lou's not the only civilian employee. There are secretaries, clerks who help the quartermaster, other nurses. And the farmers don't go around blindfolded."

Mother leaned against her desk. "But if we print anything we're breaking the code," she said in a flat voice.

Dad only nodded.

"Then that's that, isn't it?"

"I'm afraid so," Dad said. Then he added. "Sorry about the scoop, Bess."

Mother was slightly mollified the next day when the air field released news that was not already back-fence gossip. Gene Autry was coming to entertain the troops. What's more, he'd take time to speak at a war bond rally while he was in town.

Gene Autry? In Hiram's Spring? The news flashed around the playground as we waited for the first bell. We'd never expected to see a movie star outside the walls of the Egyptian Theater. While I was among the group who would have preferred Roy Rogers, none of us could feign indifference. Even Harvey McDougall, hanging around on the edge of the conversation, seemed impressed.

"Is he bringing Champion?" somebody asked.

"Sure," Sarah Jane said, "a cowboy never goes anywhere without his horse."

"Don't be dumb." Tom Schmidt said. "He's a pilot in the army. Horses can't fly on planes."

"Champion could. He can do anything he wanted," Sarah Jane said.

"Aw, girls will believe anything," Harvey snorted.

I brought the argument to a stop with inside information. "Mom said there'll be a surprise. Anybody who buys a bond at the rally gets to sign their name on a bomb they'll drop on the enemy."

"Are you kiddin'?" Harvey asked. "You getta sign a bomb?"

"Yeah, down at the band shell in the park where the rally is."

"My war stamp book is nearly full," Sarah Jane said smugly. "I can get enough money from my Mom to finish it out. So I'll be able to sign."

"A bomb? How much you gotta have?" Harvey asked.

"Eighteen seventy-five," we all chorused. "Everybody knows that." We'd been bringing nickels and dimes to school every Friday all year, trying to fill a book with twenty-five cent stamps so we could turn it in for a twenty-five dollar war bond.

With hands over hearts, we had taken the solemn pledge on the back of the book, promising "every soldier, sailor and marine who is fighting for my country" to buy bonds "to the limit of my ability until the war is won." Half my weekly allowance went for a stamp, but I still had many pages to fill. I felt a surge of envy. Sarah Jane had everything so easy.

As we all took stock of our chances to finish our books, two other classmates decided they could do it in time for the rally.

"Well, I just might do that myself," Harvey said.

"Listen to him," Tom said, and we all laughed. "He hardly ever buys stamps."

"Who wants to mess with penny-ante stamps," Harvey said. "I want a bond. I'm gonna get my name on that bomb."

The school bell interrupted our hoots of disbelief.

In spite of the late snowstorm, spring was rapidly turning toward summer. The Mason jar on Miss Dumbroski's desk was graced with a dark purple lilac spear, cut by an eager young hand before it had a chance to relax into lavender. It was nearly time to plant.

That evening I stood with Mother and Lou to give our plot in the community victory garden a preliminary look. The city had plowed a parcel of vacant land along the road up Cemetery Hill for anyone willing to produce vital vegetables. Every patriotic American was expected to join in the effort to provide "Food for Fighters Everywhere." The community garden was bordered on the north by farm fields; only a small irrigation ditch, blessed with a cottonwood some farmer had not had the heart to destroy, would separate town gardeners from their country counterparts.

"It's not bad soil, do you think, Lou?" Mother asked, as she crumbled a handful.

"Looks wonderful to me compared to Phoenix." She laughed, a sound we hadn't heard much since Ira left. "My Dad broke a spade once trying to dig a hole for a clothesline pole."

"It's probably more than we should tackle," Mother said, "with us both working. But I don't know what we're going to eat next winter if we don't do some canning." She broke off. "Listen to me, talking like you'll be right here—taking for granted you're part of the family."

"You've made me feel like I am," Lou said. "With Ira overseas— I'd really like to stay."

"That's settled then," Mother said. "Wouldn't you say so, Sis?"

"I'd say," I felt suddenly expansive, relieved of a weight I hadn't known was there, "I'd say we should take two plots. We need tons of roasting ears. And how about watermelons?"

"How about peas and green beans," Mother countered. "And squash. And red beets."

"Yuck. You can send mine to the refugees."

"That's not funny, young lady. People are starving all over the world and our troops need more and more food. Every bit we can raise is important, and I expect your help." She rubbed the soil off her hands. "In fact, I feel guilty. I really should give up my rose garden and grow something more useful."

"I'd hate to see you do that," Lou said quickly. "I know they're plowing up parks and lawns all over the country, but there may be times we need a rose much more than another tomato."

"Lou," Mother said huskily, "you always say exactly the right thing." They linked arms and walked the field, making plans.

Each Saturday Betty and I had dumped our tin-can collection on the pile in the middle of Longfellow's front sidewalk. Gleaming silver in the sunlight, the cans had crept slowly up the sides of their snow-fence enclosure.

On Thursday evening I bicycled by the other three schools to check their progress. None of their piles was above my bike seat. I was sure Longfellow's collection was level with my handlebars, but I decided to go past to see for sure. What I saw was Harvey Mc-Dougall loading up a gunny sack with our cans.

"Hey! What do you think you're doing?"

"None of your beeswax."

"It is so my beeswax. Those are our cans!"

"They're not yours. They're for the war effort."

I was taken aback. "If you know that, why are you taking them?"

"That's for me to know and you to find out."

"But you'll make us lose the jungle gym!"

"So, who cares about an old jungle gym?"

"I care. And so do all the kids. I'm going to tell everybody to-morrow morning."

"So tell. What are they gonna do? Arrest me for stealing junk?" He gave a superior laugh, balanced the full sack on his handlebars and rattled away.

I seethed with indignation. Who did he think he was? We'd worked hard for that jungle gym and he had no right to make us lose it. What he was doing was wrong. I could hardly sleep that night, my mind was so busy. I could shame Smarvey Harvey in front of everybody—just like he'd embarrassed me at the air-raid drill. I could scarcely wait. But part of my mind kept chewing on the why? Why did he want those cans? What good could they do him?

I'd lain awake so long that I overslept and by the time I got to school Friday, the kids were all inside. Nearly bursting with my news I hurried into the room to see Sarah Jane waving four fat books of war savings stamps, enough to buy a $100 bond. Then, smug with satisfaction at the sensation she'd created, she turned a sweet smile on Harvey.

"And how many are you going to buy, Harvey?"

He had his back toward me, but his ears turned red and I felt an instant's empathy. As I well knew, Sarah Jane could sink a needle in a porcupine.

"I'm making progress," he said. "Don't worry about me." Then he turned around and saw me. I saw something that looked like fear flash in his eyes, but he lifted his chin and gave me a challenging stare.

Suddenly I knew the why. He took those cans to sell to a dealer. He was trying to buy that bond so he could sign the bomb. I returned his stare, but I was seeing his legs sticking out into the aisle—the frayed cuffs of his jeans, the stretched out, holey socks, the tattered black tennis shoes he wore even in January. I heard his voice, struggling to sound out the words in a simple paragraph. When the bell rang I was still standing there in indecision.

Saturday I came in from our Victory Club meeting just in time to hear the announcer's voice alerting us to a special bulletin. I dived for the volume knob and the news blared out. "At 10:20 a.m. Mountain War Time today, May eight, 1943, the Office of War Information confirmed that Bizerte and Tunis have fallen to Allied forces."

"Mom," I shouted. "Did you hear?"

Mother came in from the kitchen, drying her hands on a dish towel. She was beaming, but her eyes and nose were red. "I know, dear. It came in on the wire this morning. Isn't it wonderful?"

The announcer was still talking. Roads east of the two cities were choked with Axis troops and tanks as they fled toward the last sanctuary, Cape Bon, a tiny peninsula sticking into the Mediterranean. The war in Africa was all but over.

Danny's safe, I thought. It's over and Danny's safe! I jumped up on the footstool and began dancing a jig. "Yippee!" I cried. "Take that you dirty Nazis."

But Mother stood near the radio, frowning. "Hush a minute."

Some one-hundred-twenty thousand Axis troops were gathering on Cape Bon, the announcer said. They might continue to fight. And the retreat had been so precipitous it had left pockets of the enemy stranded. The assignment to mop up resistant areas had gone to the 34th Infantry Division.

So it wasn't quite over. I sank down on the stool, as deflated as a pricked balloon. We couldn't stop worrying yet.

It was another five days before there was unconditional surrender in Africa. The fight-to-the-finish on Cape Bon had not materialized. Axis troops were surrendering by the truck-full, by the regiment—perhaps 224,000 all told. By the end of the month, newsreels had filmed wild celebrations in Tunis as citizens pelted Allied soldiers with flowers.

We were reminded there was a lot of war left to fight. Sicily was only 160 miles from Tunisia, Rome just 190 beyond that. But those battles would come sometime in the future. I relaxed and began to think about summer vacation.

But Mother seemed more tense than ever. She continued to watch the mailbox anxiously, and when Mr. Kelly produced a letter from Danny on May twenty-ninth, she surprised me by bursting into tears as soon as she opened it and read the date.

"But, Mom," I said. "You knew the fighting was over. You knew Danny was okay."

"Not 'til now," she said. "Not until this very minute." She wiped her face apologetically. "I know it doesn't make sense, but I kept thinking some freak thing would happen; that now, when it was all over—" She blew her nose. "Never mind. It was silly. Let's read the letter."

It was dated May eighteenth and seemed intended especially for my father.

> Dad,
>
> You've asked me to write a letter, when I could, that might do for the paper. Here goes.
>
> They told us today we're free to write about what's happened to us. It's hard to know where to begin. Much of the winter is kind of a blur and not a lot of fun to think about. Guys died to take places with strange names—Fondouk, Pichon, Sidi Nsir. But the last month is fresh in my mind and will give you some idea what we've been doing.

146

As we pushed north and east the last of April, the Germans were all dug into the hilltops where they could see everything that moved and direct fire on it. So we had to take every hill and we paid a big price.

The one I'll never forget was called Hill 609. It was the highest around and overlooked the road to Bizerte. The west end reared up like the Bluff at Mitchell Pass, only higher. The Jerries had a regular stone fort cut into the top and there was almost no way up. They knew they had to hold it. We knew we had to take it, and a lot of guys gave their lives to do it. The 34th fought hard for nearly a week to get the hill surrounded. But the Nazis weren't about to give up. They had mined the ravines and mortared all possible cover. So we'd fight our way up a few yards, then hear Jerry blowing whistles and shouting commands, and try to hold against a counterattack. Then fight to inch up some more. It was the toughest going you could imagine, but we got close enough for grenades—even bayonets—and we kept going after dark.

There were some low rock walls across the hill and once in the dark I heard some Jerries talking behind the next one up the slope. Makes your heart stop, I can tell you. But we kept going, and just about dawn some of us followed a little goat path up the back side of the cliff and surprised the Germans who were still holding out. Guess they thought nobody could make it up that way. I can't really tell you how we felt. Kind of proud that we'd done a tough job, but mostly just numb and exhausted and thankful it was over and glad to be alive. Couldn't feel much like celebrating with so many, many guys killed and wounded. And with who knew how many more hills to come.

We took Hill 609 on May 1 and our battalion held it while the others moved ahead. The next night we could hear explosions and see fires light the sky as the Germans retreated. Some of the Jerries were holding out to the bitter end, but others were surrendering by the thousands, and then we heard about the surrender and that was that.

Don't know what happens next. There have been rumors all winter that we'd get to go home when this campaign was over, but don't get your hopes up. Will write again soon.

Love,

Dan

In strange writing across the bottom of the page were the words "Mr. Greggory: Advise against publishing that last paragraph."

EVERYBODY,
EVERY DAY, 10%

The war in the Pacific littered the jungle with casualties and bombers fell over Europe in increasing numbers, but we knew, at least for now, no one was shooting at Danny. An unexpected step on the porch didn't raise the specter of a telegram; an empty mailbox could be taken in stride. When I ran home clutching the last report card Miss Dumbo could ever inflict on me, I was sure each step carried me into the blissful freedom of endless, carefree summer days.

Even Mother's reminder those days could be devoted to bike hikes, belly-flops and evening games of kick-the-can only after the victory garden had been cared for, did not dim the summer sun of my first morning of vacation. I cheerfully shouldered my father's spade and walked up to irrigate our family's contribution to the world's food supply.

But as I neared the community garden, I saw a half-dozen men in identical dark denim shirts and pants moving over the adjacent field of young sugar beets. As I neared I could see their shirt backs were marked with two white letters—P W. Then one stood up and turned my direction. His pants legs wore the same strange letters. Puzzled, I glanced around the field. A soldier with a rifle stood near the road. A guard. They were prisoners. Prisoners of war. The Germans!

The spade dropped to the street with a clang. Horror stories about the Nazis flooded my mind: the Greek boy pictured in the *Herald* starved until he was nothing but knees, ribs and deep-shadowed eyes; the twenty-nine small coffins lined up beside a bombed-out English boys' school; U-boat captains who fired their own men out torpedo tubes to fool pursuers. I backed away.

But then I noticed a man in a straw hat was busily tending his plot in the victory garden, paying the prisoners no attention. A stout woman leaned over pulling weeds in another. They seemed to feel safe. The prisoners were on the other side of the ditch and they didn't look at all like the fierce men we'd seen marching down the road from the train. They had given me bad dreams. These men moved as individuals, some working down the rows with hoes, others crawling after them, thinning the remaining beets by hand. With wide-brimmed hats they could have been the Mexican field hands I was used to seeing. A guard stood relaxed and easy between them and the community garden.

I hesitated. The street looked as it always did. Cars were coming and going. The Bluff rose to the west, the fresh grass on its flanks soft green in the morning sun. A magpie braked above the road, its wings a swirl of white and black, and dropped to examine something in the roadside weeds.

Without water our tiny spears of corn and miniature green beans would wilt and die. Mother was depending on me to irrigate this morning. I couldn't tell my father I didn't do it because I was afraid. I swung the spade back to my shoulder and walked on to our plot.

Something was happening with the carrots. I knelt and peered down the row. They had not popped up with firm green leaves like the beans, but the row bore a definite tinge of green. I was amazed the needle-thin sprouts were strong enough to push through the ground. I forgot the workers in the next field and moved on, nose to the ground, celebrating each new sign of life. The long hours we'd spent hoeing and dropping seeds were finally producing results.

Mother had shown me how to irrigate. Water in the big ditch separating the beet field from our gardens was let into a smaller, parallel ditch that ran the length of the gardens. If you took two or three shovels-full of dirt out of the small ditch bank above your plot, the water ran down your rows, which were planted at right angles to the ditch.

It sounded simple. But I soon discovered water has a mind all its own. It rushed to pool in any low spot, quickly submerging the tiny plants. It turned the tiniest obstruction in a row into an excuse to flow out in new directions. It raced through other sections, threatening to wash small roots from the ground. I felt like I was trying to herd a whole flock of the headless chickens Agnes had chased for Sunday dinner.

I was rushing around to close first one leak and then another when I heard a voice singing.

"'Oh, gif me land, lots of land, under starry skies abof—'"

It was a man's voice, low and deep. I straightened from my work and looked around, surprised anyone was that close to me. My eyes met those of a prisoner working just across the ditch. He was shorter than most of the other men and his blue eyes looked through a pair of gold-rimmed glasses.

He gave me a grin and a broad wink. "Don't fence me in," he sang, dragging out the words and pulling his round face into such a woeful expression I couldn't help but laugh.

The cowboy's musical plea for the chance to ride wide-open spaces had been on the *Hit Parade* several times and was one of my favorites. I could identify with his love for murmuring cottonwood trees and riding a range unfettered by fences, but hearing the German prisoner sing it gave it a whole new meaning, one I found irresistibly funny.

My giggles seemed to spur him on. He knew most of the words, I realized, though some of them sounded strange to my ear. He continued to work down the row, methodically swinging his hoe in rhythm to the music. I was singing along under my breath, when he got stuck for a word. "Can't stand—" he hesitated.

"Hobbles," I called out without thinking.

He gave me a wave in thanks, finished the song with another dramatic "Don't fence me in!" and disappeared down the field.

I had turned to tend my irrigation water before I realized I'd been laughing—almost talking—with a Nazi. My knees gave out and I sat down on the ditch bank in a whirl of confusion. I had liked him immediately, this man who probably had been fighting against Danny in Africa. My stomach twisted into a knot of guilt.

Maybe this singing, joking man had set up a booby trap under a pair of binoculars. Maybe he'd manned a Stuka that strafed a Red Cross truck. Maybe he'd fired a machine gun that cut down Danny's buddies as they tried to take Hill 609. How could I like him? I thought I might be sick to my stomach.

Yet he didn't seem like some kind of a monster. He seemed warm and human. He liked to sing. He could make a joke about being a prisoner. He had made me feel he wanted to be friends. My mind jumped around like a grasshopper, but I could not make sense of any of it or understand my feelings.

"Hey, girl! Watch your water!" It was the man in the straw hat. I looked up to see half our plot under water. I grabbed the shovel and plunged into the mud to shut off the flow, too busy to think about anything but saving the garden.

The benches in front of the park bandstand were always full for our weekly summer concerts, and we kids usually sprawled on blankets right in front of the white, concrete band shell. But on this Wednesday night the crowd was standing-room-only by suppertime, and valley residents kept coming until people stood nearly solid all the way back to Maple Street.

The grassy area in front of the stage, ordinarily host to a mass of small, wriggling bodies more intrigued by the piccolo player's eyebrows than the music, was roped off for a more serious display.

There, in isolated, flag-draped splendor, sat the bomb. People crowded close, chattering as they looked it over. The fire chief sat at a card table beside it. "Buy a Bond and Sign a Bomb," one sign read. "Send Your Message—Whack the Axis," read another. A can of white paint and a small brush lay ready.

Dressed in my Camp Fire uniform for our part in the program's finale, I squirmed through the crowd to where I could see the large metal cylinder gleaming dully. One end was brought to a lethal point, the other finished with a circular fin. I'd sign it right there by the point, I thought. But it looked so heavy—so permanent—I could not imagine it exploding into hundreds of pieces.

"I bet if you touch it wrong, it goes off," a little kid said.

"Yeah, I saw this movie about this bomb in London," his friend answered. "You have to hold your breath while you unscrew the end to cut some wires. Your hand shakes and you sweat a lot."

"What if somebody knocks it off that stand when they go to sign it?"

"Ka-boom! We'd all be blown to smithereens." They laughed excitedly at the prospect.

"I hope it goes straight down Hitler's chimney," a lady said.

I wished even harder I could sign it, but it was too late for that. I consoled myself that I could at least get Gene Autry to sign my autograph book.

"I'd pick Hirohito," the lady's husband answered. "Serve him right for executing those airmen they caught after Jimmy Doolittle bombed Tokyo." It had been more than a year since the fabled raid had thrilled the country, but we'd only recently learned the fate of the flight crews captured afterward.

"You're damn right!" another man answered. "Suppose you heard the Nips wiped out a whole village in China that helped Doolittle after he landed there. Women, kids, everybody!"

"And did you see where they torpedoed that Australian hospital ship last month? Killed three hundred helpless, wounded men!"

"Barbarians!" the woman shuddered.

"Bunch of yellow-bellied savages," somebody added.

The public address system came to life with a screech that ended all conversation. The mayor was urging us to be seated; the program was about to begin. I gave the bomb a last wistful look and hurried to find my Camp Fire group.

Our leader, Mrs. White, was herding us behind the band shell when the mayor's first words sent a groan through the audience. Gene Autry could not be with us as promised. Weather had delayed his flight, so he had time to give only one show. He reckoned we'd understand that show had to be at the air base.

A wave of disappointed talk surged through the crowd, but no one could argue about his choice. The boys in the service had to come first.

Mrs. White hushed our cries of dismay and herded us into the back of the band shell, where she lined us up and passed out our big, white letters and flashlights covered with red crepe paper. We crowded into the narrow passage with the other performers. The light was dim and the floor cluttered with heavy black electrical cords. We didn't pay much attention to the speeches, but I kept my ears tuned for a special announcement. The superintendent was to reveal which grade school had won the tin can contest.

Keeping still about Harvey was about the hardest thing I'd ever done. I still seethed at the unfairness of it. A dozen times I'd been on the verge of blurting out his secret. But somehow I'd never got the words all the way out. I wasn't sure why. Maybe because he hadn't seemed quite so obnoxious lately. Maybe because, before tonight, I'd always thought, "I can tell later, if I want to."

I'd fantasized exposing him at the last minute, getting the Longfellow kids the jungle gym they'd earned, becoming a hero. And as the superintendent announced we grade school kids had collected seventeen thousand pounds of tin for the war effort, I knew this was my last chance to set things right. I thought, "It's not fair. I'm going to tell!"

But my mind could still see Harvey's ears, turned red by Sarah Jane's needling, the fear in the challenging glare he'd aimed at me. My feet didn't move. The jungle gym went to William Cullen Bryant Grade School. Henry Wadsworth Longfellow Grade School received a plaque.

The Bryant kids cheered wildly. The Longfellow kids groaned. Betty, standing beside me, said, "Gee, kid. We didn't make it."

I felt a pang of regret, but underneath I was surprised to discover I felt better than I had in weeks. "Who needs a jungle gym?" I said. "That's kid stuff. What's important is the war." I was amazed to realize I meant it.

But my new maturity did not extend to Sarah Jane Rivers, who was sashaying around in a red satin blouse with a big white V-shaped collar, tight blue shorts, a sparkly red-and-white top hat and tap-dancing shoes. She'd been bragging even before school was out about the dance she was going to perform to "Johnny Got a Zero."

The new song was about the hopeless student who grew up, learned to fly and turned scorn to cheers when he shot Japanese Zeros from the sky. We'd learned it in music class, but it had been spoiled forever for me when we had to serve as a chorus for Sarah Jane's taps and turns.

After a high school girl had given her reading on "Why We Fight" and high school boys had presented tableaux of Paul Revere and his mount, WWI Doughboys, and current GIs, it was time for Sarah Jane's act. The finale came next, so we lined up just behind her, clutching our letters.

We'd rehearsed several times, filing out onto the darkened stage with the whole cast, kneeling in front with our letters held chest high, clicking off dot, dot, dot, dash with our red lights before we grandly illuminated the letters V-I-C-T-O-R-Y one after the other. I'd thought it was a pretty special part until Sarah Jane said she guessed it was okay for people not good enough to do solos.

I was thinking about that when the band stuck up "Johnny Got a Zero," and as she began tapping onto the stage she gave me such an incredibly smug look that my hand did something all on its own. It pushed her sparkly hat down over her eyes.

As she stumbled on stage, cartwheeling her arms for balance, her foot caught in the tangle of electric cords. The band shell lights went out. The music faltered and died with squeaks and squawks. We were left with the less than rhythmic sounds of Sarah Jane tapping her way into the trombone section.

The conductor evidently thought somebody had jumped the gun and killed the lights for the finale. He called out, "Stars and Stripes!" which the musicians could play in their sleep, and one by one the instruments picked up the familiar opening phrase. Somebody behind us hissed, "Get on stage! Quick!"

There was a rush of bodies down the pitch-black hall and onto the stage and a wild scramble to find our places. I was nearly run over by the back half of Paul Revere's steed and dropped my letter. I barely managed to grab it up again. We had scarcely knelt when we heard our cue—a phrase we knew as ". . .for a duck may be somebody's mother," and clicked on our flashlights. Our dot, dot, dot, dash may have been a little ragged, but when we lit our letters one by one there was silence instead of the applause we expected. Then laughter began to build.

I looked down at my chest. I was holding an "R." Two spaces down, next to the "Y," Betty was holding my "T." We were spelling V-I-C-R-O-T-Y.

Mother said later she was sure nobody noticed Betty and I trading places. Dad said I spelled like the Lindeman side of the family. Sarah Jane said it served me right. I couldn't find a thing to say back to her.

But the bond drive, even without Gene Autry, raised $1,227,634: $37.20 for every person in the county. And when the lights had come back on, and people lined up to autograph the bomb, I watched Harvey buy his bond and walk proudly up to paint his name.

I did tell on him later that night. But only to Mother. She said it was awfully hard to choose between being fair and being kind, and that she was proud I'd made the right choice. All in all, it wasn't quite the worst night of my life.

When the June 14 issue of *LIFE* magazine arrived, we devoured page after page showing the blasted buildings, crumpled tanks and great fields of captured equipment the African campaign had left in its wake. But the pages we practically wore out were twenty-two and twenty-three. The two large photographs dominating those pages showed two gnarled and twisted olive trees whose roots spread wide on the grassy slope of a hill 609 meters high.

The text compared the battleground to Midway or Guadalcanal and to the audacity of Pickett's charge at Gettysburg. It predicted a memorial would be built to honor those who died on *Djebel Tahent* May 1, 1943. I looked deep into the pictures, trying to imagine the fighting Danny had described. There was a rock-covered German grave, a small pile of U.S. shell casings and a neat stack of Teller mines awaiting pick-up. But they looked small and temporary in the expanse of sunlit flowers.

"But how can it look so normal?" I asked Mother.

"I wondered the same thing," she said. "You'd think that hill had never known anything but grazing horses and ancient groves of olives."

A few days later we learned Danny's outfit had been part of ceremonies that dwarfed our program in the park.

"Mom, guess what?" I was on the phone with the letter in my hand, most of it yet unread. "Danny was in the victory parade in Tunis!" Without giving her a chance to respond, I continued to read:

> *Wish you could have seen our regiment marching with Arabs in white turbans and red-lined capes, Polish, British, and Scots in kilts playing— you guessed it—those godawful bagpipes.*

We marched down a wide boulevard lined with palm trees and people waving flags and cheering. Fighters and bombers were roaring over. People threw roses and lilacs and kisses at us. They gave us the Victory sign and shouted "Vivé! Vivé!" I felt like I was in the movies.

"The movies!" Mother said. "Maybe we'll get to see him in a newsreel."

"I'd better go twice a week," I said.

"We'll see. Go on."

I read on, but my mood changed as I got into the next paragraph.

It was kind of a thrill, but I was so tired I felt like only half of me was there. It was the first time in weeks we'd had a chance to shower and get clean clothes. It was nice to see those people so happy, but I can't forget what it took to get there. This country is a wreck—towns bombed out, bridges gone, burned out vehicles everywhere, and shallow graves all over the place.

I heard Mother sigh.

The other day I saw four German graves beside a green field. They were bordered with white rocks, very neat, and each had the German Iron Cross on a white cross above it. "These dead gave their spirits for the glory of Greater Germany," it said. They have a strange idea of glory.

We're near Bizerte now and it's a totally ruined city. Maybe was beautiful once—lots of pink and white houses sitting above the ocean. But they're all blasted and burned now and the harbor is full of sunken ships.

My Lt. and I walked along the old walls built for protection thousands of years ago and talked about how many times men had fought over this place. He was a history teacher before he was drafted. Sure an interesting guy to talk to. Our job now is to guard the POWs—.

"POWs!" I interrupted myself. I hadn't told anyone about "Don't Fence Me In," as I thought of him, and again I felt a surge of guilt.

"Go on about the POWs," urged Mother. "Your father will be interested in this. He's been waiting nearly a month for the Army to admit there are prisoners here and clear his story."

There are thousands in this camp. Must say they're a disciplined bunch. The German officers control their men and take care of any punishment needed. Most of them are still loyal to Hitler and wear their dirty old uniforms instead of the denims we give them. Some seem to be more reasonable, men who had to fight no matter what they thought of Hitler. But some are really fanatics.

Love,

Dan

"Is that all?" Mother asked.

"Not quite." I read a note scrawled in the margin.

Please keep writing. Tell me about your garden and the trees and books and movies. I need to hear about the normal world.

THE SECOND FRONT DEPENDS ON THE HOME FRONT

The normal world Danny reached for was still with us in many ways. The meadowlarks were back for the summer, pouring liquid song into the air from atop the fence posts. Sunflowers were budding and farmers' fields boasted promising strips of green. But three thousand young men, a tenth of the county's population, were off fighting the war. The draft board dug deeper, taking men in their thirties to fill its quotas. Mother took a picture of the railroad's first female section crew. The five women posed proudly in their overalls, hair tied up in kerchiefs, rakes and shovels ready to maintain the trackbed.

The implement I was supposed to be using that Wednesday morning was a hoe. My erratic attempts at irrigation, which my father described as "teacup or tidal wave," coated parts of the garden with a crust capable of suffocating the tiny plants. I'd wielded the hoe pretty conscientiously around the carrots and corn, but I had a hard time working up much sympathy for the red beets, and helping squash into the world was not high on my list of priorities. The hoe lay forgotten as I crept toward the cottonwood tree on the ditch at the garden's edge.

Magpies make no secret of their presence; I'd been hearing their coarse chatter and raucous cries for two or three weeks. A pair nesting in the tree was feeding its brood, which set up a clamor the minute they sensed a parent arriving with a bill full of cricket or caterpillar. The adult birds swooping tirelessly to and from the tree reminded me of black-and-white bombers, ruling the air despite the dive-bomber attacks of feisty smaller birds only a quarter of their size.

Sometimes one of the parents followed me as I worked. I liked the shimmer of green and purple the sun found in the bird's pitch-black feathers as it strutted boldly along, taking advantage of the insects I unearthed. But the cries I'd been hearing this morning seemed different—the squawk was more intense, without interruption, and it kept up even when the other young birds were quiet.

At my approach, the adult birds screamed louder than ever, but retreated to continue their scolding from the upper branches. Peering up at the messy pile of sticks that held their young, I saw one shaggy black head, then another, poke in and out of the pile. But I realized now the continuing cry came from somewhere else. I looked down at the ditch bank weeds just as a young bird pulled itself under cover.

Dropping on my stomach, I reached as far as I could. My fingers closed on a ball of fluff. I sat up to examine a handful of young magpie.

It seemed scarcely heavier than a pod full of milkweed silk, but it screeched and worked its legs. I could feel its heart beating inside its coat of rumpled feathers. Except for the solid black hood and white belly, it bore little resemblance to its sleek, long-tailed parents. As it squawked, it continually opened its long, sharp beak, and I felt as if I could see clear down into its stomach. Its head looked large compared to its stubby wings, and its ragged tail twitched against my wrist.

"What'd you find, Kathaweenie?"

I jumped at the unexpected voice and looked up to see Roger Haycraft. He squatted beside me.

"Where'd you come from?" I asked in amazement.

"Just across the ditch." He laughed at my surprise. "My dad's farming this place this year."

I thought of the last time I'd seen him, whistling futilely in the twilight. "Did you ever find your dog?"

His head dipped. "Nope. Never did." He touched the bird with the tip of a brown finger. "What's wrong with him?"

"I don't know. Maybe he's hurt." We studied the bird, which alternately screamed and watched us with its bright blue eyes. "So you don't live in Bayard anymore?"

"Not this summer anyway." He glared up at the squawking adult birds, which were pecking at branches and dropping bits of twigs. "What are you going to do with him?"

I hadn't thought about that. "Can't we put him back in the nest?"

Roger shook his head. "Better not. They say the big birds will kill him because he smells like a human."

It took me a minute to realize the implications of that. "You mean I shouldn't have touched him?"

He pushed a lock of hair off his forehead. "Better not to. You got the touch of death, Kathaweenie," he teased.

I didn't feel like teasing back. "But I only wanted to help him." I could hear my father saying, "Think first, Sis, think first!" As usual, it was too late. "But if we leave him here a cat or dog will get him. Or else he'll starve."

"Guess you're right about that." Roger sobered. "Want to take him to my house? Maybe my mom will know what to do."

He showed me how to cross the large irrigation ditch by walking the narrow top of a gate used to control the water. I cradled the bird against my chest and made it across with only one frightening wobble. We walked the beet field to his house, a small white frame building in a grove of trees. But a search of the barn, chicken yard and a "hallo" into the depths of the potato cellar did not reveal his mother. We finally found a note under the sugar bowl on the kitchen table.

"Rog—They called for volunteers to help at the canning factory. Don't know how long I'll be. Maybe all night. There's fried chicken in the fridge. Dad's working the beans."

I was trying hard not to clutch the little bird too tightly, but he was now so quiet I was frightened. His head drooped against my fingers. "I think he's dying," I said, feeling a terrible surge of guilt. "We can't let him die!"

Just then we heard the squeak of a pump handle. "Maybe that's Dad," Roger shouted. We raced out the back door.

But the man drinking from the curving stream of water wore a denim shirt bearing the letters P W. He turned as we raced up to the pump. "*Vas ist los?*" he asked. It was "Don't Fence Me In."

We skidded to a stop and I sidled closer to Roger. "Where's my dad?" Roger demanded. I could tell he was scared. "Where's the guard?"

The prisoner gestured toward the side of the farmyard. Just walking into the shade were several more Germans. A guard strolled behind them, talking to a man in coveralls and a straw hat.

"There's Dad," Roger said.

I breathed a sigh of relief. But the prisoner's attention was focused on the bird in my hands. "*Ach*," he said, "hurt, is it?"

I nodded, my mind again on the warm, limp form. "I think he's dying," I said, my voice thick in my throat.

He reached out with cupped hands. I pulled back, afraid of what he'd do to the bird. But he leaned over and looked into my eyes. He was much older than Danny; the skin at the corner of his eyes crinkled almost like my father's. "Is okay," he said. "I help, maybe."

I laid the small body in his large, callused hands. Its small chest rose and fell with rapid breaths. He turned it and gently lifted a drooping wing with a blunt-tipped finger. "Ving, maybe," he said. "Ving broke."

"Is he going to die?"

The German gave an uncertain grunt. "You got bread?"

Before I could answer Roger's father was peering over our shoulders. "What you got there? Looks like a pesky magpie."

"It is, Dad," Roger said. "M. K. here found it under the tree on the ditch."

"You know I got no use for magpies. They'll peck a sore on a cow 'til it's clear to the bone. Regular cannibals. And steal everything in sight."

"But it's just a baby, Dad. And it's hurt."

"Don't matter." Mr. Haycraft took off his hat and wiped the sweatband with a kerchief. The skin near his hairline looked dead white above his tan face. "Don't want you keeping no magpie, Roger."

"But, Dad, can't I just—" Roger's plea was cut short by another voice.

"This man giving you trouble, Mr. Haycraft?"

The prisoner's arm twitched and he quickly stepped back.

Roger's father turned to the young guard. "No, no," he said hastily. "This man's a good worker. Speaks English. I'll take him as often as I can get him—heap of work to do on this place. It's just these crazy kids wanting to save a damn magpie."

The guard's round, freckled face looked at us with sympathy. "Pretty smart birds, I hear."

Mr. Haycraft gave a snort. "Plenty smart enough to cause me trouble." He looked at Roger. "You mind what I say, boy. I'm going in to get me some dinner. Expect to see you weeding beans as soon as you've eaten."

"Yeah, Dad." Roger shuffled his feet. "Be right there."

The POW was handing the magpie back to me. "Put in cage," he said. "Bread." He rubbed his thumb and index finger together. "Little bread. *Mit* v*ater, ja?*" He stroked the bird's head with his finger. "Und bugs, *ja?*" He turned to follow the guard and join others who sprawled under a tree eating sandwiches.

I watched him go, feeling strange and uncomfortable, wondering if the eyes that had looked into mine had sighted down a rifle barrel, if the hand that stroked the bird so gently had been thrust up in a salute to Hitler. Who was he? How could I feel I could trust a Nazi? Why did I want to? What would Danny think?

A minute later he was back with some crusts of bread. He handed them to me with a smile and a nod. "Smart, *ja, Hatzel* smart. You see."

I stared at the white letters on his retreating back. Hatzel? Why did he call the magpie a hatzel? Why did he know so much about birds? Why should he want to help?

A flutter in my hands brought my attention back to the immediate problem. I squatted to wet a crumb in the puddle beneath the pump. Working together, Roger and I coaxed the bird to open his mouth for a morsel or two.

"You going to take him home?" Roger asked wistfully.

"Guess so," I said reluctantly. The bird was getting more interested in the food. He reached to take a crumb from my palm and began to screech again. But taking it home meant explaining why I had it and listening to another lecture. And Roger would hardly ever get to see it. "Suppose I could keep it by the garden ditch?" I asked. "Just until it's able to fly?"

"Why don't you?" Roger brightened immediately. "I could help you feed it—" he glanced at his kitchen window—"if I'm careful. But what are you going to use for a cage?"

"I don't know. You got a box or a bushel basket?"

Just then Mr. Haycraft came out the door. He frowned at me. "Let's go, Roger. Time to get to work."

Roger jumped up and moved in his wake. "Look behind the chicken house," he whispered, and he hurried after his father.

The pile of junk behind the paint-bare shed did not offer much promise. The best thing I could find was a small cardboard box. I put the bird in it and decided it would do until I found something better. And as I looked at the wire fence that kept the chickens inside, I realized I knew exactly where to find it.

It took most of the rest of the afternoon, a trip home for some of Dad's tools and two skinned knuckles, but by suppertime the young bird rested in a weed-sheltered depression beside the ditch under my wire bicycle basket. Visits to the garden, I realized as I dropped some more crumbs and a miller moth into his yawning beak, would have to be frequent and regular. I was glad Roger could help.

Luckily miller moths were not difficult to come by. The annual invasion of the inch-long gray pests was tapering off; only a few batted against our lampshades in the evenings. But I had no trouble searching out three or four from the corners of the screen door the next morning and I fished two more out of the folds in my bedroom curtains. Feeling well provisioned, I headed for the victory garden.

But the magpie did not altogether appreciate my efforts. When I approached, it backed into the farthest corner and squawked in fear. Its cry of alarm was taken up by the birds still in the nest and the racket drowned out any other sounds. Afraid Roger's dad might be nearby, I looked around. I could see a couple of POWs working far down the ditch bank, but no sign of Mr. Haycraft.

I managed to get the bird to take a few bits of moist bread, but while I was busy opening the sack of millers, it scrambled out the side of the cage and began to hop and flutter down the ditch bank. I was after it in an instant, but even though one wing didn't seem to operate just right, it managed to keep just ahead of me. I was nearly to the gate across the main ditch when I made a lunge and caught it again.

This time it thrashed its wings and struggled to peck my hands, screaming loudly all the time. I tried to hold it gently, but I was afraid I was hurting it. I was about to let it go when a large hand closed over mine. "Hold it so," he said, curling his fingers over the bird's back to hold the wings close to the body.

The bird ceased its struggles. I didn't have to look up to know that hand belonged to "Don't Fence Me In."

I shrank away from him, but he didn't seem to notice. "You got hold down," he said, moving his other hand around the bird in a circle.

I realized he meant we needed to tie the wing down. But what could we use? I turned out one jeans pocket. In the grit in my hand lay a rock that was green when it was wet, a broken barrette and a crumpled bunch of the red paper poppies left over from the veterans' Poppy Day sale. The other pocket yielded crusts of bread and a small, sharply pointed rock I tried to believe was an arrowhead.

The prisoner reached for the rock with his free hand. "*Ach*," he said. "Indian?" He examined it closely.

"Not really," I admitted. "But it's the closest I've found."

He smiled with understanding and nodded emphatically. "*Ja.* Indian. Could be Indian."

Then he picked up the bunch of poppies and studied their paper-covered wire stems. "Dese, maybe."

Suddenly I understood what he intended. I untangled the stems and twisted three together, end to end. They easily reached around the bird. The prisoner positioned the ring deftly, so that the healthy wing was free and the injured wing was held secure. He stood up and handed the bird to me. "You call—?" he asked.

"Magpie," I said.

"Mag-pie smart," he said with a confident nod. "Talk, *ja*?"

"Okay, Mueller, you got the bird fixed. Let's get back to work." The guard's voice made me jump, but the prisoner did not seem surprised. He was across the ditch in two strides and joined the guard, who gave me a wave. It was the freckle-faced soldier I'd seen in Roger's farmyard. As they headed off down the ditch bank I heard him say, "And from now on don't be asking special favors. I don't want to get my ass chewed off."

So the German's name was Mueller. I puzzled as I carried the magpie back to the cage. How could he know about the Indians and arrowheads? Did he only want to be friends? Or was he after something else? What would Danny say—what would my mother and father think—if they knew I'd been talking to a Nazi?

For weeks now I'd been paying closer attention to the newsreels than the feature, hoping to catch Danny's face if they showed the Tunis victory parade. But today the focus was on the Pacific, and my mind wandered. The announcer introduced a special Japanese Army film the Marines had taken from a captured cameraman. Then somewhere behind me a woman screamed.

"Bobby! That's Bobby! That's my husband! My husband!" She began to sob and the audience erupted in a buzz that drowned out the movie. In a moment the screen went black and the lights came on. People flocked to where the woman sat alternately laughing and sobbing. The manager came on stage and called for quiet, which he was several minutes getting.

By then the woman had calmed enough to be escorted to the stage and, in halting phrases, she told us her story. Her husband had been listed as missing ever since Bataan fell. His last letter, written February 11, 1942, had been from Corregidor. The Japanese film showed American troops, hands in the air, surrendering the island fortress. One of the thin, bearded, disheartened faces the enemy's cameraman had recorded with such satisfaction was her husband's.

"He wrote he was fine," she said, her voice shaking. "He just wanted some cigarettes. And some cookies." She felt for a dry spot on her handkerchief and wiped her eyes. "Some cookies. I sent some, and I've written him every day since. Every day."

"That was sixteen months ago," the manager said.

She raised her chin. "Four hundred ninety-one days to be exact."

Something about the way she said it reminded me of Mother's story about a young woman who kept writing into silence. The thought propelled me out of the theater and on the run for the paper.

MORALE IS
EVERYBODY'S BUSINESS

Mother was not at her desk and Dad was nowhere in sight. Eager to tell the story, I ignored Dad's rule and pushed through the door to the shop. I came face to face with Harvey McDougall.

"What are you doing here?" I demanded.

He gave me a superior grin. "Workin'."

"Working! What do you mean? You don't work here!"

"Do now," Harvey said. "Your folks hired me to help in the shop this summer."

I couldn't have been more amazed if my parents had brought a rattlesnake home for a pet. My father wanted dumbbell Harvey for a helper? Stupid, dirty Harvey who couldn't even read worth a darn? My brain was still trying to find something to say when I heard Mother call, "Can you get this roof-stop, Harvey?"

"Sure thing, Mrs. Greggory." He hurried to the Linotype where she sat, looking small, hot and discouraged. Harvey ducked behind the hulking gray machine, which reared a good two feet over his head. In a moment he called out, "Try it now."

Mother's fingers moved over a keyboard twice as big as her typewriter's and the machine whirred into action. Smells of hot metal and machine oil mixed with hints of rubber and other odors as mysterious as the intricate complex of movements taking place.

167

I watched, fascinated as always, as bars lifted and fell, wheels revolved, belts and pulleys turned, cog wheels meshed and tiny brass letters tinkled down from a sloping metal cabinet higher than Mother's head to assemble in a neat line.

She read the four or five words in the line, said, "Finally!" and lifted a lever. The line was whisked up and out of sight and after some whirs and whooshes a hot, shining, lead slug cast with the words slid out to join a small stack of others in the Linotype's stick. Immediately the brass letters were whisked aloft, where they took a brief ride on a revolving scroll before clinking down into the cabinet to await their next call.

My father loved to demonstrate how the machine used every principle of physics, but it was a mechanical ballet I hardly ever got to watch, since Dad's rules put the shop out of bounds for me. I was too little to be any help; I was too careless around the machinery; most of all I was a girl. And now Harvey McDougall, of all people, had a seat in the front row. He had been chosen to help my father. My feelings of hurt and betrayal hardened into anger as he came out from behind the machine, looking pleased with himself.

Mother was massaging her shoulders. "Thanks, Harvey," she said. She stretched her arms and then rubbed her lower back. "I'll never learn to do this. Never." She hadn't even noticed I was around.

"What'd you hire this dirty dumbbell for?" I demanded.

Mother whirled in her chair. "Mary Kathleen! What an awful thing to say!" She glared at me. "I want you to apologize to Harvey right now. Then go wait for me at my desk. I think we need to have a talk."

"Apologize? To a thief who steals tin cans? Who cheated our school out of a jungle gym?" I was gratified to see shame wash over Harvey's face. "Okay. I'm sorry! I'm sorry I didn't tell!"

I spun on my heel and stomped out of the shop, but the stomps had subsided by the time I got to Mother's desk. I was in for a lecture and I knew I might as well get it over with, although I couldn't see why I should be in trouble for telling the truth.

But Mother wasn't interested in what was or was not true. What she gave me was worse than a lecture. She gave me "things to think about." How would I like to go to school in ragged clothes? How many baths would I take if I had to heat the water on a stove? When had I ever gone to bed hungry? How would I feel if I were twelve years old and still couldn't figure out how to read? What would I do if everybody called me a dumbbell? Especially if I wasn't dumb?

Her quiet questions settled on my shoulders like the heavy quilt my grandmother had made from Grandfather's old suits. I felt like I did sometimes at her house, tucked in until I could hardly breathe. My arguments were smothered under a blanket of guilt.

I redeemed myself somewhat by telling Mother what had happened at the theater, and she was immediately on the phone. The theater manager had invited the young wife to sit through as many showings as she wanted. Olsson's Portrait Studio offered to make a print of the frame that showed her husband. Shirley was busy fielding phone calls as Mrs. Reynolds' story swept up and down Main Street, but I felt more in-the-way than part of the excitement.

Wanting to be any place but the office, longing to talk to Betty, or Lou, or anyone who'd understand, I decided to go up to the garden and feed the magpie. The young bird needed me, if no one else did. It was all Roger and I could do to keep it fed, even though he'd started snitching handfuls of chicken mash from his mother's flock. Once, the day before, the bird had come to the side of the cage, as if he knew me, and I was eager to see if he'd do it again.

I cut through the alley behind the paper and was passing the big double doors where the rolls of newsprint were delivered when Harvey sauntered out and climbed on his bicycle. I was surprised when he began to ride slowly alongside me. In no mood to trade barbs, I refused to look at him.

We were nearly at the corner when he said, "How come you didn't tell on me?"

"That's for me to know and you to find out," I snapped.

He swerved over to kick at a pile of boxes. Then he circled back to stop directly in my path. "I mean it. How come?" He was looking at me as if he'd never seen me before.

"Because I'm about as du—." I thought about Mother's questions and swallowed the word. "You got me," I finished with a shrug.

He seemed equally at a loss. I stepped around his bike and walked on. I was just about to cross the street when I heard his bicycle behind me. Before I could react I felt a tug on one of my braids. His rusty bike fender rattled as he bounced down over the curb, but I thought I caught the words "Guess I owe you one, M. K.," before he sped down the street.

The late afternoon sun was still hot on my back as I crawled along the ditch bank searching for insects. It made me think of Danny's last letter. Mother fussed that he didn't write as often now as when he was in combat; I missed the funny things he used to tell us. Instead, he wrote about roads lined with ragged, hungry Arabs, the families walking beside donkeys piled high with their belongings. He wrote of brutal heat, biting ants, inescapable flies and mosquitoes, and something called a scorpion that crawled in your boots at night and stung you if you forgot to check in the morning before you put them on.

I wondered if a magpie could eat a scorpion without getting stung. This one seemed ready to devour whatever we offered, and he was getting better at picking up things on his own. I managed to catch a cabbage butterfly and was lucky to unearth a fat, white grub.

When I approached the cage I saw I was not imagining the bird's interest in my presence. He squawked as loudly as ever, but his free wing flashed a fan of white as he hopped over to see what I had to offer. The grub disappeared in a gulp, and after a few tries he managed to spear the flopping butterfly.

I felt a surge of pride. I thought, if only Danny could see him. Then, if only I could see Danny.

The sudden longing for my brother swelled into a pain so intense I had to curl myself around it to stay whole. He'd sent us a snapshot of himself on the beach with two of his buddies. Their bodies looked almost black above their shorts and they were squinting at the camera. I'd had a hard time deciding which one was Danny.

I hugged my legs to my chest and rocked back and forth; tears streaked down my dirty knees. I had never felt so alone.

"Ach, *Madchen*, *vas ist los*?" The voice was soft with concern. "*Hatzel* dead, is it?" He stood on the far side of the ditch, a muddy spade in one hand, leaning toward me over the water, his round face full of sympathy.

"No," I sobbed. "No, he's okay." The magpie gave a guttural chuckle as if to provide his own answer. "I just miss Danny."

"*Ja*. I see. *Und* Danny is—?"

I wiped my nose with the back of my hand. "My brother." It was getting easier to talk. "He's in the army."

"*Ach.*" He shook his head. "So many. So far away." He sat down on the ditch bank. "I haf daughter, far away. *Deutschland* is far, far away from here." He looked across the fields. "America big country." He spread his arms wide. "Big country."

"Danny's in Africa," I said. It felt better, having someone to talk to.

He closed his eyes for a moment and nodded. His voice took on a harsher tone. "*Ach, ja, Afrika.*" He picked up a handful of dirt and stared as it ran through his fingers. I thought maybe he'd forgotten me, but when I snuffled he looked up again. "*Und* your name is—?"

"Mary Kathleen."

"*Ach, ja.* Maria." He smiled. "Good name." He touched his chest. "My name Horst." He laughed. "Sounds good for cowboy? No?"

I managed a smile, remembering his rendition of "Don't Fence Me In."

He peered toward the cage, which was all but hidden from his view. "So, *Hatzel*—mag-pie—is okay?"

"He's getting big," I said, suddenly realizing the young bird was looking more and more like his parents. "He eats everything."

"Fly soon, maybe," Horst said thoughtfully, "if ving okay."

We heard voices coming our way from down the ditch. Horst stood up. "You feel better now, Maria?"

I nodded. Ordinarily I'd have been embarrassed if anyone had caught me crying, but Horst made it seem all right.

The prisoner reached for his shovel and leaned on it for a moment. "Is hard, being lonesome for brother, Maria," he said, "for daughter. But ve must vait. Keep busy, *ja*?" He shook the shovel at the ditch with a laugh and gestured toward our garden. "Tings be okay sometime. You see."

Swinging the spade to his shoulder, he walked out to join the rest of the work crew, which the guard was gathering from along the ditch. The white letters on their backs rose and fell in a ragged pattern as they crossed the field to Roger's house.

When the army finally cleared the story my father wrote after his visit to the internment camp, Hiram's Spring had the basic facts. In addition to the three compounds, another fenced area held a hospital, a chapel, and buildings for classrooms, a library, a theater

171

and shops where prisoners could work as tailors or cobblers. The camp's garrison lived in barracks in a separate, open area.

The enlisted Germans baked, cooked and served their own food, cleaned their barracks and washed their clothes. Those who worked, either in camp or out on farms, were paid eighty cents a day, as established by the Geneva Convention. They preferred their own army shorts to prison denims and liked to go bare-chested in the sun. German officers, who did not have to work, maintained discipline through an *oberfelter*, similar to a sergeant, who was in charge of each compound.

"But what about the men themselves?" Mother asked as she set the table for breakfast one Sunday. "What are they like?"

I was squeezing a capsule of garish yellow food color into a pound of lard-white margarine. The color was supposed to help us pretend it was butter, which we hadn't seen for weeks. It may have helped my parents, but as the appointed household squeezer, I rated both process and product only slightly more appetizing than cod liver oil.

"Seemed like a pretty tough bunch to me," my father answered. "Proud. You wouldn't know they'd been defeated. They were polite, but kind of arrogant. I think a lot of them still expect to win the war. To tell you the truth, if it hadn't been for the barbed wire, I'd have felt like I'd wandered into a German army base."

My hand closed involuntarily and cold margarine squished between my fingers. A drop of vivid yellow splashed out on the linoleum counter top.

"That gives me chills," Mother said. "You didn't put that in your article."

"What I put in and what the army left in were two different things," Dad said. "They don't want to alarm the civilian population."

"Do you think the camp is safe?" Mother asked.

"Oh, I think it's secure all right, although the commander wasn't real thrilled with the caliber of men assigned to his unit. Not the cream of the army, for sure. But I think they figure prisoners who've spent three or four days on a train to get here realize there's not much point in escaping."

What was it Horst had said? "Big country!" I wondered now what he'd been thinking.

Lou, who stood at the stove flipping pancakes, had been quiet, but now she spoke up. "Well, I only see the prisoners when they're sick, but I seem to have a different impression than you do, Hal. A few of them frighten me, but we have several who work in the ward, and they're very helpful. Very capable."

I was thinking of telling her about Horst when Dad said, "Oh, I don't say they aren't workers. They were all doing something—putting shelves over their beds, sprucing up around their barracks, scrubbing the floor—or doing calisthenics, playing soccer. It made me realize what a really tough enemy our boys are up against."

Horst was the enemy. Why was it so hard to remember that? Telling about him didn't seem like such a good idea.

"But some of them are just boys, too," Lou said. "We had one yesterday with a bad fever. He kept crying for his mother. And one of the wardmen brought in a pet kitten to try to comfort him."

"They let them have pets?" Mother asked in surprise.

"I was surprised, too," Lou said, "but this man had a kitten a farm wife had given him. And I hear another man has a baby cottontail. I think maybe the chaplain convinced the commander it couldn't hurt anything and might help encourage their humane impulses."

"Guess he's got to have faith in human nature," Dad said, "but the only sign of humanness I saw was the pictures above their beds—pin-up girls, like our boys, and lots of pictures of their families."

I thought of Horst's little girl and wondered what she looked like. Did she have blond braids like mine? Did she go to school? A picture flashed into my mind. What if she was one of *Hitler's Children*! The bowl of margarine went spinning across the counter.

The bowl hit the floor with a crash, leaving a trail of streaky globs. I heard Mother's cry of dismay and Dad's exclamation of disgust. Lou bent to help me clean up the mess. We had hardly started when she sat back on her heels and clamped her hand over her mouth. Her greasy fingers were yellow against dead-white cheeks. She jumped up and sprinted for the bathroom.

"Lou must be hurt," I yelled. "Maybe she cut herself."

I was astonished when Mother only smiled. "Oh, I don't think so," she said. "Probably just a little stomach upset."

Unconvinced, I ran for the bathroom. Lou was bent over the toilet, losing a breakfast she hadn't yet eaten.

THEY GAVE THEIR LIVES. IS 10% ENOUGH?

This day belonged to Schnoz. Betty and I had been planning it secretly all week. It was the right thing to do, we agreed solemnly. Knowing we'd need an early start, we met in front of Woolworths just after nine. Schnoz greeted me with unusual abandon, and I was pleased to see he'd missed me as much as I'd missed him.

"What did you tell your Mom?" I asked.

"Just that I wanted to take Schnoz for a hike because it's his last day. I didn't even have to argue."

It was getting hard to recognize the Main Street we'd known all our lives. Instead of pyramids of canned food, the old Piggly Wiggly Market's windows held signs welcoming servicemen to the enlarged recreation center. As we hurried by, someone was pecking out a jazzy version of "Don't Sit Under the Apple Tree," on the piano the Methodist ladies had lent for the duration.

A small group of paratroopers from the base at Alliance swaggered down the street in front of us, pants tucked into boots that set every boy in town to dreaming. Other airmen eyed the local girls from the hospital steps and stood aimlessly on the corners in crisp suntan uniforms. Schnoz detoured to every friendly voice that promised a pat on the head; Betty watched with somber eyes.

"Why'd your dad decide to do it?" I asked.

"He heard some kids when they rode by on their bikes and called me a crummy Kraut." She sighed. "He says this will prove we're good Americans."

A line of women snaked out J.C. Penney's door. "Nylons? Do you suppose it's nylons?" A woman pushed past us to join the queue.

Traffic was heavy. As we crossed the street south of Penneys, a Jeep horn made us jump. We turned to see the vehicle draped in bunting and two young boys grinning proudly from the back seat.

"Let's run," Betty said. "Maybe we can be next."

The posters above the merchants' booth showed us what our dollars would buy—the sleek pursuit plane that would carry Hiram's Spring's name if we raised $75,000. The picture made me catch my breath. It soared through cloud-free skies like a beautiful bird.

The poster next to it provided the "why" and brought me back to earth. A GI lay collapsed over his machine gun, a hole through his helmet, his face in the dirt, the fingers of one hand dug into the ground, the other dangling lifelessly over the gun's muzzle. "What did YOU do today for Freedom?" it asked.

I straightened, glad that today I could answer that question. I laid my two dollars on the counter. It had taken me six weeks to save it, but as I looked at the GI's helmet, it seemed a little thing to do. And the pressure of Schnoz' moist snout in my hand made giving up my ride almost easy.

Betty counted out her share and in a few minutes Schnoz' ears were blowing in the breeze as they grandly toured Main Street in the Jeep. I ran along the sidewalk, keeping up for almost a block. Schnoz stood with feet braced against the driver's seat, his nose stretched eagerly forward, too intent to wag his tail.

"I'll be damned. There goes General Patton," one of the paratroopers yelled. He snapped off a salute while his buddies laughed.

Then I had to stop for breath and they pulled away. I went back to the booth to await their return.

"Thanks, M.K." Betty's cheeks were rosy with excitement as she pulled a reluctant Schnoz out of the Jeep. "That was swell of you."

"I hope he liked it," I said.

"I think so," Betty answered. "I hope so. I don't want him to be scared."

By the time we'd walked on down to the Platte bridge, we were all hot enough to wade right in. One fall I'd waded clear across the river with Danny leading the way from sandbar to sandbar. Even now, in July, it was shrinking, much of its flow diverted for irrigation. We amused ourselves by squirming our feet into the bottom. Schnoz galumphed cheerfully around, his muzzle streaming water as he scattered minnows and nosed out crawdads.

The heat shimmering through the eroded ridges of the badlands immediately sucked away the river's cool. My eyes watered in the glare from the naked buff slopes, but Schnoz immediately trotted off up the nearest gully, and we were soon deep in what always seemed an unending maze. We never tired of exploring its twists and turns, searching its striated clay walls for fossils, pretending we were explorers in Africa, or Indians on a hunt, or Hiram Scott, crawling desperately after his fellow trappers.

For a long time I'd believed this was where I'd find my arrowhead. My eyes automatically scanned the rough bottom of the gully as we picked our way over the rocks. Schnoz blundered ahead, sniffing out holes that Betty and I gave wide berth; they might be home to a rattlesnake instead of a rabbit. I was stepping over a clod the dog had dislodged when I saw it—a reddish point with unmistakably chipped edges. At last! I pounced with a cry of delight and Betty turned back to see what I'd found.

I spat on my treasure and wiped it on my shorts. Close to two inches long, it gleamed a mottled red-brown, and the finely chipped edge reflected facets of light as I turned it in my hand. Entranced, I wondered if the last hand to touch it had been an Indian's. Had it killed a deer? Or stopped a jack rabbit? Or had rain washed it down from the Oregon Trail? Maybe it had been stuck in the shoulder of some pioneer. Its shining point evoked the sound of tom-toms and war cries and buffalo hooves. When I heard footsteps scrape the ridge above us I looked up, almost expecting to see a brave silhouetted against the sun.

Instead we saw dusty, brown boots, then the bloused pants of a paratrooper. He held a rifle in one hand and gripped Schnoz' collar in the other. "This your dog?" he asked with a scowl.

"He's mine," Betty answered in a small voice.

"Well, you better get him out of here. We're in bivouac for training. With him around we ain't got a chance in hell of secreting our parachutes." Schnoz whined and pulled against his grip.

177

"Let him go," Betty said.

I looked at her in surprise.

"Let him go!" she said in a firmer voice. "You can't have him until tomorrow."

The soldier snorted. "God knows I don't want him." He released his hold and Schnoz bounded down to us. "I want the three of you out of here now! Or I'll get me a little target practice." He swung his rifle toward Schnoz, and we fell over him and each other scrambling back down the ravine, followed by the trooper's laughter.

"It won't be like that," I said to Betty when I'd caught my breath.

She walked, head down, without answering.

"He'll have a trainer. Like we saw in the newsreel. He'll teach Schnoz to stand guard, and jump at guys with guns and all that stuff. They'll be friends."

"He won't understand. He'll think I don't want him anymore." She squatted to slide down a steep section. In a voice I could scarcely hear she said, "He'll forget me."

"Old Schnoz? He'd never do that." I caught up with her and put my arm across her shoulders.

"He'll get killed." Her voice broke.

I dared not think about anyone getting killed. "Listen, kid. You can do what I do." I walked a few steps, wondering if telling would jinx the spell. I decided sharing it with a friend might make it stronger. "When Danny went to Africa I got out his lucky baseball cap and hung it on my bedpost."

"What good's that do?" she asked tonelessly.

"Every night before I go to bed I touch it and say 'safe at home.' It's worked so far."

"Dogs don't play baseball," she said.

"So use his collar. Or his leash."

"I guess I could." She was perking up a little. "And I know what I'll say. 'Schnozy, Come Home.'"

The dog turned at the sound of his name, his expanse of snout so unlike Lassie's elegant, pointed muzzle even Betty had to laugh. She gave him an apologetic hug. We walked slowly on home, Schnoz content to be between us, our fingers touching now and then in the fur behind his ears.

I had been home only a few minutes when Betty flung herself in our back door. "Mama says we can be friends again!" she shouted.

We threw our arms around each other and danced a jig.

"What happened?" I asked.

"Mama saw us come home with Schnoz. I thought she'd really be mad, but she just asked me about it, kind of quiet like. When I told her about you buying Schnoz the Jeep ride and everything, she got even quieter. Then she said, 'So? What are you waiting for? Go see your friend.' I'm supposed to tell you thank you. And to come over some day and she'll help you make some *Kuchen.*"

The day after we tagged a bewildered Schnoz for the Camp Robinson K-9 Corps and put him on the train for Alliance, *LIFE* published a list that took twenty-three pages of tiny print. It included 12,987 names of men killed in combat during the eighteen months we'd been at war. They were listed by state and hometown, and we had to turn twelve of the big pages before we came to Nebraska.

There were three names listed for Hiram's Spring, and we knew another family had received the Adjutant General's telegram too late to make the list. *LIFE* said there were two thousand more like him, and many more missing, or dead of disease or accidents whose names were not included. I found Broken Bow in Nebraska's list, and Holstein, and Wahoo and a hundred more. It was hard to think of a town that wasn't represented.

The War Department reminded us the list was minuscule, compared to Great Britain or Russia. But we had been fighting mostly from defensive positions, the editor's noted; when the great offensive battles begin, U.S. casualties will mount.

On July 10 we learned the Allies had landed in Sicily, "the stepping stone to Italy," and Europe's soft underbelly. Dispatches told us British, Canadian and American troops had used everything from rubber boats to paratroopers in an invasion described as "a new high in military science."

What they didn't tell us was which American units had left the coast of Africa to fight the three-hundred thousand Axis troops holding the Italian island. Where was Danny? We could only wait for the mailbox or the War Department to provide an answer.

I lay beside the magpie's cage, facing a bitter truth. I'd lain there often, my mouth close to the wire, repeating the word "Hello," in my best imitation bird voice. I'd been doing it for weeks now, every chance I got, and I thought I was making some progress.

The bird seemed to have lost most of his fear; he often chattered and whistled softly when I was near. I pretended we were talking, even if all he ever seemed to say was "What? What? What? What? What?" He could make an astonishing variety of sounds, from the demanding almost duck-like string of "What?"s to a soft gargle of notes deep in his throat.

I was confident he'd soon learn "Hello," and I planned to make the phrase "Hello, Danny," when he was ready. I'd pictured Danny's surprised delight, the look of respect he'd give me.

But as I watched the bird bump against the top of the basket and catch his tail feathers when he tried to turn, reality intruded on the daydream. He was growing every day, looking more and more like his parents. The cage was no longer big enough. When he thrashed his free wing, the injured one pushed against the wire that bound it. Maybe it was healed. He was trying to fly. He wanted to be free.

The rest of the brood had already left the nest. I'd seen them flutter from branch to branch and finally launch themselves on short, ragged flights. Now they were soaring with their parents, foraging for food. My bird wanted to do the same. What would happen, I wondered, if I unwrapped his wing?

I wanted very badly to keep him, to have this interesting creature for my own. I tried to imagine how and where I could keep him. Yet I knew without asking that my parents had no time or patience for a difficult pet. And if I kept him he would be a prisoner. Like the men on Bataan. Fenced in like Horst.

I hadn't seen the German for several days. I stood up and surveyed the fields, wishing he were there to tell me what to do. Some POWs were going in and out of the Haycraft's potato cellar, but it was too far away to see if Horst was one of them. Instead I saw Roger running toward me.

When he was within a few feet of me, I grabbed my nose. "Puewee! Do you stink!"

"We're cleaning out the potato cellar. Nothin' stinks as good as rotten potatoes." He waved his hands in front of my face. "But never

180

mind that," he panted as he dropped beside the cage, "Dad knows about the bird."

The magpie shrieked loudly at the intrusion and drew back to a corner of the cage.

"Are you in bad?" I asked.

"Not yet. He just knows you keep it here. I won't dare feed it anymore. He said he'd better not catch it on our place. He's gone to pick up some stuff at the feed store, so I had a chance to come tell you."

"I was kind of thinking," I said, hating to put the idea in words, "about maybe turning him loose."

"Guess that'd be a good idea, the way things are," Roger admitted reluctantly. "Do you suppose his wing is healed?"

"Guess there's only one way to find out."

I lifted the corner of the cage. This time the bird shrank back in the other corner but Roger reached in and got him. He held it carefully as I unwrapped the poppy stems. I stroked the bird's chest with my finger. "Goodbye, magpie," I said, already missing him. "Don't forget me."

Roger tossed him into the air and his wings spread and began to beat. My sorrow dissolved at the sight of his body in the air where it belonged, supported by the white fan of his black-tipped wings, his tail a black exclamation point against the blue sky.

But something was wrong with the way he moved. His injured wing bent strangely. He couldn't seem to stay in the air. He glided down just across the big ditch.

We watched him flutter and jump down the row of beets, trying to take off. He could stay in the air for only a few feet. But he kept trying. And he was heading right for Roger's farmyard.

"He can't fly!"

"We've got to get him!"

We ran for the irrigation gate but by the time we were across the ditch the bird was far down the field. We sprinted after him, but we slid in the loose dirt of the furrows and he easily kept ahead of us.

"There's Dad!" Roger yelled. A pick-up truck was pulling into the yard. Mr. Haycraft got out. He stood watching for a moment with his hands on his hips. Then he turned, lifted a spade out of the truck bed and stalked toward the magpie. I realized with horror we were chasing it right toward him.

"Don't, Dad!" Roger yelled.

I had no idea what the farmer intended to do with the spade, but when he raised it over his head, I screamed.

"THEN CONQUER
WE MUST, FOR OUR
CAUSE IT IS JUST"

The farmer slammed the spade to the ground, but the bird darted from under the blow, screeching shrilly. Again he tried and missed, while the terrified bird shrieked and I screamed, trying to chase it out of reach.

The POWs came running up from the potato cellar and before the farmer could strike again, a hand gripped his arm.

"You don't have to do that, sir," a soldier was saying. "I'll take it back to the camp." It was the familiar guard. His voice was quiet, but his freckles stood out against his white face.

Mr. Haycraft glared at him. His breath came in gasps, but he lowered the shovel. He looked from the bird to Roger to me to the guard's determined face. "Okay by me," he said shortly. "Just get the damn thing off my place."

By now the magpie was so exhausted Roger and I cornered it easily and the guard took it with one hand. Then he turned back toward the prisoners—and we were all staring at his rifle, lying forgotten on the ground halfway between us.

For a heartbeat no one moved. Then three people moved at once. The guard dropped the magpie and sprang for the gun. The group of Germans stirred and parted as Horst and another man fell heavily to the ground. As they scuffled, the guard reached the rifle and grabbed it up. A click from the gun sounded loud in the silence and the scuffle came to an end. The surprised bird recovered himself enough to scold and the tension dissipated.

Horst got to his feet and retrieved his glasses from the dirt. The other prisoner brushed the dust from his clothing. He was a young man, a head taller than Horst. For a moment they confronted each other, talking loudly. Then the other prisoner spat at Horst's feet and turned away.

Why was he so angry? Had they both dived for the gun at the same time and ruined their chance? Or had one of them tried to stop the other from getting it? Had Horst wanted to get the gun? I tried to remember what I'd seen, but it had all happened so fast.

"I think you'd better take us back to camp a little early today, Mr. Haycraft," the guard said, "if you don't mind."

The farmer nodded and stepped into the cab of his truck. As the prisoners scrambled up in the box one by one, the scent of rotten potatoes tainted the air. The guard held out a hand for the bird, which we had again rounded up, and handed it up to Horst before he climbed in. The last I saw of the magpie he sat cradled in Horst's hands as the truck jounced out of the farmyard.

It was a week before the War Department identified the units fighting on Sicily and early August before Danny's letter confirmed the 34th Infantry was still in Africa. But in that letter we learned his outfit was back in training. Hope-filled rumors of going home, of handing the job over to other units, had been just that. "Can't say much about what we're doing," he wrote, "except it's tough and serious business."

Everyone knew what had to happen next: that Hitler had to be challenged in the fortress he'd made of Europe. The only question was when and where. Defense plants were building armaments twenty-four hours a day, seven days a week. Everything from mines to mess kits poured off production lines. Five ocean-going ships splashed down shipyard launching ramps every twenty-four hours. Planes were taking to the air at the rate of eight thousand a month. The demand for raw materials was unending.

Hiram's Spring focused its energies for another scrap drive. Merchants closed their stores to help. KGKY scheduled hourly progress reports, and promised that anyone donating especially large items would have his name and contribution read during a live broadcast from the big scrap rally that evening.

"Look again!" my father's editorial read. "Dig deeper. Think bigger. Tin cans are fine, but the war industry needs heavier metals—motors, machinery, old cars and trucks. Search your home or farm. Then think about our boys in the service, search your conscience, and look again!"

My own conscience was clear by the time I started out on my familiar route. My beloved electric train sat waiting at the curb. When I'd seen Mother put Grandma Lindeman's roaster on our pile, I'd known it was the grown-up thing to do. If we won the war, I could get another train. If we didn't—there was a new poster in the drug store window, an image that burned into my mind. Dark, brutal Nazi faces, with the promise, "If they win, only our dead are free."

It was harder with my bicycle. Mother urged me not to do it, but she didn't know the bargain I'd made with God. Dad threatened to put his foot down, saying it was silly to donate a usable vehicle. I was terrified he'd forbid me, but when he saw I was determined he suggested a compromise. Harvey needed a bicycle to run errands for the paper and get to and from work, and his was beyond repair. Would I consider giving my bike to him instead of the scrap drive?

I think he expected me to refuse. But I knew immediately seeing Harvey with my bike would be much harder than imagining it in a new life as a gun. It was like sealing my bargain for Danny's safety in blood; surely even God would hesitate to break it. When I readily agreed, Dad looked surprised, but I thought I saw a glimmer of respect in his eyes.

When I remembered that, giving up my bicycle seemed less important. I'd miss having it for bike hikes and trips to the swimming pool, but it wouldn't be anything like the way Betty was missing Schnoz. I knew she'd hoped the army would find him too lazy or too friendly to train, but so far that hadn't happened.

"Maybe Schnoz will trip over the hurdles," I said as she put the store's "Out for Scrap" sign in the window.

"Maybe," she answered without much hope. "I sent him some dog biscuits last week and somebody wrote me a thank you note that was signed Schnoz. But I don't suppose he knew they were from me."

185

"Sure he did," I said as we started off with our wagons. "I bet he could smell they came from you."

"I hope so." Betty turned backward to pull her front wheels up a curb. "I left the box in his bed all night before I wrapped it up so it would smell like home."

The donations we piled in our wagons showed me many families were digging deeper than ever before. We sweated in the August heat as we trundled load after load to the nearest intersection. There were bowling trophies, pans and tools still good for years of use, a perfectly good blue scooter.

Everyone was sacrificing except the Rivers. We stood staring at the hated gate.

"It's too bad we can't give that to the scrap drive," Betty said.

"Yeah," I said. "Wouldn't that be great? They need big things like that."

"Mama says some people make a big show of being patriotic, but when nobody's around they ask if she has any coffee under the counter. Or offer her a dollar for a twenty-five cent pound of hamburger."

"I was at the paper the other day when Mrs. Rivers called about another one of her fancy parties. Shirley said she must have a pantry full of sugar."

"Papa said when he was out buying eggs from one of the Rivers' renters, he saw four brand new tires stacked in the barn."

"Dad says he owns half the county. And Sarah Jane rides up to school in that big, black car every day, even when it doesn't snow." I felt anger building inside me. How could they be so selfish when our soldiers needed help? Didn't they care about boys like Danny?

Betty picked up her wagon tongue. "We'd better get done. Mama wants me to help clean the meat counter tonight, and she'll be cross if I'm late."

I followed her down the street, but before we turned the corner I looked back at the gate. I felt an idea scratching at the back of my mind, but it was going to take some thought.

Evening deadlines made supper at our house catch-as-catch-can. Sometimes, with Lou working late or helping out at the rec center, I fixed myself a sandwich and took it down to the paper. Food tasted better in the bustle of the office than alone in the breakfast nook. But tonight when I headed for the paper I didn't bother with the sandwich. I wasn't looking for company. For the first time in my life, I wanted to talk to Harvey McDougall. And I didn't have much time. The rally was due to start at twenty hundred hours, army time.

Everybody in town was there: the mayor, the director of Civil Defense, the Navy mothers and Red Cross volunteers, the Veterans of Foreign Wars and American Legion. With the high school cheerleaders and band, it felt like the pep rally before the homecoming game.

But instead of a huge bonfire, the center of attention was a growing pile of scrap. A large flat-bed truck from the lumber yard sat at the ready. The voice of the master of ceremonies booming from the loudspeaker was one I'd heard on the radio every noon of my life; it was strange to see it came from the anemic-looking bald man standing on the makeshift stage.

But tonight his voice had a vibrancy I'd never heard before. He was our Scrap-Happy Pappy, he insisted in high good humor. He paced from one end of the platform to the other, cajoling the crowd, celebrating pledges, leading the cheers when a truck brought in the latest contribution.

I made my way toward the stage, my heart thumping until it nearly drowned out the cheers. Could I really do this? I hadn't imagined so many people. What if someone recognized me? What if—why hadn't I thought of this before?—the Rivers were here?

A Boy Scout ran up with the latest pledge called in to the fire station across the street. "Mr. Herbert Williamson donates a Model T Ford!" Scrap-Happy Pappy held the card high in triumph. "Hitler cannot af-Ford to ignore this." The crowd groaned and jeered good naturedly.

I checked the sky. It still held some light, but a few stars were visible and the shadows were deep beneath the trees. Harvey and his friends would be in action soon. I wished again there'd been a way for us to synchronize our timing.

Scrap-Happy dispatched a truck to fetch the Ford, and someone boosted a little girl to the stage. She had a card in her fist, but she refused to relinquish it until the announcer held her up to the microphone. Then she sing-songed a victogram I recognized from "Terry and the Pirates."

187

Scrap iron is a mighty weapon
Haul it in, keep smartly steppin'
Turn in every scrap you can,
To lick the Nazis and Japan.

When the applause died down, Scrap-Happy announced the pledge—the corrugated metal roof from her father's tool shed. "This man is going to make do with a wooden roof for the duration," he crowed. "Can you top this?"

Another truck pulled up beside the pile and four men in Elks bowling shirts heaved an old cultivator onto the heap. The cheerleaders lifted their megaphones and led the victory chant.

The sky was nearly dark. Surely Harvey was ready. I didn't dare wait longer. I darted up to the stage, handed up my card and dived back into the crowd. For once I was glad I was short. I didn't stop until I was behind a big woman with a baby buggy. I peered around her bulging elbow and was relieved to see the announcer leaning down to collect a couple of other pledges. Maybe I could be anonymous after all. I tried to look like I'd been right where I stood all evening.

I held my breath through cheers for a stock tank Scrap-Happy promised would sink Hirohito in the drink, and a steam-powered combine destined to thrash the life out of Hitler, before I heard the words I was both terrified and longing to hear.

"Listen to this, folks," Scrap-Happy bellowed. "You won't believe it. Lawrence T. Rivers is donating the big iron gate on his front walk!" He was too astounded to think up a pun.

Exclamations of surprise rippled through the crowd. "I'll be damned," said a man behind me. "This war is good for something."

I waited for calamity to strike, for a voice to yell, "It's a lie! Catch that girl!" But someone began to applaud and the yells and whistles grew into the loudest cheer of the evening.

I almost grinned in spite of the ice pick piercing my stomach. Now if Harvey's crew got the gate off without getting caught, if the truck could come and go before the Rivers realized what was happening, if—it was the biggest if of all, yet I'd worried about it the least—if Mr. Rivers would choose to give up his gate rather than face public censure by reclaiming it.

I got the answer to the first two "ifs" after endless minutes when a truck ground its way through the crowd. The grand gate lay supine at the feet of the Elks bowlers.

The answer to the second came immediately after. Mr. Lawrence T. Rivers' long, black Lincoln screeched to a halt at the curb and the door flung open. He stalked through the crowd toward the stage, his mouth set in a grim line. I shrank into myself, trying desperately to disappear. *Jail,* I thought. *I'm going to jail!*

But as people recognized him they began to cheer. He looked around, apparently bewildered at the reception. His pace slowed. He took in the band, the cheerleaders, the size of the crowd. One man gave him a slap on the back. Others grabbed his hand as he went by. The band struck up "For He's a Jolly Good Fellow." Bug-eyed, he was pulled through the crowd and hoisted onto the stage, where the manic Scrap-Happy Pappy enveloped him in a hug.

"This man just gave the Axis the gate," he chortled. "Now I guess he has something else to say to us."

Mr. Rivers' jaws opened and closed twice before he could manage a weak smile. "I came to say," he croaked, "I came to say—" The smile gained ground. "I came to say—" his voice was stronger, "what the hell good is a fence without a gate? Why don't you come over and take the fence along with it?"

The delighted crowd roared its approval. My knees gave out and I sank to the ground with a fervent prayer of thanks. But I didn't stay there long. A feeling of joyous satisfaction swelled until it lifted me to my feet and very nearly off the ground. It had worked. Mission accomplished! I'd done something right. Something that mattered. That fence would make hundreds of bullets, maybe thousands...or hand grenades . . . or depth charges . . . I fairly floated off to the alley where I was to meet Harvey and retrieve Dad's tools.

Even that went as planned. Harvey was grinning so widely his teeth gleamed in the dark as he came toward me. He handed me the sack of tools as we passed, just like members of the underground.

"We got the whole fence," I hissed.

"I know." He raised two fingers in the victory sign. Then he curled his index finger to meet his thumb, nodded at me and said "A-OK."

I walked on, feeling a glow a whole report card full of As could not have produced. Harvey McDougall and I were allies, I realized with surprise. There was no telling what might happen when there was a war on.

I stopped by the store, where Betty and I held a whispered celebration of the Rivers' comeuppance, and the next morning I wrote Danny of my triumph. But I warned him "mum's the word" in his letters home. Much as I longed to take credit for the incident the whole town was talking about, I had the feeling my parents might question my way of inspiring the Rivers' patriotic fervor.

I tried to keep my good spirits under wraps, but even so, Mother seemed somewhat suspicious. "Isn't it remarkable Mr. Rivers decided to give his fence to the war effort?" she mused the next day as we started dinner. "When I interviewed him this morning he seemed to have a hard time explaining just what brought it all about."

I was suspiciously poking something called a victory patty, which consisted of carrots, potatoes and ground liver. I tried to buy off the gods by taking a big bite.

"And no one at the radio station could remember just who turned in the pledge," Mother went on.

I realized my father, who had just come up from his workshop, was giving me a long look. Swallowing, which had been problematic, became impossible. Had I hung the wrenches back up in the wrong order? Miss-sorted the screwdrivers? But he said nothing.

"You didn't happen to see who gave the pledge, did you, Sis?" Mother asked. "I know you were there last night."

I thought fast. "No, Mom, I didn't see anybody do it," I said carefully. I felt like a bug on one of her prize roses. I waited for the whoosh of insect spray.

Just then my father spoke up. "Guess we shouldn't look a gift horse in the mouth. Half a block of six-foot iron fence can do a lot more good where it's going than where it's been."

Mother looked at him as if he'd stuck his finger on the nozzle of her spray gun just before she could push the plunger, but he kept right on talking.

"And without it, maybe Rivers will find out how much ordinary people are sacrificing to fight this war."

The victory patty was tasting better. I could swallow it if I held my nose.

Mother looked nonplused, and their conversation turned to some kind of disturbance at the Liberty Cafe. I was left to spiral down like a spider on a silken thread, allowed to live another day, but never out of range of the Flit gun's contents. I had a father who could read upside-down and backwards, and a mother who could read my mind. Even on the home front, life could be dangerous.

HARVEST HEADACHES
FOR HITLER

The victory garden, which seemed a novelty in May and a challenge in June, had by the end of August become more demanding than ten Miss Dumbrowskis. I felt like the frantic Mickey Mouse in *Fantasia*, overwhelmed by a deluge of ripening crops. As the August heat deepened the red of the tomatoes, Lou and I spent evenings relieving the pungent vines of those ready for the canning kettle.

Lou hadn't seemed herself all summer. I had supposed she was worrying about Ira, who was flying missions over Europe, until the day I mentioned her unusual behavior to my practical friend Kay.

"Is she pinning the waistband of her skirts?" Kay asked archly.

I wondered how she knew we'd spent fifteen minutes the week before searching through dresser drawers for one of the household's scarcest treasures.

At my nod, Kay answered with the certainty of one who'd been changing her little brother's diapers for close to a year. "She's got a bun in the oven."

This made no sense to me at all, since Lou never had time to bake, but Kay laughed at my ignorance and explained further. "She's in the family way."

When my response was "Whose way? We've got lots of room," Kay gave an exasperated groan and came right out and told me Lou was going to have a baby.

I was horrified. Even with my sketchy knowledge of human reproduction, I knew a woman had to do "it" with her husband before she could have a baby. I wasn't entirely sure what "it" was, but I didn't like what I'd heard, and I couldn't believe Lou and Ira were guilty of such behavior.

And when Kay counted the months since Ira had left on her fingers, I realized they must have done "it" in Danny's bed! I wondered if Mother knew what was going on. Now everybody in town would know! It was two weeks before I could look at Lou without blushing as red as the tomatoes that piled in baskets and boxes around the kitchen as August turned into September.

When the tomatoes were joined by bushels of peaches and a lug of apples from the fruit market, Mother gave up evenings at the paper and joined the canning crew. We moved through a kitchen so saturated by the unending scalding, boiling and steaming that I felt I was wading through a colored fog.

To lighten our drudgery we tuned in the *Lux Radio Theater* and other shows. On the second Wednesday in September I waited for the stirring theme that meant *Mr. District Attorney*, "guardian of our fundamental rights to life, liberty and the pursuit of happiness," was ready for action.

I was squishing the skin off my ten-thousandth scalded tomato, and pondering the fundamental rights of children enslaved in their mother's kitchens, when I heard President Roosevelt's voice.

I always thought he sounded as if he were seated on a throne. He began talking about the critical need for the nation's third war bond drive, and I paid little attention until I heard his voice rise in excitement. "At this moment," he said, pausing dramatically, "Allied troops are moving through the dawn up to strange enemy coasts."

Mother dropped her hot pad on the stove. "Italy," she said, "it's got to be Italy." She ran to the living room to turn up the radio.

"But the Italians surrendered this morning," Lou called. "I heard Eisenhower on the radio."

"I know." Mother was kneeling, her ear close to the speaker, Lou and I froze, listening for something more, but the president ended his speech without another word on the invasion.

Mother came back to the kitchen, looking frustrated. "Why didn't he tell us more? It must be Italy—the English landed on the heel a week ago."

I couldn't understand what was going on. "But if Italy surrendered, why would we invade it?"

"Because the country's full of Germans," Mother said, "and some of the Italians still support them."

"The guards out at the camp were all excited about the surrender," Lou said. "Some guys were saying with the Italians on our side we can push up through Italy in no time, and the war in Europe will be over by Christmas." She stretched a rubber ring over the neck of a pint jar. "Somebody else was betting the German people will overthrow Hitler and sue for peace."

"You mean the war's over, Mom?" I tossed a tomato into the air and impaled it on my paring knife. "We can quit canning tomatoes?"

"Oh, I don't know what it all means." Mother collapsed on a stool. "Do you suppose that could really happen?" She peeled bits of tomato skin off her forearm. "If only—" Then she shook her head. "It's just too good to be true. I'm afraid to believe it—get my hopes up."

"Oh, come on, Bess. Good things have to happen sometime," Lou said, giving mother's shoulder a squeeze. "Why not believe it?"

Her optimism made anything seem possible. Mother began to smile. "You're right," she said. "Why not? Let's have good dreams tonight for a change." She pulled me into a three-way embrace redolent of hot summer sun, ripe fruit, and hope.

Four days later the AP wire at the paper tapped out a shocking, unthinkable word: evacuation. Even without Italian allies, the Wehrmacht was about to overwhelm our beachhead near Salerno. It was a "see-saw bloody battle" for "battered, heroic U.S. troops" and the outcome was "precarious." While British forces raced to link up with the threatened Americans, Berlin radio boldly predicted they would force a second Dunkirk and push the Allies into the sea.

I taped a new map to my bedroom wall and found Salerno in small print at the ankle of Italy's boot. Did Danny's pin belong there? Just above it in larger print was Naples. It was marked with a black swastika. So was Rome, a little farther north. And swastikas dotted the map all the way into the Alps.

Again we lived for the latest report from the front. The Germans claimed they'd already killed or captured twenty thousand Americans on the Italian shore. I began touching Danny's lucky baseball cap before I got out of bed in the morning, beginning, as well as ending, my day with a whispered, "Safe at home."

The new bond drive focused on the Italian front. The war department lectured us for our "foolish, childish, over-optimism" and asked us to re-dedicate our efforts on "Back Salerno Day."

The high school auditorium was packed and stuffy, but I had no trouble keeping my attention on the stage. The band from the Casper Air Base had opened the program with songs that reminded me America was the greatest country in the world. Our Army Air Corps was unstoppable; our Marines the first to fight for freedom. I waved the small flag given me at the door and sang along, but I longed to get up and march, to celebrate being an American.

But, speakers began to remind us, it was too soon to celebrate. The enemy was strong. Our troops out there fighting evil needed help. Giving ten percent of the family paycheck was no longer enough. The men being pounded into the Salerno beach by German 88s and tanks were giving so much more. How could we refuse to help them?

I watched the final and most-honored speaker make his way across the stage to the lectern. His uniform was sharply creased; his tie tucked smartly into his shirt; the medals on his chest flashed in the spotlight. But his right trouser leg was pinned up around his thigh and his crutches thumped hollowly on the wooden floor. Lou's fingers tightened on the armrest between us.

He'd come all the way from Denver to tell us his story. He played nervously with the microphone cord as he told us about his last mission over Germany. It had been a successful mission, he said. He'd watched their bombs fall through the sky and counted the bright circles of fire when they met the ground right where they'd been aimed. He'd seen gratifying smoke billow from what had been a factory.

The audience breathed out in satisfaction.

But he wasn't any hero, he said, only a tail gunner in a Flying Fortress that had been unable to keep up with its squadron. Shooting down five out of six attacking German fighters was luck as much as anything, he said, luck and the skill of the pilot who'd got them back to England. Luck and maybe a little help from the Almighty. Four other planes from his squadron hadn't made it.

He said nothing about his missing leg. He didn't even ask us to buy bonds. He didn't have to. The airbase band struck up "Comin' in on a Wing and a Prayer" as he swung slowly back to his seat, and the crowd soberly applauded.

I watched tensely as he struggled with the crutches and the folding chair and breathed a sigh of relief when he was safely settled. I stared at the stump of his leg. What does it look like, I wondered. Is there a bandage? Does it hurt? Does it bleed? What does he do with his other shoe? I tucked one leg back under the seat, trying to imagine how it would be to know it was gone forever.

Then Lou was pulling me to my feet to sing "God Bless America," and the crowd spilled out into the lobby, where we queued up at tables in front of the trophy case. When we got to the head of our line, I noticed Lou was endorsing her army allotment check. "But you said that check was for baby clothes," I said.

"Babies don't care what they wear," she answered. "I'd rather help Ira."

I fished out the two dimes and five dull-gray war pennies I had in my coin purse to buy a savings stamp. But I also had something more, the crisp new dollar bill Grandmother Greggory had sent me for my birthday. I took it out and laid it down on the table alongside the coins.

"It's not knowing—not knowing—this everlasting not knowing wears me out," Mother said the first Sunday in October. "If he were still in Africa, we'd have heard by now." She gave the handle of the meat grinder a forceful turn and watched stoically as a rare piece of ham spiraled out in ground form.

Lou, who was chopping pickles, looked up. "I know how you feel. A dozen times a day I wonder what Ira's doing. Is he just taking off, or already over Germany, or landing safely after a mission—" She leaned forward so as not to drip pickle juice on her bulging smock.

We were fixing sandwiches for the canteen at the North Platte depot. Having snacks ready for every serviceman who rode a train through the town, 175 miles downriver from Hiram's Spring, had proved to be more than the women of North Platte could manage.

With trains rolling in day and night, as many as five thousand men needed to be fed every twenty-four hours. Nearly every town in western and central Nebraska was helping out, finding some way to make cookies, cakes and sandwiches for the boys.

"And yet," Lou continued softly, "would it really be any easier if we knew?"

Mother didn't answer, and I thought about it as I lined a shoe box with wax paper. *LIFE's* "Picture of the Week" showed three dead Marines on a beach in New Guinea. They'd been lying there some time; waves had nearly buried the legs of one in sand, water lapped at the out-flung arm of another.

I'd seen drawings of dead Americans, paintings of battle scene casualties and numberless pictures of dead enemies. But this one made my stomach contract and I knew immediately it was different. I realized why when I read the editorial beside the picture. The editors explained this was the first photograph they'd been allowed to publish showing Americans fallen in battle. It was time, the War Department had decided, to let us see the names on the casualty lists belonged to real men.

Lou brought me a plate of sandwiches, and I packed them in the box. I decided she was right. Until we heard differently, I could believe Danny was still safe in Africa. If he was running across a beach like that, or lying—I cut off the thought. If somebody was shooting at him, I didn't want to know.

I jumped as the telephone rang shrilly. Mother wiped her hands on her apron as she hurried to answer. The box of sandwiches blurred before my eyes and I saw a body rocking gently in the surf. She came back looking stunned.

Lou's face went white. "Ira?" she asked hoarsely. "Danny?"

"No, no," Mother said quickly. "Nothing like that. It was about Agnes."

"Your hired girl? What's happened?"

"What about Agnes?" I asked. I grinned as I pictured her dueling with the wringer.

"That was her sister," Mother said. "She thought we'd want to know."

"Know what?" I insisted.

"There was an explosion at the munitions plant in Maryland. Agnes and seven other people are missing."

"Missing? You mean they don't know where she is?"

"No, dear." Mother seemed to be searching for words. "I mean she was—caught in the explosion."

I had the lid on the shoe box and was tearing wax paper for another before I realized what she was telling me. "You mean she's dead? She's all blown to smithereens?"

"Oh, honey," Mother stepped behind me and wrapped her arms around my shoulders, "I shouldn't have told you. Try not to think about it."

The sandwich fixings whirled with images of dead bodies in the surf and the khaki-wrapped stump of the tail gunner's leg. Agnes wore flowered house dresses and got dreamy when she listened to Helen Trent and fell in love with Homer. How could she have anything to do with bombs and death? In sudden fury, I twisted from Mother's arms and threw the box of wax paper across the room. "I won't think about it! I won't! Because it didn't happen. It's a big lie!"

Pushing past her, I eluded Lou's outstretched hand and ran from the kitchen. I didn't stop until I got to the clothesline, where I hugged the pole and began to cry.

The troops at Salerno had held, but it had taken all of September for the Allies to advance forty miles into the smoking ruin of Naples. My father was writing headlines about a river called the Volturno before we finally heard from Danny.

Oct. 1

Dear Folks,

Guess you know by now we're in Mussolini country. Got in the game late, so got ashore without much trouble. Action hot and heavy before we got here.

Where we are is beautiful. The valleys are full of crops—tomatoes and tobacco. (Never saw that growing before.) Lots of little villages on hilltops—terraces cut into the hills—olive groves.

People are in pitiful condition and awfully glad to see us. Kids and women stand in line with pails to get our garbage. Give them anything extra we have. I try to go through the line again for them. Really tough to see the little ones.

Got a quick look at a couple of ancient temples when we landed. Just like pictures in my Latin book. And old stone towers kind of like the lighthouse at Lake Minatare. This country is all so old. And so full of mountains. And rivers that are a lot deeper than the Platte. And rain. And mud. And the Krauts are as tough as ever.

Please write soon.

Dan

P.S. Got a new outfit fighting with us. they're kind of pint-sized, but it sure doesn't show on the battle-field. I don't think I'll give anything away if I tell you their favorite place to eat in Hiram's Spring would be the Liberty Cafe.

"The Liberty Cafe? What's he mean?" I asked Mother when she'd finished reading.

"I think he means they're Japanese boys," Mother said. "Billy Tanaka's grandson was drafted last winter. He's been training in Missouri, Billy told me last time I was in for coffee."

I tried to picture a Japanese in an American uniform. It was hard. I kept seeing Tojo's buck teeth and squinty eyes. "How do the other soldiers know he's not a spy?" I asked. "He'd look just like the enemy."

"I think they've put all the Japanese boys together in one unit."

"But would the other soldiers trust them?"

"Oh, Sis. You ask questions I just can't answer. I'm not sure anybody can. Maybe that's what they're finding out in Italy."

THE JAPS STARTED IT. WE'LL FINISH IT.

School, which had once dominated my life, seemed less and less important. I was in sixth grade now, a status I'd often longed for, but I could hardly remember why.

My class was bigger than it had ever been, and our teacher, an elderly woman called back from retirement, seemed hard put to know what to do with us. She called us "kiddies," which made us snicker, and before long even Sarah Jane Rivers was imitating her behind her back.

When Tom Schmidt brought his uncle's war souvenirs to show, her blue-veined hands fluttered to her throat and she backed away. We kids crowded around his desk, all wanting to be first to touch a real Japanese saber, to try on a Jap marine's belt.

"Look," Tom said, "see all these rust marks from the buckle?"

We leaned close to observe several thin, orange smudges across the fabric, each an inch or so from the last.

"My uncle says this shows how his outfit on Tulagi starved the Japs out. They had to keep hitching in their belts so they wouldn't lose their pants!"

We laughed in delight. When I tried it on, I had to suck in my breath to bring the buckle close to the last rust mark.

He wouldn't let us touch the most-treasured item—a Japanese flag with a dark stain across one corner. "Jap blood," he told us importantly. We were too impressed to say anything at all.

I'd looked forward to seeing Roger Haycraft again, but he was still out helping his folks harvest. Harvey McDougall was in the other sixth grade, and I was surprised how much I missed him.

With so much going on in the world, it was harder than ever to care about spelling lists and gold stars, and I joined whole-heartedly in the uproar when we found out school was dismissed for a harvest recess. With the military and defense industry vacuuming up all able-bodied workers, the crops were in danger of rotting in the fields. All but the smallest children were called to help. The farmers needed all the hands they could get, regardless of size.

It was barely light when we gathered on the school sidewalk the next morning, waiting for the farmers to pick us up. I stuck my sack lunch under my arm and plunged my hands into my pockets to keep warm. It was exciting to be up so early, to be going out to work, to know I could do something for the war effort that really counted. I talked with Betty as we waited, but when the farmers arrived, I found myself boosted into a different truck. Most of the kids were younger than I was. I didn't know any of them very well.

As the truck pulled out of town and picked up speed, the wind whipped my braids. I scrunched down behind the cab and wondered if I might see Horst in the fields. I'd been carrying my arrowhead in my jeans pocket for weeks, eager to show him I'd found a real one. But I hadn't seen him since the day he'd driven off with the magpie in his lap.

There were often prisoners working at Roger's farm, but the guard was never the one I knew, and Horst was never among them. It made me wonder again about the gun. Was it Horst who was trying to get it? Had he wanted to escape? I didn't want to believe that, but a piece of my mind kept asking the question.

The truck bounced off the main road to the edge of a field and we piled out. The sun was pushing above the horizon. Frost glinted on the brown tumble weeds and sparkled from row after long row of drying potato vines. The digger had already lifted about half the field; it churned away in the distance, spewing dirt and potatoes in its wake. Our job was to get the potatoes from the ground into gunnysacks, so they could be hoisted onto trucks and taken to storage.

The farmer stood with hands on hips, shaking his head as he surveyed the helpers his hired hand had just delivered. "God, you're a little bunch, aren't you?"

I was insulted. After all, I was eleven now. I stood as tall as I could.

"Well," he said. "Can't be helped. You're too little for the belts. You'll have to use the baskets." He pointed to a pile of wire baskets and we each picked one up. "That's half a bushel. I pay nine cents a bushel."

Nine cents a bushel! I was going to be rich!

"You fill this up, see? And dump it in the sack. Okay?" He assigned us each a row and we were quickly on our knees, pulling some potatoes from the uprooted vines, picking others from the loosened dirt.

By the time I'd spent the morning struggling to dump full baskets into the sacks that waited along the row, I was scaling down my financial expectations. I hadn't realized how heavy potatoes could be. Or figured out how to hold the sack open while I dumped the basket; half of those in my basket ended up on the ground again. Nor had I realized how sore my knees would get. Or known that potatoes and sandburs are best friends. The burs needle-like spines stabbed right through my cotton gloves, and I'd have to stop to pull them out. Once I stepped on one and discovered the shoe sole which had been paper-thin had worn clear through in a tiny spot. Mother would be upset. I wondered when my next coupon would be good for a new pair.

By mid-afternoon the sun was hot on my back and my throat was dry from breathing in dust. The row I was on looked endless. Some of the smaller kids were throwing clods instead of working. I longed to quit. Then I felt ashamed. The farmer was depending on us. The country needed food. I bent to the job again. We worked until it was almost too dark to tell the potatoes from the clods.

When Mother called me the next morning before dawn, I could scarcely move. Every part of me protested. My fingers were cracked and sore, my lips chapped, my knees bruised. It was all I could do to drag myself down the street to the school.

It was the fourth day before I began to feel better, and that was the day I finally saw Horst. I was working on a different farm by then. I'd taken off my shoe to adjust the piece of cardboard I was using to cover the hole, when the farmer's wife brought out a jug of water and noticed what I was doing. She clucked and fussed and insisted I come up to the house and see if I could wear any shoes her kids had outgrown.

Embarrassed beyond words, I followed helplessly. She sent me back out to work in a pair of ugly, brown high-tops I was determined to change at the first opportunity. I ducked behind a piece of big machinery to get that job done and there was Horst, up to his elbows in the engine compartment.

"*Ach*, Maria!" He was as surprised as I was but his smile was wide. "The little gardener. I missed you." He sat back on his heels and wiped his hands. "Sit a minute."

I sat and we began to talk. I explained why I was there, but the first thing I wanted to know was about the magpie.

"Did the soldier keep him? Does he take good care of him? Did he ever learn to fly?"

"Whoa your horses!" Horst laughed. "Soldier had to go avay. I got magpie now. He's okay. But no fly."

I remembered the moment the black-and-white wings had spread against the sky. I felt sad.

"Is okay," Horst said. "He like me. He say '*Ach, gut*' when I feed him."

The thought made me smile. "Can he say 'Hello'?"

"No. You want him say 'Hallo'? I teach him 'Hallo, Maria!'"

"I was going to teach him 'Hello, Danny.'"

Horst's smile faded. "Your Danny okay?"

"I don't know. He's in Italy."

"*Ach*, Italy." His face was somber. "I know. We hear radio, see newspapers."

I drew circles in the dirt. Lou had been right. It hadn't made it any easier to know where Danny was. The news made crossing rivers sound as hard as taking mountains. I'd been trying not to think about it.

"Don't worry, Maria." Horst's voice was gentle. "He be okay."

I didn't trust myself to talk.

"You know something, Maria? I gif you lucky piece." He reached into his pocket and pulled out a small gray medal on a leather thong.

It glinted dully in the sun as I turned it in my hand. An elfin mountaineer waved cheerfully from the front. As I studied it, I decided he'd just climbed the trail that twisted up the cliffside on

204

the back of the medal. I felt like that when I got to the top of the Zig Zag Trail.

"It keep me safe," Horst said. "You rub it for Danny."

I shut my eyes and tried that. It did make me feel better. I thanked Horst and slipped the medal into my pocket, deciding I'd rub it every day. Two charms had to be better than one. My fingers touched the arrowhead and I pulled it out. Impulsively, I dropped it in Horst's hand. "This is for you," I said. "I found it in the badlands this summer."

"No, Maria," he protested. "This yours."

"Fair trade," I said. "Even Steven." And I hurried away before I could change my mind.

Saturday morning Lou turned from the calendar and gave Mother and me a determinedly cheerful smile. "How about helping me celebrate my anniversary? I'd like to take you to dinner. Hal, too, if he can spare the time. My treat."

I didn't need two invitations. Dad, as usual, was too busy to get away, but Mother agreed to take a long supper hour and meet Lou and me at the Liberty Cafe.

It was exciting to be downtown at night. I stared at the sophisticated young women in high heels who strolled on the arms of their dates. We had to walk in the street to get by couples lined up at the ticket booth of the theater. Others window-shopped the diamonds in the jeweler's display or crowded into the drug store for a soda. Men in khaki lounged on the fenders of parked cars and joined the hopeful line of stags leaning against the bank.

The cafe seemed quiet after the street, but several booths were occupied. Billy greeted Mother like an old friend and scurried about getting us seated. Then he hovered in the background while a teenaged Japanese boy who spoke perfect English took our order. I had a hard time deciding between a strawberry soda and a chocolate malt, but the malt finally won out. Mother added a hamburger to my order.

"You have some new help, Billy?" Mother asked when he came to make sure everything had been handled properly.

"Sister's boy from Olegon," he explained. "Lost home. Was in camp. Now come here."

"The relocation program?" Mother asked. "Oh, Billy. I didn't know. But I'm glad he's here now."

Was this one of the aliens? I poked Mother and whispered the question, but she hushed me with a frown as the boy returned with our food on heavy white china. I took one bite and decided I liked everything about eating out. The hamburgers tasted better than at home, and the malt was larger than I'd dreamed, a big glass with more yet in the metal container it had been mixed in.

Lou had been chattering away with Mother about her wedding day, but when she began talking about her work at the prison camp, I listened with more interest.

"I'll be glad when harvest is over," she said. "One of our best orderlies is working in the fields."

"Do you really get along with them all right?" Mother asked doubtfully. "Aren't some of them difficult?"

"Only some," Lou answered. "There are a few hard core Nazis who make trouble when they can. They threaten the men they think are too friendly with the Americans—accuse them of being disloyal to Hitler."

Mother leaned across the table and lowered her voice. "We hear rumors men can be beaten up, for things like writing letters against the war or playing American music. But the camp commander won't admit to anything like that."

Lou looked like I felt when I was trying to choose between the soda and the malt. "You and Hal have done so much for me, Bess. I really shouldn't say anything—"

Just then the door burst open and a young woman ran into the cafe. She clutched a folded newspaper in one hand and her gray coat swung wide as she whirled to survey the room. Her gaze fastened on our booth, where Billy was clearing dinner plates.

Conversations around the room died as she rushed toward us. I knew I'd seen her somewhere before. Suddenly I remembered where. She was the young wife who'd seen her husband in the newsreel about the Corregidor surrender.

"How can you people live with yourselves?" she shouted, flinging the paper down on our table. Lou's water glass toppled noisily into her plate and water splashed across the white cloth. I shrank back into the corner of the booth and we stared from her tear-streaked face to the newspaper. It was from Denver.

"But that's not even our paper," Mother protested in a shocked voice.

"No! Not you! I'm talking to this Jap!" She picked up the paper and brandished it in Billy's face. "Look at this! Look at this!" She held the front page open and slapped her hand against it.

Billy looked stricken and backed away. I caught a glimpse of a picture that took half the page. An emaciated man in ragged shorts stared dully at the camera; his bony arms hugged skeletally thin legs.

"Look what you're doing to these men! Just look!"

Billy, who was shielding his face with one arm, had been backed against a table in the center of the room. "No, missus! Not us! Not us!"

"What do you mean not you?" Her lips twisted in hatred. "It says right here, 'Japs Brutal to Prisoners.'"

Billy shook his head helplessly. "Not us, Missus! We Amelican!" His face contorted and tears began to course down his brown cheeks.

The other tables of diners seemed frozen in their seats.

"Please! Mrs. Reynolds!" Mother was halfway out of the booth when the kitchen door swung wide and our teenage waiter hurried toward Billy.

"Get away from my uncle," he said, moving swiftly toward the angry woman. Several frightened Japanese faces grouped in the doorway behind him.

But Billy straightened and kept himself between the boy and the hysterical woman. He spoke sharply over his shoulder in Japanese and the boy stopped short. He stood indecisively as Billy motioned him away.

The old waiter's face took on a look of resignation as he turned back toward Mrs. Reynolds. Bowing slightly and murmuring apologies, he appeared ready to accept whatever abuse she had to offer.

"Bobby's starving! I know he's starving!" Mrs. Reynolds began to sob. She turned at Mother's approach. "And I can't do anything about it!"

She was a head taller than Mother, but somehow Mother gathered her into her arms. "I know, dear, I know," she murmured as she held her. "It's awful to be so helpless."

Mother turned her gently and began walking toward the door. "Wouldn't you like us to take you home?" She nodded over her shoulder at Lou and me, and we gathered up our coats. When we had paid the bill, we found them standing on the sidewalk and I helped Mother into her coat.

Lou stepped to the other side of the still-sobbing Mrs. Reynolds, and I followed along behind. We had to make our way through a group of paratroopers who had congregated near the door. They looked curiously at the distraught woman and one of them peered through the cafe window. I saw him nudge his buddy. Then I stumbled into a woman in a fur wrap.

"Watch where you're going, kid," she snapped.

Embarrassed, I hurried after Mother. The crowds were no longer exciting. Hiram's Spring seemed as foreign and threatening as the crush of people in Denver's Union Station. I wanted only to be safe at home.

We woke early Sunday morning to the ringing of the phone. By the time I'd stumbled downstairs to see what was wrong, Dad was pulling on his clothes.

"There was trouble at the Liberty Cafe last night," he told Mother. "Some drunks smashed the place up pretty good."

"Oh, no! Was anybody hurt?"

"I don't think so. I've got to talk to the police."

He had his hat on and his hand on the back door knob when someone rang the doorbell. Mother opened it to find our young waiter from the night before. "Please! Can I talk to Mr. Greggory?"

Dad walked back toward the living room. "What is it?"

The boy moved to the center of the rug, looking uncomfortable. "I've come to speak for my family," he explained, "to ask you not to write about our trouble last night."

"Oh, dear." Mother's hand went to her mouth. I remembered the argument about Father Sato's family and my stomach plunged.

WHOSE BOY WILL DIE BECAUSE YOU FAILED?

Dad stared at him. "You mean at the cafe? You can't be serious. Doors and windows broken, booths upset, food thrown around the kitchen. I can't ignore—."

The boy broke in. "This is their desire. They feel such news will dishonor the family and their adopted country."

Dad frowned in disbelief. "But your family did nothing to deserve this. How can it be your dishonor?"

"You have to understand, sir." The boy seemed to be searching for words. "Because our elders cannot be citizens, they cannot own property. My uncle has been in this country since 1917, but he can lease his cafe only through his son, who was born here."

Mother spoke up. "Is that true? I had no idea."

The boy gave her a grateful look and turned toward her. "You see what they're up against? They're under constant suspicion. They've been questioned by the FBI. My aunt was so frightened she burned all the family pictures and documents they had from Japan. Even with sons fighting in the army, they can't cross state lines without permission."

Mother said, "Our son's in Italy. I think there are Japanese boys in his division."

Dad's tone was sharp. "Bess, please—"

But the boy continued to appeal to Mother. "They're trying so hard to prove they're good Americans. To see their restaurant's troubles on the front page would cause them great distress. And great fear."

"You see, Hal?" Mother reached a hand toward Dad.

The boy seemed to sense success. His words tumbled out. "It will make everyone think of us as Japanese—not Americans. Some people may think there was reason for the attacks—start more rumors—cause more trouble."

I thought of Mrs. Reynolds' hate-filled eyes, of Billy's stricken face. Surely Dad could understand the danger.

"That's what I was talking about, Hal," Mother said. "They're almost afraid to breathe."

"Bess," Dad's mouth made a thin line. I was finding it hard to breathe myself. "I have to remind you this is not your affair and not your decision."

Mother looked as if she'd been slapped. She bit her lip and sat down on a chair. The boy looked from one to the other in consternation.

Dad blew out his breath in a long sigh. He took off his hat. "Sit down, son," he said.

The boy perched on the edge of the davenport and Dad pulled a chair over so they could talk eye-to-eye. "You will have to tell your family that I cannot grant your request."

The boy's shoulders sagged and I saw Mother wince. I couldn't believe Dad was saying no.

My father seemed to be choosing his words carefully. "What happened, happened. I couldn't be sorrier. It's a rotten deal for your folks." He looked earnestly into the boy's face. "But pretending it didn't happen—trying to hush it up—won't help anybody. Never has, never will. People in this community have a right to know what goes on. That's my job. I cannot make exceptions."

I felt a surge of hatred for my father. Why couldn't he forget his rules for once? Why did he want to see people hurt?

Mother, her face set like stone, let the crestfallen boy out the door. She had scarcely pushed it shut behind him when she hissed at Father. "How can you be so unfeeling? What if they're right? What if this leads to more trouble? How will you feel then?"

"I'll feel," my father's voice was tired, "like I did my job." He stood up and put on his hat. "And you might realize it's not always easy."

As he opened the back door he added. "And you also might have more faith in this town and its people." The door shut behind him with a bang. And the Liberty Cafe's troubles made the front page of the next day's paper.

I'd been so busy helping the farmers harvest their potatoes that it was late October before Mother reminded me our own crop was still in the ground. I wanted nothing less than to face another potato, but the next Saturday I was crawling along a drearily familiar, if shorter, row.

My mother and father had spent their noon hour digging them. They were as silent and tense as they'd been all week. Mother had told me shortly, when I asked, that the Liberty Cafe was closed; the broken windows and door were boarded over.

I wondered how Billy's family had felt about my father's story, whether there had been any more trouble, whether the cafe would open again, but the subject was not discussed in my presence. At meals, even here in the garden, my parents spoke to each other only when absolutely necessary. I was relieved when they went back to work and left me to finish sacking the crop alone.

I wasn't entirely alone. Far down Mr. Haycraft's field, a crew of POWs was topping beets. I could see them bend to pick up the beets, and the lift and fall of their large knives. The beets just across the ditch, already topped, lay in long columns, ready to be tossed in a truck and taken to the sugar factory.

The beet harvest was just getting started, but already a huge, long pile of beets towered beside the factory and smaller piles grew at beet dumps on farm roads around the county. To me, the beets looked like big, dirty-white tops, but they were much too large to imagine them spinning. I figured one must weigh more than a dozen potatoes, and I was glad I didn't have to pick them up.

That job was keeping the prisoners busy. I looked up as an empty truck lurched and rattled across the loosened soil toward me. Mr. Haycraft was driving, and a POW rode in the back. I thought at first it might be Horst. The man was about the right age, but when the farmer stopped and the prisoner jumped down, I saw I was wrong. This German was darker than Horst and a little taller.

But he seemed to have the same cheerful nature. He was whistling, and I grinned when I realized the tune was "Pistol Packin' Mama." He scooped up a pitchfork full of beets and heaved them into the truck.

I turned back to my job, eager to be finished. I'd just decided I'd put my gravy on bread for the rest of my life when an unusual sound made me look up.

Another prisoner held the man who'd been whistling against the truck by a handful of shirtfront. And I knew this man. It was the young blond who'd fought Horst for the gun.

The older German's eyes were wide with fear. The blond man's face was so fierce I wanted to run, but I was afraid to move. I shrank as close to the ground as I could. I saw the young prisoner's arm move in two short punches to the other's belly. He released his hold on the shirt and the man sagged against the truck. Then Mr. Haycraft approached from the other side of the truck and the young POW began pitching beets into the box as if nothing had happened.

It was over so fast I almost wondered if I'd really seen it happen. But the slow, pain-filled movements of the older prisoner told me it had. He said nothing to Mr. Haycraft, but he winced as he lifted a forkful of beets toward the truck. Why were Germans fighting each other? What had made the young German so angry?

I tried to think what Lou had said that night at the Liberty Cafe. So much had happened since it was hard to remember. She'd said something about American music. Was it the song that had made him angry? Was the young man one of the Nazis who made trouble?

I stared after them as they moved off down the field, joined now by the rest of the crew who'd finished topping. The sun was still high in the sky, but I felt as I had the night I first saw the Germans marching from the train; in addition to their shorts and songs, they brought with them into the valley something dark and evil.

November was as cold and dry and gray as the leaves its winds scoured out of the gutters. It was as if all the colors of life had bled from the landscape. The noon news said Italy was cold, too, yet anything but dry. The Allies were creeping north, but the pace was agonizingly slow. The mountains there had numbers, too, and day after day we heard about struggles to cross the Volturno River, which seemed to curl back and forth across the direction of battle like a malevolent serpent.

I was almost glad to be back in school, where I could find other things to think about. Roger was back, and Betty brought a picture of Schnoz, a proud K-9 graduate with what his trainer described as "an extraordinary sensitivity to foreign smells."

Yet as I walked home through the chill afternoons, I stepped very cautiously. The phrase had come to me suddenly, out of nowhere, one day when Betty and I were fooling around on the way home.

"Step on a hole; break your mother's sugar bowl," she chanted as she planted a foot on a hole in the concrete.

I lifted a foot. "Step on a crack—" I froze. My mind was supplying the rest:

'Step on a crack; Danny won't come back.'

My knees buckled.

"What's the matter, M.K.?" Betty knelt beside me.

I couldn't tell her. I didn't dare put it in words. I could only tell her I was scared. She didn't have to ask why. Since then I'd tried to push the phrase out of my mind. But the more I tried not to think about it the louder the voice became. I could not bring myself to step on a crack. I began walking on the grass instead of the sidewalk.

The empty mailbox was a daily source of pain. I was nearly always home from school by the time Mr. Kelly limped down our block. He now rang the doorbell when he had a letter from a loved one in the service, and in more and more Hiram's Spring homes someone hovered near the door, listening for his familiar tread on the porch. I started running out to the end of our sidewalk when I saw him coming down the other side of the street. He'd answer my unasked question with a shake of his head.

I'd been avoiding cracks for more than a week when he gave me something besides a shake of his head. He smiled broadly and waved a letter in his hand. "Come on over and get it, Sis," he called. I flew across the street and had it open by the time I was back in the house.

Oct. ??, 1943

Dear Folks,

Taking time out, so have a chance to write. Hard to find things I can say. War's a funny business. Days of tough going and days you're sitting around an orchard eating apples, talking about home and laughing at the way a farmer's dog barks every time a Long Tom goes off, even though it's been going off for days.

I knew what a Long Tom was. A great big cannon *LIFE* said was one of our best weapons. It seemed strange a dog would be anywhere around one to bark. And to think of soldiers sitting around eating apples.

The other day I heard the sky rumbling and it took me a couple minutes to realize it was thunder, not artillery.

So far all we've seen is rain, rain and more rain. And drizzle. And fog. Mud up to our knees. Rivers flooded. Have crossed one ▮▮▮▮ times.

Did he mean the Volturno? I hated that name. It made me think of the vultures I'd seen in a book about Africa.

Don't think much about being dry anymore.
Discovered the other day if you ever get clean socks you have to change them fast. Our poor dogs have been wet so long they swell up as quick as you take your boots off and you can't get them on again.
Lots of guys out with trench foot.
Trucks can't get anywhere. We've been packing our food and water and ammo in by hand. Have to climb trails over the mountains at night. Hell of a way to fight a war. Blankets sure felt good last night. First we've seen in three weeks. By the way, the

214

new outfit I mentioned? Tough as they come. You couldn't ask for better men beside you.

Our squad has kind of adopted a little kid. He just started following us. Dirty, scrawny, but a great scrounger. Amazing what he comes up with. We don't ask where he gets it. We're teaching him some English and he learns pretty fast. He gives us some laughs and we can sure use them. We call him Georgie.

The houses are all stone, and most of them are pounded into rubble. But they seldom burn, so you can see things people left behind. Makes you realize what only means cover to you was somebody's home.

Hope you're all OK. I feel like home is so far away.

Love,

Dan

I went back and read the part about the little kid again. I felt a surge of jealousy. Would he make Danny forget me? What did he do to make him laugh? I wished I could be there and scrounge things up for Danny and his buddies, be part of what was happening to him. Why couldn't he have blankets at night? Why didn't they have enough socks? Why would his feet swell up? Why wasn't the army taking care of him better?

Yet it was a relief to hear from him—to know he was all right when he wrote the letter. I decided to take it down to the paper so Mother could read it for herself. I hoped maybe seeing the letter would make her and my father feel better, so they wouldn't be so cross with each other.

I took a short cut down the alley behind Main Street and had just entered the block that contained the Liberty Cafe when a door opened and a man came out to dump some trash. I was too far away to be sure, but it looked like the young waiter. I hoped he wouldn't see me; I didn't know what he might say.

The letter failed to work any magic. Mother read it through two or three times and passed it wordlessly to my father. I thought maybe she was going to cry. He read it without comment and sat staring at the wall.

"But it's funny about the dog, isn't it, Mom? And him thinking thunder was guns?" The longer they were quiet the more anxious I became. "And he likes the little boy who finds them stuff and makes them laugh."

I wasn't getting any response, but I couldn't stand the silence. "And that part about the Japanese soldiers is good, isn't it? What good fighters they are?"

Mother roused herself at last. "Yes. I suppose Billy would like to hear that. But I don't even know how to get a hold of him." She turned a bitter stare on Dad.

Why had I mentioned the Japanese! "I think I do," I said quickly, hoping to forestall an argument. "Maybe I should go show him."

I grabbed the letter and hurried out without waiting for an answer. I had only the vaguest notion why showing Billy Danny's letter would make any difference, but I had to try something. Maybe it would make him feel better about our family. Maybe he'd forgive my father. If Billy and Mother could be friends again, maybe she wouldn't be so mad at Dad.

The closer I got to the cafe's alley door, the sillier the idea seemed. They probably wouldn't even want to talk to me. They might yell at me and chase me out. It took all my courage to pull the door open and step inside.

Everyone was busy working and no one noticed me for a moment. One woman was scrubbing the kitchen walls, another the floor. I could smell paint and hear a hammer pounding in the dining room. Expecting anger and dismay, I saw cheerful faces and heard somebody whistling.

"Missy Gleggory!" Billy was smiling at me. "You come see we make you chocolate malt?"

I stared at the activity around me. "You're going to open your cafe again?"

"Yes." He was nodding vigorously. "Yes. Open next day. Two days."

"But your nephew said you were afraid—my dad wouldn't listen—his story—aren't you mad at us?"

He laughed. "No, no. Not mad. People see paper. All time calling. Telling solly. Asking when we open up?"

The news was better than three chocolate malts. My parents didn't need to be mad anymore. I wanted to hurry back with the news, but first I needed to show Billy the letter. When I explained, he gathered the others and I found myself sitting on a high stool, reading the letter sentence by sentence, while the nephew translated for the older Japanese.

I had to explain the part about the Japanese troops, and when they understood there were smiles and nudges and satisfied nods, and it had to be read and translated all over again.

Then Billy insisted on walking back to the paper with me to thank my parents for sharing the letter and offered to share any news his family received from his grandson in Italy. When he told my parents of the supportive calls they'd received and the decision to reopen the restaurant, my mother's eyes filled with happy tears.

After he'd left, she turned to Dad. "You were right, Hal. You had more faith in people than I did. How did you know?"

"I didn't," my father answered. "I still don't. This war is pulling people every which way. There's a lot of hate floating around out there and it's easy for some of it to get misdirected." He leaned back in his swivel chair and looked directly at her. "Bad things could still happen. But most of the people in this town are good, decent people. You can trust them with the truth."

It was a long speech for my father, who seemed more comfortable voicing his thoughts in writing.

"I wish—" Mother's voice was low, "I'd trusted your judgment—understood."

My father looked both gratified and embarrassed. "I've been at this a few more years than you have, Bess. And I didn't learn it half as fast." Then, quickly, as Mother beamed, "You have that city council write-up done yet? I need to know where it's going to fit."

I'd just fixed my after-school jelly bread when the doorbell buzzed. I hadn't been watching for the mail, since we'd just had a letter, but sometimes we did get two or three close together. I hurried to the door to see what Mr. Kelly had for us. I opened it to a high school boy in a Western Union cap two sizes too big.

"Your name Greggory?" He pushed a form at me to sign. I watched my hand write Mary Kathleen Greggory. Then I watched it take the yellow envelope. I closed the door and leaned against it.

I felt dizzy and sick to my stomach. My heart was pounding in my ears. The envelope was burning my fingers. I dropped it on the chair by the door and stumbled to the telephone. The operator had to ask me three times what number I wanted.

"Mom?" My voice was strangled.

"Sis? What is it?"

"Mom? We got a telegram."

She gasped. "Have—have you opened it?"

"No."

"Don't touch it. I'm coming home."

I hung up the phone and backed into the kitchen. I didn't stop until I'd climbed into the far end of the breakfast nook. It was as far away from the front door as I could get.

Was it my fault? Had I forgotten to say, "Safe at home?" Had I skipped a day rubbing Horst's lucky medal? Had I stepped on a crack? I tried to think. I'd been so careful. Then suddenly I saw myself running back to the house after Mr. Kelly handed me Danny's letter. I hadn't paid any attention at all to cracks! It was! It was my fault! It had to be. How could I be so careless? How could I make Danny be killed?

When Mother ran in the back door, Dad was right behind her. "Sis?

Where—?"

I pointed at the front door. My father strode ahead of her and I heard him tear the envelope open. I clapped my hands over my ears.

MAKE THE LIGHTS
GO ON AGAIN

Then I heard him yell, "Bess! Bess! It's all right. He's only wounded! He'll be coming home."

Mother screamed, "Oh, thank God! Thank God!" and began to cry.

It took several seconds for the words to penetrate my mind. Not dead? Danny was not dead? Did I dare believe it? I hadn't killed him after all? My backbone turned to rubber and I almost wet my pants. Danny was all right! He was coming home!

I found the strength to uncurl and stagger into the living room. My mother and father were locked in each other's arms. Mother was sobbing into Dad's shoulder and his eyes shone with unshed tears. They swayed together for several moments before they remembered me.

"How soon?" I asked. "How soon will he be home?"

Dad reread the telegram. "It doesn't say. It says he suffered significant injury to his right foot and will be evacuated to the USA after treatment."

Mother was drying her tears. "Significant? What do you suppose that means? Oh, Hal, I wonder how bad it is."

Dad pulled out his handkerchief and blew his nose. "I'd guess it's pretty serious," he said reluctantly. "I wish they'd given us more information."

They began to speculate about what might have happened, but I had all the information I needed. Danny was alive. And he was coming home.

"Let's see. There'll be six of us." I counted to myself as I got Mother's good dishes out of the china cupboard.

"Actually seven," Lou whispered to me as she spread the lace tablecloth. She patted her belly and smiled contentedly.

She'd brought two of the guards from the POW camp home for Thanksgiving dinner. "They don't get as many invitations as the airmen," she'd explained.

I knew Mother thought she should quit working, with the baby less than two months away. But Lou said she'd go crazy just sitting around, and the doctors were anxious for her to stay as long as she could. I knew a trip up the twenty-eight stairs to visit Dr. Erickson meant endless hours in the waiting room, and Mother admitted hospitals from as far away as California were running ads for nurses in the *Herald*. When Lou reminded her a prisoner of war camp was at the bottom of most job-seekers' lists, Mother threw up her hands.

"Lou, you can't take care of the whole world. Think of your baby."

"I am," she insisted. "I'm thinking of our baby and the world that baby's going to live in. I've got to do what I can to make it better."

Mother shook her head in rueful admiration. "Well, I hope the baby takes after you. You'll have every stray dog and hungry cat in town at your house."

Lou began to laugh. "I hope so," she said. "I hope we do."

Remembering the conversation, I realized one of the soldiers she'd invited to dinner had a lost-puppy look to his eyes. It seemed an effort for him to say "yes" or "no." The other had a vivid red scar that curled down from his left ear to his collar.

"If you think that's bad, you should see the Nip that gave it to me," he teased when he caught me staring. He kept us entertained at dinner with stories about the prisoners. How they wanted "potatoes, potatoes and more potatoes" to eat, and said our white bread upset their stomachs. How some men had begged hollyhocks and iris from farmers wives, so they could plant them in their barren compounds. How strange it felt to see an artistic POW painting a large mural of a covered wagon passing Chimney Rock, and to learn many of them had dreamed as boys of becoming American cowboys.

Was that why Horst knew about arrowheads? I remembered dropping mine into his greasy, calloused palm. But that image was suddenly replaced by the young German's clenched fist. "But aren't there some bad ones, some mean ones?" I asked.

The soldier looked uncomfortable. "I guess. But it's hard for us to know who they are. What goes on in the compounds at night is pretty much their secret."

Lou spoke up quickly. "But they're all getting training in democratic ideas. They're seeing American movies. And some of them make beautiful wood carvings and other crafts. There's going to be a public sale before Christmas. And maybe a concert. They've formed a wonderful chorus."

"I know the church women are planning to take out a tree," Mother said. Then, with a shake of her head, "People from Hiram's Spring sharing Christmas with German soldiers. Aren't we living in a strange world?"

Two days after Thanksgiving, we learned more about what had happened to Danny. It came in a letter addressed in strange handwriting.

Nov. 16, 1943

Dear Mr and Mrs Greggory,

I'm sure by now you have received word that your son, Daniel J. Greggory, was wounded in action the night of Nov. 9. I want to extend my sympathy to you and to assure you he is receiving the best of care.

I want you to know that Daniel has served well and bravely, many times risking his own safety to help others. Our recent action has been against Germans strongly entrenched in the mountains here. On the night he was wounded, the battalion was under intense fire. He was responding to an enemy break-through in his company's lines.

A number of men were killed or wounded and some were taken prisoner. Daniel was trying to reach one of the wounded men when he stepped near an enemy mine.

Our chaplain recently visited Daniel in the field hospital and reports his physical wounds do not appear to be life threatening. He will probably be sent to a hospital in Africa, and from there home. He is, of course, terribly shocked and fatigued and needs a long rest to recover his equilibrium.

Perhaps you should also know that shortly before he was wounded he witnessed the death of a young Italian boy in whom he had taken particular interest. It seemed to affect him deeply. Daniel is rather special to me. He seems so bright and interested in things. We often talked about history, and he was the sort of young man I loved to find in my college classes.

These boys endure so much. I don't know how they last as long as they do. It makes me humble to be serving with them.

Sincerely,

Lt. Edwin B. Landolt

I thought it was a wonderful letter. The officer said Danny was bright, which anybody with half an eye could see. He said Danny was brave, which I'd never doubted. He'd risked his life to help another man. He was a hero, just as I had always known he would be. I had a lot to tell the kids at school.

I was sorry about the little Italian boy, but I couldn't wait for Danny to be home, where we could take care of him and make him feel better. Where he could tell us all about his adventures. Where I could make him laugh.

The rumble of Mollie's tires on brick streets pulled me from a deep sleep. It was dark. My arm, curled under my head, felt wooden and lifeless. I rubbed it as I sat up, thinking we must finally be in Beatrice, our day-long drive to Grandma's house nearly over. Waking in the back seat to the sound of tires on brick and Mollie's companionable squeaks, audible again after the motor slowed from highway speeds, always told me summer vacation was really beginning.

But my sleepy eyes were seeing too many lights for Beatrice, too many other cars, too many tall buildings. Then a street car rattled past and I remembered. We were in Denver, on the way to Fitzsimons Army Hospital to see Danny. I'd been sitting on the edge of the seat ever since we'd left Hiram's Spring, breathing down my father's neck, trying to push the Ford down the highway. I couldn't believe I'd gone to sleep.

We'd had only two brief post cards in the nearly six weeks since he'd been wounded and neither came from him. They were brusque, official forms in which someone had inserted his name and rank. The first came from Africa, informing us he'd been evacuated to the USA for further hospitalization. On the bottom there was a card we could tear off to send him a message.

"Five words?" Mother said. "What can you say in five words?"

We spent half an hour trying to find five words that could begin to express our feelings. I liked "Can't wait till you're safe at home." But it was seven words. Mother liked "You have our love and prayers." But it was six. Various versions of "Get well soon," sounded trite and trivial. "Love from Dad, Mom, Sis," didn't say much.

It was Dad, drawing on his years of writing headlines, who finally found the combination that said the most. "You write it." He handed the fountain pen to Mother.

"No, we should each write part."

When we put the card in the mail, it read, "*God's love,*" in Mother's graceful script, "*and ours,*" in Dad's neat backhand, "*always.*" The last word in penmanship whose perfection would have amazed Miss Dumbroski.

The second card, postmarked Denver, confirmed Danny's presence at Fitzsimons and indicated he was "making normal improvement." It had come only yesterday and we didn't bother trying to choose another five words. By the time my parents had left the office, they'd been given more than enough gas coupons to deliver our message in person. However, no one had good tires to offer. Our right-rear gave out with a tired sigh west of Pine Bluffs, and

223

when what passed for our spare refused to hold air, Mother and I had waited hours by the side of the road while Dad hitched a ride into town to get a patch.

Now Dad was saying, "It will probably be too late to visit."

"I don't care," Mother answered. "I won't sleep unless we try."

After we were past the big buildings, Dad kept driving down the same wide, straight street. I saw a number of motels; all of them had No Vacancy signs glowing. Then the road narrowed and we were completely out of the city, riding through dark countryside once more.

"Do you think we're lost?" Mother asked. "Maybe we passed it."

"Couldn't have," Dad said. "They said straight east on Colfax."

Finally we saw lights ahead and turned left into a little lane where Mollie bumped over frozen ruts. Then Dad turned right and braked to a stop beside a small gate house. The soldier who came to Mollie's window said we were too late for visiting hours. Yet he seemed to want to help. "Try the Red Cross headquarters," he said. "Maybe they can at least get you a place to stay."

As Dad followed his directions, weaving along paved streets and stopping at traffic lights, I realized this hospital was nothing like the one at home. We passed building after building, almost as if we were driving through a small town. Then a huge building loomed ahead, lights glowing in floor after floor after floor of windows. We parked in the large lot in front of it.

"Oh, my," Mother breathed.

"That's the main hospital," Dad said. "Now to find Red Cross."

I was glad the Red Cross headquarters, when we found it, was not nearly so large and frightening, and that the woman summoned to help us was short and plump, wearing a polka-dot dress that reminded me of my Grandmother Greggory. But her dress made me smile. Small slips of paper were pinned all down her left bosom and on down her skirt. She winked at me. "How do you like my filing system? When I get all these things done, I know it's time to go to bed."

"You'll be up all night," Mother protested.

"That's all right. I'm just running a little behind today," she said cheerfully. "Now, what can I do for you?"

She could not get us in to see Danny. What she could do was find us three beds in the post guest house. That turned out to be exciting, because it was not a house at all. It was a two-story barracks. "Just like the quarters the soldiers live in," she promised. "We had to do something. Motels are scarce out here and they're just as full as the rest of Denver. You're really lucky we have any beds empty."

As most of the other visitors were already settled for the night, we crept into our beds. I bounced a little to see if I could make the cot creak like Danny had described in his letters from training camp. It did. I felt warm clear to my toes. Tomorrow, I thought, we'll see him tomorrow.

As we walked several blocks to and from the post exchange for breakfast, I watched a continuing stream of cars and trucks, and I was tickled to see mules pulling several delivery carts. Just like North Africa, I thought. There were dozens of soldiers in khaki and both men and women dressed all in white. By daylight the hospital looked even bigger than the night before. Its yellow brick was bright in the December sun. I counted ten stories in the central tower and six in the two wings.

Gawking up at the soaring flag pole in front of the main entrance, I nearly ran into a distinguished-looking man in high boots with spurs and a leather strap across his chest. "Easy, there." He put out a hand to steady me. "I don't want to have you as a patient."

By the time I'd followed my parents through the marble-columned entry and the massive doors had closed noiselessly behind me, I felt like I needed a hand to hold me up. Everything was so big, so spotlessly clean, so official looking. I was surprised people could talk out loud.

"Danny's in an outlying ward," Dad reported after he'd checked at the information desk. "His doctor will meet us there."

"Is something wrong?" Mother sounded alarmed.

"I don't know. They said Building C-13."

We walked out into the sunshine. The air was warm and dry. Dad pointed the way and I skipped ahead. When I saw that C-13 was a building much like the one we'd slept in, I decided Danny must be almost well. He didn't need to be in the big hospital anymore.

Impatient with my parents' pace, I circled the building, hoping I might see Danny in a window. All I saw were the slats of Venetian blinds, but in back I discovered stairs up to a little wooden porch.

A back porch. And Venetian blinds just like home. The building seemed even less like a hospital.

Inside we waited at the nurses' station that faced the door. Halls led off in both directions. I peeked down one to see long rows of white metal beds. A lady wearing a white cap with a gray veil that brushed her shoulders was reading a letter to a man in one bed. She had stiff white cuffs like the Pilgrims. A nurse in a white cap more like Lou's moved among the beds. She stooped to crank one up and lingered to talk with the patient. Maybe that's Danny, I thought with a thrill. We were so close. Why couldn't we just go on in and surprise him?

But the doctor, when he came, wanted to make me wait even longer. He held a long, quiet conversation with my parents. I caught a few words—fatigue—state of mind—matter of time. Then he turned to me and asked if I would please let them go in first.

"Your brother is still quite ill," he said. "We don't know how he'll respond to visitors. We want to take this slowly. You wouldn't want to upset him, would you?"

My mother and father were led off down the hall. I was so disappointed I had to blink back tears. But the disappointment sank into worry. So Danny wasn't almost well. How could seeing me upset him? I wasn't some "visitor." I was his little sister. What was wrong? What was wrong?

I couldn't bear to sit there and wait for an answer. I remembered the back door. Hurrying outside, I circled around to the bottom of the stairs. There was no one around. I stole up the stairs and entered the porch. Then I let myself into the building.

The nurse at the desk was talking on the phone. She didn't turn as I edged toward the hall. No one seemed to notice me enter the ward. I walked down the aisle between the rows of beds so closely placed their white rungs reminded me of a picket fence, vaguely aware of antiseptic air, men lying under white sheets and the murmur of voices.

I did not immediately see Danny. Instead I saw a man standing by one of the beds, a man who looked much like my father. But older. Immensely older. I had taken two or three more steps before I realized it was Dad.

Mother stood beside him, clasping a patient's hand in hers, raising it, pressing it against her cheek. The man in the bed had to be Danny. But it didn't look like Danny. There was nothing under the sheet where his right leg should be. But worse than that, far worse I discovered when his gaunt face turned toward mine, was the incredible, bottomless pool of emptiness in his eyes. We were strangers, staring at each other.

I remember Dad reaching toward me and Mother's voice in the distance. But I was backing away. Then I bumped into someone and a metal tray went crashing to the floor. The man jerked his hand from Mother's and threw himself over on his stomach. Then he was on his knees, digging, digging, burrowing into the bedding like a frightened animal. And I was running, running, down the aisle, out the door, across the grass. Running. Running. Until I could run no more.

THIS IS THE ENEMY

My mother—my father—Danny's psychiatrist—filled the air around me with words. As they talked, I was aware their mouths were moving, they were smiling reassuringly, their hands were reaching toward me. But I could not feel their touch. I couldn't hear what they were saying. I could see only the haunting emptiness of Danny's eyes, hear only the crash of metal on the tile floor, believe only the frantic hands digging in the bed.

It didn't matter what they said. The Danny I knew was dead. Part of me was just as dead. My brother was gone. There was a broken stranger in his place; I couldn't bear to see him again. All I could feel inside was an ache too deep for tears. I was glad when we were back in Mollie, on the road home.

We drove miles and miles and miles without a word, creeping through the frigid plains. I wanted to keep driving forever, to remain suspended between the past and future, isolated from the pain. Mother looked pale and exhausted. She lay her head back on the seat and closed her eyes. Dad took his eyes off the road only to light a new cigarette from the old.

The hospital had sent Danny's barracks bag home with us. It lay beside me on the seat. I stroked the scuffed and dirty canvas. Its reality was somehow comforting. Danny had packed it, carried it, when he was strong and whole. I could imagine him swinging it to his shoulder. I curled up on the seat and used it for a pillow. It helped me think of him the way he was before. Maybe he'd laid his head on it just like I was. Maybe he'd sat on it to write us a letter. Maybe there was a letter in it right now, one he hadn't had a chance to mail.

I loosened the draw string and slipped my hand inside. I could feel a jacket, softer material that might be underwear, then the buttons of a shirt. I worked my hand deeper and came on a shoe. I jerked away and plunged my arm down the other side. I felt something knitted, like a stocking cap. And that was a sock. But there was something in the toe. It felt like a little book.

I pulled my arm back out and sat up. It was a book, held together by a rubber band. A folded piece of paper was stuck under the rubber band. The edges of the cover were bent and worn and some of the pages had been rippled by moisture. I pulled the paper out of the way and tried to make out the title. "My Life in… Serv…" it said. A diary. It was Danny's diary.

Was the note about the diary? I unfolded the paper. The printing was big and kind of jerky, not at all like Danny's, but it began with

Nov. ??

Dear Dad,

We're heading into the mountains and it looks like Africa all over again, only worse. If you ever read this (with Sis at home and Mom at the office, I don't dare mail it home) I want you to know I'll last it out as long as I can. You always taught me to do my job. I'll try not to make you ashamed.

Why should Danny think Dad or anybody could ever be ashamed of him? Why didn't he want Mother or me to read it? What had happened to him over there? I lay back down on the barracks bag and opened the book. He'd started it back in Africa.

Feb. 19

No way to be ready for this hell. And maybe
no words to describe it. But maybe trying will keep
me from going off my rocker. And I guess someday
I might want some kind of a record.

Moved up in the dark to relieve the French.
Groped around and fell in a foxhole. No sooner dug
in than Rommel broke through down south.

Kasserine. I remembered how frightened we'd been when the
Germans broke through.

Ordered to withdraw. Mass confusion. Nazis
hit before we can move. Mortars drop like light-
ning bolts. Artillery blinding, deafening,
brutal. Shells shriek in. Can't see for smoke.
Ears bursting. Ground heaving. Feels like my heart
will explode. Keeps on and on. Can't think or
breathe. Know now what puking fear is like. God,
what feelings. Hugged the ground until my
muscles cramped, my jaws ached. Thought every
shell was aimed right at me. Never felt so helpless.
So alone.

Then retreat. In shock. Ears ringing. Everybody scared spitless he'll be last—be left.
Racing back, miles and miles. Dark as pitch. Stumbling, falling, trying to carry gear. Trip over stuff
guys dropped. Pushed on all day and into night.
Too tired to go on. Couldn't stop.

My God! What's happening? Why can't we stop
them? Are the Jerries going to beat us?

Danny? Scared to death? The drone of Mollie's motor echoed
with the heartbeat in my ears. I didn't want to read any more, but I
couldn't stop. As I turned the pages the entries got shorter and
harder to read.

Feb. 24

Time out. Dirty Germans plant mines everywhere. Afraid to take a step. They've thought of everything. There's a wooden one the detectors miss—'til it blows off your foot. And one that jumps out of the ground and sprays every guy close with shrapnel.

His leg? Was it a wooden one that got his leg? A damn cheater wood mine that didn't even give him a fair chance? The dull, dead ache inside me began to stir and swirl around a darkening core.

March 5

Move up in the dark. Sweat out walking blind. Jerry catches us in cactus field. Rifles, machine guns, mortars. Panzers churn at us straight from hell. My buddy gut shot. God damn them, damn them all!

Some of the entries were dirt-streaked and hard to read, some were mostly about the cold, or one of his buddies, or the battlefield, but others jumped out at me.

April 5

Jerry drops flares to find our holes. No place to hide. Feel like clay pigeons. Frigging Stukas scream down to slaughter us at will.

April 28

Sons of bitches use their own dead for booby traps. Bomb and strafe our ambulances. Don't think any of them deserve to live.

The black core in my chest squeezed tighter and whirled faster. I welcomed its hot, hard presence. Danny hated the Germans. Every one of them. All the posters and billboards and ads were right. The Nazis were monsters; Hitler's bullies would blow up their dead buddies, laugh while they starved little kids and hang old ladies from the gallows.

And Horst was one of them. How did he make me think he was different? I was angry at myself for trusting him—for thinking his medal could keep Danny safe. Maybe he knew all along it would be bad luck for Americans. Maybe that's why he'd acted friendly, to trick me into jinxing Danny. I felt a wonderful, warm, liberating surge of hatred and hugged it to me; it swelled to fill the emptiness; it blocked out the pain. I fed on its strength.

May 2
Finally took fucking 609. Gave up hope of making it through. Don't know why I did. Didn't really care. Never knew blood could smell so strong. Afraid to sleep for dreams. Yet all I want to do is sleep.

May 11
Have seen things I can't write about—will never be able to talk about—pray to forget.

The Ford's tires hummed on the dry highway. My mother slept. The smoke from my father's cigarettes mingled with the smoke of the battlefield as I began to read about Italy. The dark core whirled and hummed inside me, its shell impervious to pain, keeping me safe, keeping me whole.

"She's reacting so strangely. I can't reach her, Lou. I don't know what—"

Mother's voice broke off when I walked into the kitchen the next morning, and I pretended I hadn't heard. I began to hum "White Christmas" to show her I was fine. I didn't need any more empty words, even from Lou. I needed only what I held inside.

Instead of offering explanations, Lou surprised me by asking, "How about coming out to the camp with me this morning, M.K.? We need some help getting the hospital tree decorated. The concert and craft sale is tonight and we're supposed to look nice for any visitors who might drop in. I'm getting a little bulky to climb up on a chair to trim a tree."

I was all ready to say no when I remembered—her hospital was full of Germans. I smiled at the thought of seeing them sick and hurting. And I could watch the others all cooped up behind their fences, under American guns, beaten in spite of all their dirty tricks. Maybe I'd get a chance to spit through the fence to show them what I thought of them.

As we climbed on the homemade bus that served the air base and the internment camp, I gave Lou a helpful boost up the stairs.

"Umpf," she groaned. "I'm glad I have only one more month of this."

An airman offered her his seat, and she dropped heavily onto one of the wooden benches that ran down each side of the make-shift vehicle. In the spirit of "making do," a local entrepreneur had created a badly needed bus by slicing a sedan in half and welding a section from another car between the front and back. The Amalgamated Express could seat eight people comfortably, crowd in sixteen when it was necessary, which it always was these days. I'd longed for a chance to ride in the strange looking vehicle, but today all I cared about was its destination.

I was feeling better and better. I carefully balanced the box of tree ornaments Mother had donated and thought about the possibilities. Maybe I could do more than spit through the fence. Maybe I could spit in their food when Lou wasn't watching, or spill their medicine. I began to hum again and Lou smiled and patted my hand.

The camp, divided in neat rectangular sections that spread beneath a huge orange-and-black water tower, looked much as I expected. The guard at the gate near the road looked at Lou's badge, carefully examined my box of shiny baubles and cleared us to pass through the administration area. I could see long lines of barracks in the prisoners' three living compounds straight ahead. When another guard let us through the double fence that surrounded the hospital and workshops, I gloried in its height and the threatening way the barbs angled in at the top. The guard towers loomed above, just as I'd imagined. It was a wonderful place. Just right for Germans.

But when we entered the barracks behind the "Hospital" sign, the atmosphere was not full of tension and pain, like I'd hoped. I

234

heard a murmur of voices, the sound of laughter. A balding prisoner, whose belly swelled the front of his POW uniform, was pushing a floor waxer across the tile, singing "Clang! Clang! Clang! goes da vaxer."

Danny was lying in Denver, nothing but an empty shell, and this fat, old Nazi could sing silly songs from Judy Garland's latest movie? Where was God? How could he let the world be so unfair?

"Do you want to walk through the wards with me, so you can see what I do all day?" Lou asked. "Maybe you'd like to be a nurse someday."

Someday? I like to be a nurse right now, I thought, as I followed her dutifully. I could give them the wrong medicine or jab the thermometer down their throats or—

"Some of these men were in pretty bad condition when they got here," Lou said.

What was I supposed to do? Feel sorry for Nazis?

She put her hand on my shoulder and turned me toward a German in one corner. "That man playing checkers over there was hurt like your brother was, M.K."

I shook her off. That Nazi had nothing to do with Danny. She hadn't seen him. She had no idea!

"Listen to me, Mary Kathleen! Battle can do awful things to men's minds, but they can get over it. Don't you see?"

What I saw were Nazis. Warm and dry and safe. Being fed. Being cared for. Ready to have Christmas. Christmas! Nazis who'd strung trip wires through grape vines and haystacks and door hinges so they could blow Americans to bits. Nazis who'd sent rockets screaming in on Danny, half a dozen at a time, like lethal rain that fell for hours. Who'd made him cry when he tramped on a dead buddy's hand. Who'd booby-trapped a pair of binoculars and blown little scrounger Georgie into pieces too small to bury.

I turned my back on Lou and stalked out to do the tree. This wasn't working out the way I'd imagined. I couldn't really do anything to hurt them. The sooner I got done, the sooner I could catch the bus back home.

I reached in my box for an ornament. The one I picked up was from the year Danny's Scout troop had painted pine cones and sprinkled them with silver glitter. He'd made so many Dad threatened to prop the tree up with a two-by-four, and that Christmas became "The Year of the Pine Cones."

Danny didn't even know what Christmas was anymore. I hung it as fast as I could. I couldn't think of things like that; the pain had almost slipped into my black core.

Then the door opened and Horst stood in front of me, a box of handmade decorations in his hand. "Maria!" he exclaimed. "My little gardener."

My box of ornaments crashed to the floor. "Don't talk to me," I yelled. "You dirty, rotten, stinking, goddamn Germans have killed my Danny!"

His expression of surprise dissolved and he looked stricken. "*Mein Gott*," he muttered. "*Nein, nein.*" He reached toward me. "*Ach, liebchen.* So many hurts there are. Forgive us, *bitte.* Forgive."

Forgive! I jerked away from his pleading hand, and as I backed away I found the words I needed. Staring him hard in the face I hissed, "It is not," I spat the syllables at him with icy deliberation, "It is not—ever—to be forgiven."

I felt the warmth of a body behind me and turned into Lou's arms. "There, there, darling," she crooned. "Maybe now you can cry."

The tears started to come, but I clenched my jaws and swallowed the sob. I couldn't. I didn't dare. I had to stay hard. I stiffened my back, and when I heard the door close behind Horst I asked Lou to take me to the gate so I could go home.

Lou said nothing to me when she came home for supper. She simply handed me an envelope. I couldn't imagine what it was. I opened it to handwriting different from any I'd ever seen.

> *My dear little Maria,*
>
> *I am in sorrow about your brother. I know your heart is hard to us, but my hope is understanding someday will come.*
>
> *For my Deutschland's leaders I have shame. Forgive us, leibchen, if you can.*
>
> *Your friend,*
> *Horst Mueller*

I read it through once and stuffed it in my pocket. I made myself concentrate on Danny's lifeless eyes; I reminded myself how he'd searched for enough of Georgie to bury. In a moment I knew what I wanted to do about the letter.

The hardest part was convincing Lou I should go out to the camp program that night. I'm not sure she believed I wanted a chance to tell Horst I was sorry, but once the lights on the big water tower came in sight, I quit worrying about it.

Yet I was worried about something else when I'd sat through the concert in the theater without seeing him. And as we crowded into the officers' mess hall to see the craft items, I wondered if I'd have to find some other way.

The event had attracted dozens of townspeople. Some of the church ladies were putting little gifts in a basket, but many people were just staring around to see what they could see. They pointed surreptitiously and whispered together.

I worked my way along tables filled with neat displays. There was a ship built in a vinegar bottle and a large, dark, wooden bowl inlaid with triangles of lighter woods. I saw several miniature scenes carved from wood—a man playing an accordion, another walking with a small brown dog, another standing by a suitcase marked "PW." A whole basket of tree ornaments cut and shaped from the ends of tin cans gleamed in the light and attracted many buyers.

But I heard a woman say. "Huh! Why aren't those in the scrap drive?"

"Same reason they get butter while we color margarine," her companion answered.

Then I saw the man I was looking for. He stood straight and stiff behind a display of animals carved from soap. His blond hair shone in the light bulb that dangled from the ceiling. He stared, stone faced, over the heads of two women who were exclaiming about the carvings.

I edged closer, my breath coming fast. I picked up a carving of a bear, and my hand didn't even shake. When I put it down again, Horst's note was beneath it. I backed away and watched the Nazi slip the note into his pocket without a flicker of expression.

It was done. My hot, black core hummed with satisfaction. I was smarter than any of them. I didn't have to hurt them myself. I could make them hurt each other. I wished I could be there to watch Horst get beaten up.

Two days later I sat in the waiting room of the community hospital on Main Street, swinging my legs in agitation. Mother had disappeared up the stairs, but by hospital rules I was still a child. We'd received the call a couple of hours before. Lou had been rushed from the internment camp to the maternity ward.

"But it's not time yet," I protested.

"Sometimes babies come early," Mother said, but I didn't like the crease between her eyebrows when she left the information desk or the way she hurried up the wide staircase.

I hated being where I was. It made my stomach tie itself in a hard knot. It was too much like waiting at Fitzsimons. I stared at the small white hexagons in the tile floor until they swam together and climbed atop each other. It was better than seeing Danny's eyes. Anything was better than that.

I thought of the hospital's back stairs and how exciting it had been when Lou and I ran up to wave goodbye to Ira. I knew I could find them again. But back stairs were even more frightening than waiting rooms. I stayed in my chair.

The early dusk began to dim the room and the woman at the desk plugged in the little Christmas tree. Not long after that the shifts changed. I was glad for a chance to watch something different. Nurses began to stream down the stairs, pulling on their coats and tying scarves under their chins. Two paused near me in the vestibule, evidently watching for their ride.

"Boy, that would be some shock, wouldn't it?" one asked. She was using one door-glass as a mirror to put on her lipstick.

"I'll say!" The other shuddered. "To have a guy stagger in with his eye gouged out? Gives me the willies." She searched her purse, pulled out a comb and peered into the other oval glass. "No wonder she went into labor."

I sat straighter in my chair.

"Really!" The first nurse rubbed a little lipstick off her teeth. "I'd have a cow! Even if it was just a German."

My hands closed on the arms of the chair.

The second nurse was concentrating on parting her hair. "I thought the weirdest part was about the magpie. Who'd be weird enough to strangle a magpie? And hang it around his neck, yet."

"God knows. There's Jack. Let's go. We only have a couple of hours to get ready for the party."

Cold air rushed in as the doors swung shut behind them. It wrapped itself around my ankles and my knees and my chest and my head. It blew into my ears and pushed its way into my lungs. I could feel it freezing my hard, hot core.

I don't know how long it was before Mother found me sitting there. "It's all right, darling," she was saying. "Lou's fine. She has a healthy baby boy. He's just a little smaller than he would have been."

A baby? I'd almost forgotten. I tried to smile.

"You're just completely worn out, aren't you, dear?" Mother smoothed my hair. "It's been such a terrible week. Let's go home. After all, it's Christmas Eve."

I'd forgotten that, too. But the words seemed meaningless. Is this how Danny feels, I wondered, like he's standing off alone in the dark somewhere? And he can't talk to anybody? Can't tell anybody the awful, awful things that are in his heart?

FOR THIS WE FIGHT

I didn't even get under the covers. I didn't dare close my eyes. I was afraid to sleep. I wrapped Grandma's quilt around me and sat staring at the stars, sharp and crisp in the winter sky. I'd sat there before, watching for Santa Claus, thinking about the exciting day to come. Now I couldn't bear to think at all. The magpie fluttered on the edge of my mind and Horst stood in the door, pleading for forgiveness. I tried to push them away, but when I did darker images threatened to overwhelm me. When I thought my parents were finally asleep, I crept downstairs.

The living room was still bathed in the colored glow of the Christmas tree lights. My father, in his maroon bathrobe, knelt by the tree, tightening something on a gray bicycle. He heard me and turned. "Oh, Sis! You caught me!"

I stared. "A bicycle? Where'd you get a bicycle?"

"You know," He stood up, looking kind of flustered, "from Santa Claus."

"Not even Santa Claus can get bicycles nowdays."

"Well, this is—second hand, you might say. Kind of put together—like the Amalgamated Express."

"You mean you made it? From different parts?"

"It may not be too good," he warned. "I got the parts from junk yards. I don't know how well it will ride." He ran his hand over the back fender. "I'm sorry it has to be gray. That's the only color of paint I could find."

My father had made a bicycle? For me? I couldn't believe it. It must have taken hours and hours. How could he find the time? Why on earth would he spend it on me? I was reaching for the handlebars in joyous disbelief when a dreadful image of Horst's brutalized face flooded my mind. I sucked in my breath and backed away, sick and dizzy.

"No! No! No! I can't take it."

"What *are* you talking about?" He sounded irritated.

"I can't take it. I don't deserve it. I've done something awful."

He didn't respond for a long moment. Then he sighed. "I guess you'd better tell me about it." He put down the wrench and reached for my shoulder.

At his touch, the tears began to come. I cried for the magpie that would never learn to say "hello." I cried for Horst, who had been my friend. A friend I'd hurt so badly I could never, never be forgiven. But most of all I cried for the brother I'd lost, for the old Danny who used to whistle and make jokes, and for the new Danny who was in such pain.

My father pulled me against him and held me as I sobbed, and when I had finally run out of tears, he led me over to the davenport and quietly asked me what I needed to tell him.

The words came slowly at first, then in a torrent. All about Horst, from the time I heard him singing "Don't Fence Me In" to the last time I saw him in the prison hospital. All about the young magpie with the broken wing who learned to say "Ach, gut." About reading Danny's diary and how it made me want to hurt all Germans. And finally—I had to tear the words from my chest— how I had caused Horst's unthinkable injury.

"Mary Kathleen!" His voice was shocked, and I cringed away from him. But he said, "You read that diary? We didn't even know. You couldn't even talk to us?"

"I didn't know!" I was sobbing again. "I didn't know they'd do something so awful! I only wanted him to hurt. Like I was."

"Of course, you didn't know." He began to explain, in his exact-ing way, that I could not hold myself responsible for a depth of evil beyond my understanding.

"I hear things about this prison camp, and others, that I can't print," he said. "I think you need to know them now. Can I depend on you not to talk about it?" He looked at me. I wiped my nose on the sleeve of my pajamas and nodded.

"Most of the Germans are relieved to be here, to be out of the war and receiving good treatment. But others remain staunch Nazis, still determined Hitler is going to win. They think helping Americans is traitorous."

He was talking to me like I was an adult. I nodded again to show I understood.

"There have been beatings, hangings, men driven to suicide because they feared for their families at home. It doesn't happen a lot, but it happens. The Nazis take control of a compound. They hold trials at night and issue death sentences."

He laced his long fingers in with mine.

"You said this prisoner was friendly to you. He helped you with the magpie. He worked hard for Mr. Haycraft. I think he may have worked with Lou in the hospital. It sounds as if he liked our music." He looked at me for confirmation and when I nodded he continued. "The other Germans could see these things. And from what you told me about the fight over the rifle, I think he must have been fighting to keep the gun from the young Nazi."

"You mean maybe Horst was trying to keep me and Roger and his dad safe?" I suddenly felt worse again. "And I made the Nazis hurt him."

"Mary Kathleen," (I realized it was the second time he'd used my name) "you're growing up. I can't pretend that what you did was right. How much it had to do with what happened to Horst we'll never know—he may already have been marked for punishment. But giving them the letter probably contributed to what happened. It was wrong. And hard as it is, we all have to live with the mistakes we make."

I lay my head back on the davenport and closed my eyes against the pain. "Won't I ever be able to forget?"

"When I was young, M.K., and grieving over something bad I had done, my mother used to remind me of her 'anything-everything rule.'"

"What's that?"

"Well, first you admit what you did. You've already done that. That's a big step, and I'm proud you had the courage to tell me." He squeezed my hand.

"Then you do anything you can to make it right."

Despair washed over me and I clamped my arms across my chest and rocked back and forth. "But I can't do anything to make his eye right again."

"No, you can't," he said bluntly Then his tone softened. "But remember, you had no idea he'd be injured so badly. You mustn't blame yourself for that." He turned my face toward him and made me look at him. "Mary Kathleen, every one of us has done something when we're angry or hurt that we'd give our lives to change. But some things can't be undone. That's one of life's hardest lessons."

"Oh, Dad. I wish I could tell him how sorry I am. I wish I could ask him to forgive me."

"Maybe I can help you do that. I'll see what I can find out." I felt his lips brush the top of my head. The thought of being able to tell Horst I was sorry made me feel a little better. "What's the 'everything' part of Grandma's rule?" I asked.

"You do everything you can to make sure it never happens again."

"How can I do that?"

"By remembering what you learned. And by trying to change whatever it was that caused you to do the wrong thing."

I could not imagine a time I wouldn't remember. I let out a long, shuddery sigh that turned into a yawn. "Then what?"

"Then you move on. You have to move on. And now, Punkin, that's what we're going to do. You're exhausted. Let's get you to bed."

We walked to the stairway. I trudged up the steep stairs, feeling I could hardly lift my feet, and when I looked back from the top he was still standing there, watching.

Danny called us about four o'clock on Christmas afternoon. He sounded rather strange and far away. He didn't have much to say. But he said that when he was better he'd be coming home, and when he told me goodbye he called me "Sis." I didn't need to hear another word.

EPILOGUE

I wish I could tell you the Liberty Cafe was never again the victim of prejudice.

The truth is the police were called several times to protect it from the misguided anger of drunken servicemen. Eventually the military placed it out of bounds, and Billy's grandson and other Japanese-American boys home on leave from the 442nd Combat Team, who served so gallantly in Europe, could not enter it to visit their families.

I wish I could tell you that I heard from Horst again, but by the time the holidays were over and my father could reach camp authorities, he'd been sent away for medical care and for his own safety. The army wouldn't say where. Nazi fanatics, called *Lagergestapo* by other prisoners, operated more freely in some camps than others. They beat, drove to suicide and killed POWs they condemned as traitors in a reign of terror that intensified from September 1943 to April 1944. Most civilians heard little or nothing about the matter; some who did were unconcerned if Germans' "fiendish, ruthless blood" was shed.

I wrote Horst a letter, but I never received an answer. My father said I'd done all I could about the "anything" rule. It was months before I quit watching the mail, quit wondering and hoping.

Children are not designed for lasting grief and eventually the memories receded, but lurking in the backwaters of my mind was the dark knowledge of something I'd never told my father: That on Christmas Eve, when I heard the nurses talking at the hospital door and realized it was Horst who was injured, I felt an instant of deep, singing joy. Real regret—composed at first of guilt and fear—was slower to come.

I can tell you that Danny gradually found his way back to us. It was as if the mine had exploded in the pool of his soul, splattering his being. Slowly, ever so slowly, the drops that remained trickled back to center. The man they created inevitably lacked some of the sparkle of the vital boy who'd gone off to war. He'd been wrong about that, that long-ago September Saturday on the Bluff. Part of him was gone forever.

When the G.I. Bill made college possible, Danny earned a degree, changing his major from journalism to history and eventually becoming a college professor. He married a girl he met during his therapy sessions and the two of them, childless, often opened their home to foster children.

Bur Danny never talked about the war. Only when his much-loved nephews pestered would he go back to those days, and then he would dredge up a funny story about boot camp. He never talked about his real war, never spoke to me of his diary, never wrote his story.

And I never managed to find the right time or words to talk to him about my friend Horst. My grief about Horst seemed disloyal; I dreaded stirring coals of memories better left gray. I told myself it was for Danny's sake, but I realize now I was protecting myself as much as him. My boisterous confidence in his unequivocal love was gone. I'd learned to weight the risks, guard my tongue, shield my soul—all the skills adults use to get along in the world. Too afraid to risk condemnation in his eyes, I forfeited the chance for understanding.

Danny fought through his shadows and emerged gentle and steadfast. No woman ever had a better brother, but we never talked about the thing we most needed to. Our family and many others, emotionally exhausted, chose to let unasked questions, unfathomable answers, unresolved issues hang, like clothes of the dead in a dark closet, too painful to touch.

Time has spread its soothing salve on the wounds of the Second World War. Those who served on the home front are more inclined to remember the enveloping sense of unity and purpose than the shortages and long hours. Women like Lou, whose family circle became whole again, remember the joyous homecomings rather than the sleepless nights. Some of them, like Lou, continue to offer compassionate care to the world's forgotten.

My mother, who had learned to cook when she had to feed her family, now learned to be a nurse to help Danny recover his physical strength. Later, she returned to the *Herald* to cover the school board and civic issues. Eventually she won a position on the school board and worked for the educational needs of students like Harvey.

My father, always certain work is the best therapy, had Danny working the phones for the paper as soon as he could function. He accepted Danny's need to move from journalism to history with difficulty, but he took pride in the academic writing his son produced. In later years he mellowed a little—I was astonished at the patience he showed his grandchildren—but he never relaxed his standards. He remained editor/owner of the paper until the day he died.

Sixty and more years later, balding, portly men stand in mute recollection on Pacific isles. Others walk the paths of memory in cross-filled cemeteries in Europe. Germans who topped Nebraska sugar beets return to those fields, renew acquaintances with farmers whose crops they harvested, and visit with a few comrades who chose to immigrate to the United States and make the Valley of the Nile their permanent home. Long-time residents with names such as Yamamoto and Sakurada and Nagata recall only with reluctance a time the valley was a fearful place to live.

Yet recently I have been drawn back to the valley to stand beside the dirt road that fronted the prisoner of war camp and watch prairie dogs burrow in what became the city dump. I hear the magpies chattering down by the river. In late May a clump of purple iris blooms. I finger the medal Horst gave me and think of the man who reached through the barriers of evil to offer comfort and friendship to a frightened child. I know, now, the words on his good luck token mean, "He protects you."

I remember with undiminished pain how that friendship was twisted by the malignant power of hatred. Then I think of the shaved heads and leather jackets I see so often in the shopping malls—and tremble for children whose ignorant parents decorate their ears with swastikas. I learn of synagogue libraries torched and a cross burned on a suburban lawn—shooters in schools, malls, churches and theaters and whole peoples in peril because they are of the wrong religion—and shudder at the parallels of history. I hear again the hate-driven boots that stride through German squares on the evening news—and taste fear for Horst's family, and for my own sons. Can telling my story be enough to satisfy Grandma Greggory's "everything" rule? Dare I move on? And what of the world?

If we who were taught the power of this malignancy do nothing, from whom dare we seek forgiveness? I stand by the road and remember. I feel the pain. I rub Horst's medal and begin to pray.

The End